"You're looking at me strangely," she said softly.

"You're beautiful," he said, because all he had was honesty in the wake of her courage and passion. "I mean, you have to know that."

"I do," she said, and any other time, it would make him smile, her cool acknowledgment. She had heard it hundreds of times, he was sure. Men had been telling her she was beautiful her entire life, and she was smart enough to know what her beauty meant, how it changed people's perceptions, for better or worse.

"But here." He reached out and pressed his fingers against her collarbone, his palm on her breastbone, above her heart. His hand moved to her forehead, tracing over the elegant wing of her brow. "And here?" His fingers rested lightly on her temple. "Way more impressive."

And that's when Grace, true to form, surprised the hell out of him. Because instead of scoffing or pulling away or laughing him off, she tilted her head up and kissed him.

By Tess Diamond

SUCH A PRETTY GIRL
DANGEROUS GAMES

Coming Soon

BE A GOOD GIRL

SUCH A PRETTY GIRL

PAPL
DISCARDED

TESS DIAMOND

AVONBOOKS

An Imprint of HarperCollinsPublishers

SUCH A PRETTY GIRL. Copyright © 2017 by Supernova, LLC. All rights reserved. Printed in the United States of America. No part of this book may be used or reproduced in any manner whatsoever without written permission except in the case of brief quotations embodied in critical articles and reviews. For information, address HarperCollins Publishers, 195 Broadway, New York, NY 10007.

First Avon Books mass market printing: October 2017

Print Edition ISBN: 978-0-06-265582-0
Digital Edition ISBN: 978-0-06-265583-7

Cover design by Nadine Badalaty
Cover photographs: © Yolande de Kort/Trevillion Images (girl); © ILINA SIMEONOVA/Trevillion Images (street)

Avon, Avon & logo, and Avon Books & logo are registered trademarks of HarperCollins Publishers in the United States of America and other countries.
HarperCollins is a registered trademark of HarperCollins Publishers in the United States of America and other countries.

FIRST EDITION

17 18 19 20 21   QGM   10 9 8 7 6 5 4 3 2 1

To my mom who taught me to read mysteries.

ACKNOWLEDGMENTS

A book takes a village . . .
   Thank you to Tessa Woodward; Elle Keck; and Noreen Lai; my agent, Rebecca Friedman; and my husband and kids for playing outdoors while I finished this book.

CHAPTER 1

We'll be arriving in about fifteen minutes."
Grace Sinclair looked from the limo
window to the driver. Checking her phone
for the time, she sighed in relief. She hated being
late.

"Thank you," she said, slipping the phone back
into her vintage Prada clutch.

"What kind of event are you going to?" the
driver asked. He was a middle-aged man with
black hair and dark eyes that had brightened
when she made her way down the stairs of her
town house earlier that evening. "Seems fancy."

They were en route to the Hirshhorn Museum
and Sculpture Garden. Tonight the venue was
hosting not only great works of art but a prestigious black-tie event for the DC elite.

"An awards dinner," Grace said.

"For you?" he asked. "You're mighty dressed up."

Grace looked down at her body-hugging silk

halter dress. The silvery material clung to her curves like a metallic skin, leaving everything—and nothing—to the imagination.

"My second book won the Callahan Award," Grace said as the limo turned into the flow of busy DC traffic.

In the rearview mirror, Grace could see the driver's eyebrows rising. "You a writer?"

She nodded. "But writing's just a side job," she explained. "I work for the FBI."

"The FBI?" He whistled, low and skeptical. "You're not off chasing bad guys, are you? You're such a pretty thing—you might get hurt."

The hairs on Grace's neck prickled in irritation as he laughed, a little too hard and a little too long. She was feminine, yes, but she packed a hell of a punch—she made sure of it.

"I'd be more concerned with the bad guys getting hurt, if I were you," she said. "I'm a profiler."

"Like on TV?" he asked, mockery evident in his leering grin.

Grace smiled, but he didn't notice the wolfish edge in her expression. "Just like that," she replied coolly.

Her focus narrowed. Her eyes tracked past the driver's face, settling on the crumpled ice-cream wrappers in the trash can on the passenger-side floor.

She was far from a Sherlock Holmes—profiling wasn't as easy as examining the dirt under someone's fingernails and deducing they'd planted some zinnias that day. And it was no magic trick—that was just cold reading and con artistry.

Profiling was about details and knowledge. About psychology and behavior. About paying attention to cues and clues, physical and verbal. It wasn't about just being able to notice such cues, but being able to identify them. To analyze them. To string them together into a solid sketch of a person.

Her driver was probably the youngest in his family. Always out to prove his worth. He equated being louder with being better because it was the only way to get any attention. Likely a poor relationship with his parents—particularly his mother—leading to his own weak parenting skills. The way his hands were clenched on the steering wheel and the irritated line of his shoulders as he maneuvered the limousine through the nighttime traffic told her he hated his job—and resented his passengers too.

Some people—the nicer ones—would say her driver had old-fashioned ideals. His wide eyes roving up and down her clingy dress had revealed an obvious attraction but also a hint of disgust that was quickly tamped down. His passive-aggressive comment about her looks made him feel like the big guy. Something he desperately needed, clearly, since he was stress eating.

Her gaze drifted to his left hand where a wedding ring should be. The strip of untanned skin was a dead giveaway. Recently separated or divorced. She'd bet all her money that the reason was infidelity—on his part. He didn't respect women. He thought they were inferior—a woman in power made him feel nervous and inadequate. He was the kind of man who felt as if women owed him something—someone who both resented and lusted after the opposite sex.

Good for his ex to have escaped, Grace thought with some satisfaction. Life was too short to waste it on a man who couldn't appreciate a woman's worth.

The driver pulled up to the front of the museum. Grace waited as he jumped out of the car and made his way over to open her door. Ignoring his proffered hand, she got out herself, moving toward the immense gray circular building.

"Oh, by the way," she said. He turned, clearly expecting a tip. So she gave him one: "If you want your wife back, you'd better stop with the stress eating. Not that she'll have you, after the fling with . . . who? The stripper? No, the camgirl. Am I right?"

His ruddy face—he'd been drinking too much, evidently—went white. "What the—"

Grace smiled, tapping her temple mysteriously. "Just like TV," she said, before turning to walk up the path to the museum.

THE HIRSHHORN ITSELF was a work of art. Perched on four legs, the striking round building with a lush plaza in the center housed some of the most celebrated modern art in the world. But the sculpture garden on the grounds had always been her favorite of the museum's many collections.

She showed her ticket, then made her way to the sculpture garden, the long skirt of her dress fluttering behind her. Already, people dressed in their finest were milling about among the sculptures. Strains of Mozart—a string quartet playing a minuet—floated through the air, and waiters circulated with hors d'oeuvre trays and champagne.

Smoothing the crown of intricate braids she'd painstakingly plaited into her waist-length hair, she tried to summon a real smile. This was her world—the one her parents occupied; the one she'd been born into. Glittering, beautiful, cultured, accomplished. She'd always been told she was these things—praised by private tutors, then boarding school teachers, and finally, top-notch professors.

She had been groomed to bring honor to the

Sinclair name. To continue the proud tradition of wealth, privilege, and power. Her mother was a society wife, but Grace was an only child, which meant a life of debutante balls and hanging on some politician's arm was not an option. Her father wouldn't dream of his only heir reducing herself to such pursuits.

She was meant for more. She was meant to be her father's perfect puppet, to do as she was told, to excel at whatever career he deemed right for her, and to be the perfect Sinclair.

The pressure had been crushing and any parental love deeply lacking. She supposed she could've bent to her father's will, but she'd always been stubborn. She'd been drawn to another world, where she discovered a different, darker kind of challenge: the criminal mind.

Her mother had been horrified at her career choice. Her father had quietly raged, as was his way. But the pull to know, to pick apart, and to understand had been too strong for her to ignore. The FBI had its eye on her since her sophomore year in college and recruited her right after graduation.

Quantico was everything she'd ever dreamed of and more. She'd graduated at the top of her class and climbed the ranks at the Bureau. A year into the job, she found herself on the hunt for a serial killer who tried to cover his tracks by staging his murders as suicides. It'd been one of those cases that got under your skin. During the evenings, alone in her motel room, she'd found it hard to block the horrific images of the victims from her head. She'd needed some sort of reprieve—and it came in the form of fiction. Every night, she'd sit down at her computer and distract herself by writing the adventures of Agent Rachel Jane.

Writing books gave her the kind of control over people's fates that she didn't always manage to find in real life. In Rachel Jane's fictional world, the bad guys always lost, the good guys always won, and her sexy leading man, Agent Matthews, was always devoted and faithful.

Nothing like the real world at all, really, Grace thought with amusement. But it was comforting to lose herself in such a black-and-white creation when in reality she experienced nothing but gray. The first in the series had been a bestseller, and the second was an award winner. The third novel, she'd completed last summer, and it had debuted at the top of the bestseller list, staying there for weeks. Much to her publisher's horror, she hadn't yet begun another book, but she'd been focused on the real world—and the very real criminals in it.

"Grace!" A voice distracted her from her reverie. She turned, her face breaking into a grin when she caught sight of a blonde woman making her way through the crowd.

"Maggie!" Grace reached out for a hug. "Let me look at you," she said. "Oh, my gosh!" she exclaimed, holding her friend at arm's length and smiling in admiration. The deep purple Gucci gown she'd convinced Maggie to buy was a hit. "You look gorgeous," she said.

"Thanks to you." Maggie grinned. She was petite, with an explosion of blond curls framing her heart-shaped face. The rich purple silk set off her blue eyes perfectly, and the deep V-neck accentuated her curves. The only jewelry she wore was a vintage charm bracelet Grace had given her a few Christmases ago.

"Your closet is as boring as those cookie-cutter beige housing developments." Grace shrugged. "Someone has to drag you farther down the color wheel—it might as well be me."

"Well, you were right on this one," Maggie said. "I Skyped with Jake as I was getting ready, and I thought he was going to leap through the screen."

Grace laughed at the image this put in her head. Maggie's boyfriend, Jake O'Connor, was a mountain of a man, a Special Ops veteran with a devil-may-care attitude that fit nicely with Maggie's controlled, organized personality. It'd been a long time since she'd seen Maggie this happy in a relationship. "How's he doing?"

"Good," Maggie replied. "He asked me to tell you congratulations. And that he was sorry he couldn't make it."

"Is he going to be in California long?"

"Another week or two," Maggie said.

"I bet you miss him."

Maggie smiled, a small, private smile. "Maybe," she said. "Anyway, enough about me. Tonight's about you! Though I guess all the award winning is getting kind of boring."

"Never," Grace replied, lifting her chin with an exaggerated air that made Maggie chuckle. "You know how I like to win. I just wish I could forgo all the ceremonies."

"But you love getting dressed up," Maggie said.

"I don't know," Grace said, shrugging. "The older I get . . ." Here Maggie, two years her senior, snorted, but Grace grinned and continued, "I just . . . I feel like something's missing. And it's not a man," she said quickly as Maggie opened her mouth. "I'm a modern woman. I don't need any arm candy to feel complete."

"Need and want are two very different things," Maggie said. "There's nothing wrong with wanting a man in your life."

Grace wanted to smile at the optimism in Maggie's voice. She was so glad that her friend had found Jake. And being in love with him had changed Maggie for the better.

But Grace had been changed by a man once, and only once. And it had not been for the better.

Instead it had been a lesson she could never forget. It had shattered her soul, and all these years later, she still felt like she was scrambling to pick up the pieces. She wouldn't wish that kind of destruction on her worst enemy. And she'd promised herself she'd never make herself vulnerable enough for a man to get close enough again.

So she kept to her rules about men in her life: never let them get attached—getting attached herself was never even on the table—never let them spend the night, and never, ever sleep with anyone twice.

It was clean. Neat. Orderly. How she liked her life. How she *had* to live her life, because it was safer.

"No wanting or needing a man for this lady." Grace shook her head brusquely. "Not right now. It's silly anyway. I just need a new case. Something juicy to concentrate on. The book tour was only three weeks long, but my face still hurts from all the smiling."

The women moved deeper into the sculpture garden as they talked, navigating gracefully around both the statues and people. "This is my first time here," Maggie remarked as they passed a bright red abstract sculpture that was clearly influenced by early Cubism. "It's very impressive."

"It's an amazing collection," Grace agreed. "Some of my favorite pieces are here."

"Did you see that big sculpture that looks like a bunch of pipes hung midair?" Maggie asked, gesturing behind her.

"That's the *Needle Tower*," Grace said. "You don't like it?"

"I think modern art might be a little beyond me," Maggie confessed with a laugh.

"Nonsense!" a voice boomed out behind them.

"Frank!" A short man with gray hair and the droopy face of a bulldog walked up to them, and Maggie smiled, reaching out to embrace him. Frank Edenhurst, perpetually rumpled, had already wiggled loose from his bow tie, letting the ends hang down.

"Or should we call you Mr. Assistant Director?" Grace asked. After a harrowing case involving the kidnapping of a senator's daughter, Frank had recently been promoted at the Bureau. He'd been the one responsible for bringing Maggie back into the FBI—and Grace would always be grateful to him for it. She'd missed working with Maggie—who was always the most valuable member on any team she was on.

"Only if you want to get on my good side," Frank joked, his homely mug lighting up with a megawatt smile that hinted at his sweet side. "Congratulations, Grace. This is quite the to-do."

"Thank you," Grace said.

"We are very proud of her, aren't we?" Maggie asked, putting an arm around Grace's shoulders.

"Damn right," Frank said. "How'd that case in Delaware work out?" he asked Maggie.

"It was touch and go there for a while," Maggie said. "Didn't you read my report?"

"Why would I do that when you can just tell me now what happened?" Frank asked.

Grace laughed, shaking her head. Frank was notorious for his hatred of paperwork. "I'll let you two talk," she said. "My publisher's trying to flag me down anyway," she said, catching sight of the man waving at her over by a cluster of bronze statues. They nodded, and as they fell into a conversation, Grace made her way across the walk but was held up by a pair of politicians she knew from her parents' society dinners.

"Grace, congratulations," said Senator Cleary, a silver-haired man who was a longtime friend of her father's.

"Thank you, Senator," she said. Cleary was a vain man who could never resist looking in a mirror. It was almost second nature for Grace to take advantage of it. "I must say you're looking very dashing tonight."

"You're far too sweet to an old man like me," he said, but he preened a little under her warm flattery.

"Hello, Congressman." She nodded at his blond companion. The man was as corn-fed as they came, a staunch old-school Democrat and family man from Iowa who actually stood by his values. She was amazed he'd managed to last in DC this long. "How are the twins?"

"Tearing up the field at Iowa State," he said proudly.

"Go, Cyclones!" she said with a disarming wink, rewarded by his wry grin. "Now, gentlemen, I must leave you. Duty calls."

"Tell your father hello for me," the senator said.

"I'll do that," Grace nodded, flashing him a brief smile as she turned away, though she couldn't remember the last time she'd talked to her father, let alone seen him face-to-face. Six months ago? Seven?

She managed to walk across the garden without too many more entanglements. Jonathan Ames was waiting by one of the museum's groupings by Rodin, the unconventional nineteenth-century Frenchman whose sensual, rough-hewn style challenged the smooth perfection of his era.

"Darling." Jonathan Ames held out both his hands, swooping in to kiss her on one cheek, then another. His brilliant sage-green tux should have been loud and out of place in the sea of traditional black suits, but his outsize personality managed to make it work. "My superstar." He beamed at her, his bright white teeth gleaming. "I really wish you'd leave that nasty FBI work behind and write for me full-time. Think of the awards you'd win! The money! Think of the absence of danger! I'm begging you!"

Grace rolled her eyes good-naturedly at his drama. Jonathan's excess enthusiasm had almost put her off choosing to go with his house when demand for her first book escalated to a four-publisher bidding war. She'd wondered if someone so cheerful and bombastic could understand the darkness of her world. But she quickly learned that beneath the drama, Jonathan was serious and passionate. And when that passion was funneled into his authors' work, amazing things happened. Her first book spent twenty weeks on the *New York Times* bestseller list, and her second lasted twice as long. The third had been released just months ago. Grace had had to talk Jonathan down from an eight-week book tour to a jam-packed month.

Her boss had been reluctant to let her go until one of the media specialists pointed out it was good PR for the Bureau, especially since it'd been announced that Grace's second novel had won the prestigious Callahan Award for Crime Fiction.

"I'd go crazy if I was in front of my computer at home all day," she told Jonathan.

He tutted, then pursed his lips in disapproval. "You're crazy, darling. It'd be sublime. You could move to New York, mingle with the literary elite! You're killing me, with all this 'I have to stay in DC and save the world from serial killers' talk."

"But I *do* need to stay in DC and save the world from serial killers," Grace said patiently. "There are a lot of bad guys around."

"And I love that it's your personal mission to get them all," Jonathan said. "It's a PR dream. But I do worry about you."

Grace reached out and patted him on the shoulder. "You'll survive," she assured him. "I'm not your only writer."

"Thank God they don't all have your penchant for darkness," he said. "I'd be a mess. Now go! Shoo! Mingle with your adoring public. I've got networking to do." He waved her off.

Grace descended down the sculpture garden's path, picking up a glass of champagne from a nearby waiter and taking a sip.

"Grace, it's so nice to see you," said a woman's voice behind her.

Grace turned around abruptly, her face breaking into a broad smile as she saw who it was: a stately woman with glasses that matched her fiery coiffure. She wore a sari-inspired dress, the gold trim glinting in the lights set out in the garden. "Dr. James, I can't believe you came."

"Please, call me Clara, dear. We're years past your student days," said her former professor warmly, embracing her. But Grace couldn't quite think of her on a first-name basis; she'd always held this woman, friendly as she was, in awe. "And of course I came. You were one of my best students. I'm very pleased for you. And Martha would've been so proud."

Grace's heart sank, her breath catching in her throat. Grief was a funny thing—just when you thought you'd mastered it, it crept up on you. Martha Lee had been a pioneer in criminology—not just as a psychologist, but as a woman in-filtrating a field that was notoriously male dominated. She was a woman with a keen mind and an even sharper eye. Grace had considered it the greatest privilege of her life that Dr. Lee had taken a liking to her. She'd become Grace's mentor, even written her recommendations to the Academy, which she'd retired from in the '80s to teach.

For years, Grace and Dr. Lee kept in touch, with emails, phone calls, the occasional lunch. Grace had just been finishing up her third book last year when she got the news that Dr. Lee had died in a car crash. It had been a hard blow—Dr. Lee had always been so full of life, it was nearly impossible to think she was gone. After the funeral Grace had returned home to her empty house. She'd found herself restless, unable to settle until she sat down in front of her computer and finished the final chapter of her book, almost as if Dr. Lee had been guiding her.

She'd dedicated *Trust Is a Bitter Game* to her memory. A small token for a woman who had done so much, for sure, but Grace knew she would have been pleased.

"I saw the dedication," Dr. James said, reaching out and squeezing Grace's arm. "It was very touching. And I know her husband appreciated the gesture. When I had dinner with him a few months ago, he mentioned that you'd sent him a signed copy. He keeps it in her library, with all her other books."

Grace blinked, trying to tamp down the emotion twisting inside her. "That's incredibly sweet of him," she said. "How is he doing?"

"I'm sure you can guess," Dr. James said. "It was so sudden."

Grace nodded. "It didn't feel real when I first got the news. She was always so strong. Like she was unbreakable. She never let anyone belittle or speak down to her. She taught me so much. I am very lucky to have had her in my life."

"We all were. She was a brilliant criminologist and wonderful human being," Professor James said. "You know, I think some of your other professors are here tonight." She looked over Grace's head, scanning the crowd. "I see Carthage over there. He taught you, didn't he? I seem to remember you transferred from University of Maryland?"

"I did," Grace said smoothly, not looking over her shoulder to see where Professor James was gesturing. She couldn't stop the slight stiffening of her spine, and her smile froze on her face. But she couldn't flinch—she wouldn't. "Dr.—I mean, Clara, would you excuse me? My publisher's waving like crazy, so I think it's time for the speeches."

"Of course, dear," Professor James said. "Go. And congratulations!"

Grace hurried away, her throat tight, her fingers clenching around the crystal champagne flute as if it were the only thing keeping her sane. She didn't go up to the stage; the speakers hadn't been called up yet. She needed . . .

She needed space. Shelter. Something other than this crowd.

She walked as fast as the long skirt of her

dress allowed and ducked into the now empty plaza at the center of the museum. The rest of the party had filtered into the sculpture garden, drawn there by the lights, the wine, and the art.

She stood in the center of the plaza, turning in a slow circle, taking in the immense circular concrete edifice around her. There was something cavernous about the tall gray walls, the way they surrounded her so completely. A protective space.

She took another sip of champagne, hoping it'd calm her nerves. It took her a moment to realize that her clutch was buzzing. She flipped it open and pulled out her phone.

"Hello?"

"Grace, it's Paul."

Special Agent Paul Harrison wasn't just her boss—he was a good friend. Once upon a time, he'd been Maggie's fiancé, but the two of them hadn't been well-suited. One of the worst things about being a profiler was not being able to shut off the analyzing. Grace had seen the signs from the start, but she couldn't do much but help them both when it fell apart. Maggie had recovered faster than Paul—she had so much trauma in her past, her survival instinct kicked in. Paul had taken longer, but Grace had been encouraged when he recently mentioned dating again.

He was such a great guy, any woman would be lucky to have him in her life.

"I know you have your event tonight," Paul said. "Congrats, by the way. But you made me promise to call you if anything came up, remember? If I'm interrupting . . ."

"No," Grace said quickly, even though she could hear the mic check sputtering. She'd have to step up to the stage and begin her speech soon. "What's going on?"

"There's a case. You don't have to come if—"

Her stomach leapt. A case. Exactly what she needed. "I can come," Grace said. "It'll take about an hour, though. I still have a speech to give. And my publisher sent a car, so I'll have to go home to pick up mine and change."

"Actually, if you don't mind, I've sent someone to come pick you up," Paul said. "One of my new agents. He has your go-bag from your office too so you can change. Does that work?"

Grace smiled to herself. Of course Paul had covered every detail. He was such a Boy Scout—always prepared. "You think of everything," she told him. "That's perfect."

"He'll be outside the museum waiting for you when you finish," Paul said. "You two can get to know each other and head over."

"I look forward to it," Grace said. "I'll see you in about an hour."

"See you then, Grace."

She hung up, and with one more bracing breath, she headed back into the garden, where her colleagues and fans were waiting.

CHAPTER 2

Gavin adjusted his tie for what felt like the hundredth time. It was a loop of dark blue silk his little sister had gotten him when he'd joined the FBI. The family dinner that night to celebrate had been raucous—three generations of Walkers under the same roof. His brother Daniel had even flown in from Texas for the occasion, and Sarah had pulled him out on the porch to give him the gift.

"I know you don't like to dress up, but all the FBI agents on TV wear ties," she'd said.

Gavin smiled at the memory. His kid sister was thoughtful and sweet to give him a sort of talisman to wear as he left behind his old life as a cop for the new challenge of FBI work.

There were times he still couldn't quite believe he'd done it. He'd given up the dream of this kind of elite work when he'd left the military. He'd spent ten years at DC Metro, the first two on bomb squad and the last eight working homicide. He'd loved his work, but there was always that part of him that was seeking something different. That itch under his skin, the one that had made him a great soldier, that would've made him a greater intelligence officer if he hadn't . . .

Gavin sighed. There was no use dwelling on what-ifs. Especially now that he'd finally taken such a leap.

When he'd run into Paul Harrison at a mutual friend's barbecue last year and got to talking about his FBI work, Gavin had felt that now familiar restlessness that he'd managed to ignore for a decade. But this time, he had decided to do something about it. He'd met with Harrison several times and just weeks later, with a job offer in hand, found himself resigning from the police force. His military background was considered quite an asset, combined with his years on the force. So he flew to Georgia for the intensive training former police officers underwent to become special agents, then to Virginia for more training. And now he was officially one of them. He belonged to a special investigative team—even though he hadn't met all of them yet.

Twenty minutes ago, he'd gotten the call from Harrison to stand by for instructions. So he'd put on a suit and made sure his weapon was loaded before sitting down to wait.

He wasn't nervous. There wasn't a lot that shook him. The Walkers were a steady lot—it's why they all became cops. He knew what to expect with this work, even if things were a little different with the Feds. But when it came down to it, murder was murder, no matter who he worked for. And he'd spent his entire career tracking down killers and bringing them to justice.

He'd been on the job for ten years and he'd seen horrific things in that time. The very worst of humanity, murderers and rapists and those who sought to destroy with bombs and explosives. But he'd also seen the very best of people: communities coming together around survivors and their families . . . the strength of a mother who relentlessly advocated for her dead son when no one else believed he'd been murdered . . . and the outpouring of love from others that often came with such tragic loss.

His grandfather always used to say he'd search for a silver lining in everything, and maybe that was true, Gavin thought with a wry grin. It had both helped and hurt him in his work. He had an idealistic streak, and he knew it. But where there was idealism, there was hope. And hope and homicide could be a dangerous and disheartening mix.

Gavin pulled at his tie again before stopping himself, his restless hands going to his hair—which an ex-girlfriend once affectionately called *floppy*—instead.

His phone rang, Harrison's name flashing on the screen. Finally.

He picked up. "This is Walker," he said.

"It's Harrison. I've just got off the phone with our profiler," Harrison said. "She'll be ready in about thirty minutes, if you can pick her up at the museum. You two can head over to the scene together. The forensic team has already been dispatched, and I'll be waiting for you when you get here."

"Got it," Gavin said. "Any details about the case?"

"All I've got is female victim, early twenties, dead from a gunshot wound. She had a government ID on her, which is why we've been called in. Zooey and the rest of forensics should be arriving in about fifteen minutes, so we'll know more then."

Gavin nodded. "Traffic shouldn't be bad. I'll head out now to pick up Agent . . ."

"Oh, I guess her name would help," Harrison said, laughing at himself a little. "Special Agent Grace Sinclair."

Shock, the anticipatory, warm kind that hits you hard and fast, filled him. He could almost hear the husky voice in his head, feel the teasing scratch of nails down his back.

"Did your paths ever cross when you were working homicide?" Harrison asked.

Gavin swallowed hard. "No," Gavin said. "I don't believe they did."

Technically, that wasn't a lie. He hadn't met Grace on a case. They'd never worked together.

"She's quite exceptional," Harrison said. "I'm sorry I wasn't able to introduce you two when you met the rest of the team, but she's been touring for her book."

"Right," Gavin said. Those books. He hadn't been able to resist buying the first one when it came out, and after reading it, he'd wished he hadn't. The love scenes between Grace's heroine and her lover had evoked memories he'd worked hard to forget. When the second was released, he'd managed to stop himself from flipping through it, for his own sake. But every time he saw it in a bookstore window, he remembered that night—he remembered *her*.

Some memories—some women—they stuck with you.

And Grace Sinclair was a woman no one forgot. If he'd seen her walking down the street one day, just gotten the barest glimpse of her, her face would have haunted him until the end of time.

But he'd gotten more than a glimpse. He'd had her in his arms, in his bed. He could remember the softness of her skin even now. The laughter in her voice as he unzipped her dress, the dark tumble of her hair when it came free of its pins.

Eighteen hours, give or take. That's how long he'd had her. To touch, to kiss, to listen to as she extolled the virtues of jazz and art, her eyes sparkling with a fire she didn't let many people see. But dawn came, the sun rose, and when he woke, she was gone. It was her way. There were rumors, of course, about her. DC was a small town in a lot of ways, a gossipy one. He'd heard them all. But this was where his damn silver-lining thinking got him in trouble. Because a part of him had taken Grace to bed certain as hell she'd still be there in the morning. That it would be more than one night. That he'd for sure be an exception.

". . . museum, Walker?" Harrison was asking.

Gavin cleared his throat. "What was that?"

"Do you have directions to the museum?"

"Yes. I'm on my way now."

"I'll have the crime scene address texted to your phone. I'll see you two there."

Harrison hung up and Gavin set his phone down, his thoughts scattered in a dozen different directions. But then he reached out, his hand closing around his gun in its holster, and his mind cleared. He fastened it to his belt, his shoulders straightening and his mind clearing as a sense of focused purpose filled him.

This was going to be complicated, but there was a job to do and a killer to find.

The job came first. Always.

CHAPTER 3

The speech had gone well, Grace thought as she headed out of the museum and toward the steps leading to the street. They'd laughed in the right places and showered her with congratulations before she'd managed to slip away. The fanfare that came with being a popular author was nice, and she enjoyed the process of writing and putting her characters through their paces, but it was the real-life background work—the nitty-gritty of profiling in the aftermath of horror—that made her heart sing.

Night had come, and it was time to get started. She could feel the familiar tightness in her stomach—a mix of anticipation and dread that rose inside her with every crime scene. She paused at the top of the steps, scanning the street below. A black SUV was parked at the curb, still running. This had to be the new agent—Paul had taken on a few new team members while she'd been on her book tour. She hadn't had a chance to meet them yet.

Gathering a handful of her skirt, she raised it slightly as she made her way down the steps. She was about halfway to the street when the door of the SUV swung open. A man walked around the vehicle and leaned against the passenger door.

Grace froze midstep the second she recognized him. It wasn't . . . It couldn't be. He wasn't with the FBI. Surely she would have heard about it if he'd been recruited . . .

But the proof was there right in front of her. Gavin Walker. Six feet five inches of pure frustration. Her heart picked up a beat, but her steps down the stairs were steady as she approached him.

Back then, he was a homicide detective working for the DC police. The last time she'd seen him, he was fast asleep and very naked. She'd slipped out of his place with a speed and silence that came only with practice, her thighs still pleasantly aching from their night spent together.

That had been two years ago. He'd called the next day, wanting to get together, and she'd ignored the ringing phone, because that's what she did. Those were the rules.

She hadn't expected how hard it was not picking up that phone call. Temptation wasn't something she experienced often—or dealt with well. She'd tried to bury that feeling—and the memories of her night with Gavin—deep in her mind.

But that was very difficult to do when he was standing there looking just as handsome as ever.

He smiled as she made her way down to him. That broad, cocky smile was one of the reasons she fell into his bed. It had twisted her up then, and even now she could feel her body responding to it. Her skin prickled under his warm gaze; she was suddenly acutely aware of how her dress fit her, the summer air against her bare back. But Grace kept her face emotionless—she couldn't let him see how off-center she suddenly felt. He'd just use it to tease her.

"Detective Walker," she said coolly. "Are you playing chauffeur these days?"

His brown eyes twinkled in the streetlights. "It's Special Agent Walker now," he said.

"So I see," Grace replied, coming to a stop in front of him. This close, she was intensely aware of his size. She was a tall woman who enjoyed her heels—she wasn't used to having to look up to men. But he was built like a warrior of yore. The span of his shoulders, the strength that seemed to ripple around him made her want to shiver . . . not in fear but in anticipation. If she closed her eyes, she was sure she'd drift back to their night together, how his hands spanned her waist, how he picked her up like she weighed nothing.

She needed to pull herself together. It wouldn't do at all for him to realize how much seeing him affected her. *She* didn't even want to think about that.

She smiled. "I must admit, I'm a little surprised," Grace said. What was his real reason for being here? Paul had surely told him who he was picking up. Had he volunteered? Was this just another one of his teasing games? Or was it more?

"Did I go against your profile of me, Grace?" he asked, folding his arms across his chest, leaning against the SUV like a cowboy in a Wild West saloon.

She glared at him. "Not at all," she said smoothly. "You clearly always desired more for yourself. Your ambition would let you climb only so high at DC Metro. I'm more surprised you got on Paul's team. He's notoriously choosy with his recruits."

"Harrison's a good guy," Gavin said with a casual shrug. "He likes rules. I like rules."

Grace snorted. The last thing in the world she'd say was that Gavin Walker liked rules.

He was the kind of man who didn't break them but who was more than willing to bend them. His keen mind and sharp senses had made him the youngest homicide detective DC Metro had seen in decades. And now here he was—an FBI agent. On her team.

Dammit. This introduced the kind of awkwardness Grace tried to avoid in her life. She didn't mix business and pleasure ever. And now pleasure—and oh, what pleasure, she could still vividly remember the searing heat of his hands on her skin—was standing there, expecting her to work with him.

Why hadn't she bothered to ask Paul about his new hire? Grace mentally cursed herself for being so distracted by the book tour. At least she would've had some prior warning before she walked out of the gala and into Gavin Walker's orbit again.

"I've got your go-bag in the SUV." Gavin jerked a thumb behind him. "Crime scene's in College Park, so we should get going."

Grace's brow furrowed. The last thing she wanted was to get in the SUV and spend thirty minutes in traffic with him. But it seemed she had no choice.

"I'll change in the back," she said, reaching for the door just as he did the same.

Their hands brushed against each other, his

skin warm and just on the edge of rough on his trigger finger. An electric shock traveled down Grace's spine and he grinned when she moved her hand, allowing him to open the door for her.

"Ladies first," he drawled.

Inside, her go-bag was sitting there innocently as Gavin hopped in the driver's seat, started the SUV, and headed toward the freeway.

Grace glanced at her bag and then back at the driver's seat, heat rising in her face.

"I promise I won't look," he said, and her eyes met his in the rearview mirror.

"Liar," she said.

His eyes crinkled with mirth before shifting back to the road. "My mama raised me a gentleman, I'll have you know."

"I'll believe that when I see it," Grace said, yanking her bag open and pulling out the skirt and slightly wrinkled indigo blouse.

Keeping her gaze on the rearview mirror to make sure Gavin was being a gentleman, she hiked up the long skirt of her ball gown, pulling on the pencil skirt from her bag underneath it.

That, unfortunately, was the easy, less revealing part of her quick-change scheme. She unzipped the side zip of her gown and reached behind her neck, where the silver ribbons were tied. The SUV stopped at a light, and her throat went dry as she lifted her eyes to the rearview mirror and Gavin's were staring right back at her.

She arched a brow. "What was that about being a gentleman, Walker?"

His brown eyes flickered with a promise that made her skin tighten. "You make it hard, Sinclair," he said, his voice rough.

Her eyes still on his, she pulled the tie keeping her dress up. It was a silent dare: *Are you the man you say you are?*

Or are you the man I think you are?

Just as the silvery material began to slip down her chest, his eyes returned to the road. He cleared his throat, and she watched as his fingers clenched the steering wheel—hard.

She smiled to herself, shrugging on the blouse and pushing her gown down her waist and to the floor of the SUV.

Once her clothes were in order, she waited for the next stoplight and then crawled from the back seat to the front.

"So, are you going to fill me in?" she asked, tucking away a stray strand of hair that had come loose from her braids.

"Harrison didn't give me too many details," Gavin said as they merged onto the highway on-ramp. "His last text said something about a sniper attack."

Grace frowned at the address on the GPS. "At a Chinese restaurant?"

Gavin shrugged. "Stranger things have happened."

"How many casualties?" Grace asked.

"One."

That made her brow furrow even more. Snipers usually liked to cause more damage than that. They liked chaos, to put people on edge, to create mass hysteria with just a few bullets.

They fell quiet as he drove them to the crime scene, time ticking by until finally, he broke the silence: "What's that big profiler brain of yours thinking?" Gavin asked.

Grace glared at him, not liking his tone.

"What?" he asked.

"I realize that you come from a type of police work that's all about gut instinct and gumshoeing it, but you're not a detective anymore. You're playing with the big guns. And I'm the biggest gun on Paul's team. You should keep that in mind."

Gavin whistled. "Is that a threat?"

"It's some friendly advice," Grace said. "Paul never would have recruited you if you didn't have what it takes. But part of working on a team like this means respecting each other's specialties."

"So you think I don't respect you," Gavin said, flipping the turn signal on and changing lanes. Their exit was coming up.

"I *know* you don't respect what I do," Grace said.

"You're wrong," he said simply.

It startled her. She'd expected a bigger protest, some male blustering. Instead he just calmly took their exit and turned onto the main street of College Park.

She could see blue and red lights getting brighter and larger as they pulled up to a pair of police cordons. Gavin flashed his badge at the officer standing in front of them, who motioned them forward.

Grace reached for the door handle when his voice stopped her. Made her turn back to him. "I respect what you do, Grace. It's not how I do things, not how I see things. But I respect it."

She looked at him, searching for any shred of deception in his face or voice.

"But you don't respect what I do," he continued. "You said *gut instinct* like it was a bad word. That's not very nice."

There it was again. That damn teasing in his voice. It riled her up. It pissed her off.

It made her . . . want things.

She looked him up and down, slowly, deliberately. And when she met his eyes, they were hot, gleaming in the flashing lights of the police cars all around them.

"Do something worthy of my respect and I will," she said.

Without another word, she opened the car door and marched toward the crime scene.

CHAPTER 4

Gavin watched her stride across that parking lot like a queen.

Grace Sinclair was a living puzzle. So beautiful she could've gotten anything she wanted by just standing there and batting her eyes. But instead she wielded that beauty like a weapon. Used it to lull people into a false sense of security. A man was helpless against a woman like that.

God, it had been agony to keep his attention on the road as she changed in the back seat. He could hear every rustle of fabric against her skin, the excruciating sound of her zipper being drawn down. It had taken all he had in him not to turn around. Or pull the damn SUV over and crawl into the back seat with her.

And she knew it. Of course she did. She knew everything.

He hadn't been joking when he'd mentioned

her big, bad profiler brain. She was brilliant, the kind of smart that went over his head. In the desert, he'd learned to rely on his gut and his instincts first, because in a world of spies, that was often the only thing he could trust. It was a black-and-white worldview: us and them. Bad and good. Right and wrong.

But Grace saw things differently. She saw the shades of gray. She saw the root of evil. She sought it out with no fear, always digging, always curious. She put herself in those bad men's shoes, day by day, and it amazed him that kind of darkness didn't rub off on her.

"Are you coming?" Her voice interrupted his thoughts. She'd turned in the parking lot, about thirty feet ahead from him.

"Yeah," he said, hurrying over to catch up with her. "Hey, we should probably talk about what we should say," he told her.

"What we should say?" she asked, looking at him, confused.

"About us. How we met. How we know each other. Harrison's already asked me if we've crossed paths when I was a cop."

"I'll handle it," she said.

"Are you sure?" he asked.

"Don't worry about it," she said.

They walked toward the restaurant, only to be intercepted by Harrison.

"Walker, nice to see you again," he said, holding his hand out. Gavin shook it. "You two get to know each other on the ride over?" he asked.

"We already know each other," Grace said.

Gavin frowned. He'd been prepared for a lie. He wasn't the kind of guy to brag about his sexual exploits. Or to throw her under the bus like that to her boss.

"Oh, yeah?" Harrison said, handing her a pair of gloves. "How?"

"I slept with him two years ago," Grace said casually, snapping them on.

Gavin coughed, trying not to turn red as he watched Harrison's mouth drop open. Grace's matter-of-fact manner was almost funny, but he knew better than to laugh.

Grace rolled her eyes. "Men," she muttered.

"Yes, we're so indiscreet," Gavin deadpanned.

And there it was: a glimpse of that playful fire in her eyes. It was just a flash and then it was gone, but he'd seen it.

She was amused and refusing to show it.

Her mouth curved disapprovingly instead. "Where's the body?"

"Um, this way," Harrison said, clearly thrown. Gavin shot him an apologetic look and got a puzzled smile back. "Let's get to work," Harrison said. "We can get into . . . er, history later."

The street was lined with old brick buildings,

a Chinese restaurant with blinking neon signs at the very end of the street.

The smell of grease and sweet-and-sour pork curled in his nose. A group of police mingled on the sidewalk ahead, making sure the perimeter was secure.

"So, what do we have?" Gavin asked Harrison.

"Female. Early twenties." Paul led them to the crime scene tape blocking off the alley next to the restaurant. "Jogger, from the looks of the outfit."

"She was probably using the park trail," Grace said.

"Kind of late," Gavin said.

Grace shrugged. "Some people like running at night. I do."

"You've got self-defense skills, though," Gavin said.

"Maybe she did too," Grace pointed out. "The weapon used was a sniper rifle, wasn't it?"

Harrison nodded. "Forensics has determined that from the angle and the bullets, it looks like a sniper."

"Is Zooey here?" Grace asked. "Have you met her yet, Walker?"

"The blue-haired one, right?" Gavin asked. "We got to talk a little when I met the team. She was telling me about some experiments with maggots and decomposition. It went a little over my head, though, I'm afraid."

Paul smiled. "Zooey's a little kooky, but she's the best there is."

"She is not kooky," Grace said. "She's original."

She moved in front of them, staring up at the tops of the buildings. Gavin followed suit, wondering what she was thinking, what was putting that frown on her face.

So he asked. "What are you thinking?"

She looked from the roof to him, her gray eyes widening in surprise at his question. "Snipers are meticulous," she said, looking back up at the top of the laundromat across the alley from the Golden Lantern. "Do we have forensics up there yet?"

"Half of Zooey's team is headed up there," Harrison said.

Gavin stared up at where Grace was fixated. "This doesn't feel right, does it?" he asked.

"I'm not much for gut feelings myself," she remarked, but her eyes were still flicking from building to building, and he knew she was drawing the same conclusion as he had the second he'd seen the alley.

"This place had terrible sight lines for a sniper," Gavin said.

She raised an eyebrow, looking at him out of the corner of her eye. "And how would you know that?"

"I'm not just a pretty face," he told her. She

snorted. "I did four years in the Army," he explained. "I was a sniper." Her eyes flickered and his stomach clenched. Was she buying it? "The angles here are all wrong. It's too tight a space." He lifted his arms, to show how narrow the alley was.

Her mouth—painted a deep, distracting red—quirked up. She knew he was right and she wasn't too proud to admit it, but it would take her a second. That way she had more control.

Grace liked control. He didn't need to be a profiler to know that. He was pretty sure the only place she let go of that exquisite control was in the bedroom. Perhaps that's why she never stayed. It was too much risk. Too much to lose.

"You're right," she said. "No pro would choose this place," Grace agreed.

"You think it's just random, then?" Gavin asked. He looked over her shoulder, down the alley, where the forensic team was swarmed around the body, taking samples and pictures.

"Anything missing from the body?" Grace asked Harrison.

He shook his head. "Our unsub didn't even bother to make it look like a robbery. She's still got her engagement ring on—and that thing's big. He could've snatched it, easy."

"You said she had government ID on her, though," Gavin said.

"That's why we're involved," Harrison said. "Her name is Janice Wacomb. She's a secretary at the Department of Transportation. Since she was a federal employee, we got called in by the local guys."

"So she goes out for a run," Grace said, back to staring up at the roofs of the buildings. "It's a normal night for her. She gets in her miles in the park and then heads over here. Maybe she had a takeout order? Do you have people talking to the restaurant employees?"

"I've got people asking questions there right now," Harrison said.

"If they get anything, yell for me," Grace said. She turned to Gavin. "You ready?" she asked.

"It's not exactly my first crime scene, Sinclair," he said, using her last name because he knew it annoyed her.

Her mouth did that cute twisting thing when she was frustrated.

"Okay, then," she said. "Show me what you got."

It was a challenge. And Gavin never backed down from one of those.

"With pleasure," he said.

They walked down the narrow alley toward the body lying on the pavement ahead.

CHAPTER 5

Janice Wacomb was on her back, her gray sweatshirt stained with blood, her eyes staring blankly at the sky.

Grace felt something tighten in her chest, like a fist around her heart. She couldn't say how many dead bodies she had seen—but each crime scene was like the first time.

"Anything new?" Paul asked the petite woman in white coveralls crouched near the body. Her neon blue hair looked practically radioactive in the bright lights. It was pulled up in a series of spiky buns topped with a vintage crocheted hairnet.

Zooey straightened, squaring her shoulders. "Just getting some hair samples. Pretty sure they're canine, though." She smiled at Grace and Gavin. "Love the lipstick, Grace. Agent Walker, it's nice to see you again."

"Gavin, please," he said. "It's good to see you too. How are the maggots?"

Zooey's face lit up. "They're *great*!" she said. "I've introduced a new set to this corpse that—"

"Zooey," Paul said, sounding like a stern father.

Zooey sighed. "Okay. So here's the situation: This doesn't look professional to me," she said. "It's messy. Snipers—at least the ones who are trained—aren't messy. At least in my experience."

"It's a bad spot," Gavin agreed. "No good places for a sniper's perch."

"Brawn and brains, be still my heart," Zooey said, fanning herself. Grace suppressed a smile at her antics, though she couldn't blame her. Gavin was the full package.

"Gavin's spot on," Zooey continued. "It's a terrible place for a sniper attack. Which is why our unsub missed. Look." She gestured at the dumpster ten feet away from the body. "One of the bullets hit there and ricocheted into the wall. And then over here." She pointed to the wall behind her, where two big chunks of the brick were missing. "He missed three times just to shoot her twice."

"Why would he choose such a long-range weapon if he didn't know how to use it properly?" Grace mused, stepping closer to the woman's body.

Gavin did the same and their shoulders touched as they crouched down next to Janice.

Her sweatshirt—a gray zip-up hoodie—was well-worn, fraying at the edges of the sleeves. Her running shoes weren't flashy, but they were a good brand. She probably ran every day. This was someone who exercised to exercise, not to be seen. Maybe that was why she'd been running so late? Maybe she'd decided on a few quick miles before picking up some greasy Chinese and just walked into the wrong person's crosshairs? Or were her late-night runs a habit, and she'd been targeted?

There was something nagging at the back of her mind as she stared at the body. That feeling you get when you've forgotten something right in front of you. What was it?

"What do you see?" Gavin asked her quietly.

Grace's eyes traced over Janice's body, taking in the subtle differences and signs. "She's an experienced runner," Grace said. "She's probably done a few marathons. Maybe one a year. Look at how worn her shoes are. She favors her left leg over her right. She's probably right-handed, or maybe it's from a sports injury. She's neat, organized. Look at her nails." She pointed at the sensibly short fingernails, painted a pale, inoffensive pink. "Running was her stress relief. Like a form of meditation for her. Her guard would've been down. She didn't see it coming."

"And the shooter?" Gavin asked.

What about the shooter? Grace stepped away from the body, scanning the area. Where would he go? Where would he feel safest?

"Zooey, can you tell where the unsub's perch was?" she asked.

"From the direction of the missed bullets and the way she fell, I'd say he was somewhere on the laundromat's roof." Zooey pointed toward the building to their right. "The team I sent up should be looking for evidence by now."

Grace looked up at the flat roof, then back at Janice's body, her mind putting it together.

"You said she had her phone on her?" she asked Paul.

"Zooey's got it."

Zooey handed her the phone with a gloved hand. On the lock screen, the reminder Jog— 8:30 PM was still flashing.

Okay. So running this late was a regular thing. As a secretary, Janice would have been someone who liked routine and schedules. She probably had her day mapped out to the minute.

Which meant the shooter would have to carefully plan this, to get into the right window of time. He'd have to watch her for days, maybe even weeks or months, to get her routine down to a *T*.

Was he someone she knew? Why else choose a weapon he obviously wasn't skilled with? Because she'd recognize him if he approached her? Because she'd run away if she saw him?

"Had she ever filed any police reports?" she asked Paul. "Harassment? Stalking? Sexual assault?"

"Nothing," he replied, shaking his head.

"Maybe he didn't want to be seen because she knew him," Gavin suggested. "Or maybe he's just really inexperienced."

"Or shy," Grace said.

Gavin's brow knit. "The shy ones are always the ones who lose it the most in the end," he said.

"That—" Grace started, automatically ready to argue, but then she stopped and took a deep breath. Paul had enough on his plate; he didn't need her bickering with Walker just because he rankled her. "Has that been your experience?" she asked finally.

His eyes twinkled with amusement. "It has," he said. "And hey, it might be the trifecta. He could be a shy first-time killer who knew her."

"But why?" Grace asked, not really to him but to herself. That was always the question. The *why* would lead to clues to the *who*. "Why would he want her dead?"

She glanced back up at the roof, where forensic techs had gathered, searching for evidence. Maybe this was guilt—then the lack of skill would make more sense. Especially if it was the unsub's first kill. He'd want the distance, the removal from the moment.

He wouldn't want to see her eyes. He might have obsessed about that. Chosen the long-distance weapon to avoid a face-to-face, even if it made for a harder kill.

"We should check the gun stores," Gavin said.

"Yes," Grace said. "We should look at the last six weeks of video surveillance. He would've acquired the rifle recently."

"Who are we looking for?" Paul asked.

"Male," Grace said, circling Janice's body again. There was something off about her, and she couldn't quite place it. Was it her hair? No, it was in a no-nonsense ponytail; even the elastic was brown and ordinary, blending in with her hair. "He probably has a white-collar job, a nine-to-five. So he has relative freedom at night. He's smart but cowardly. He might not have very good social skills—especially around women. That would explain the need for distance when it comes to killing. This isn't a guy who makes women comfortable. This is a guy who triggers their internal alarm bells. So he's had to work around that in order to fulfill his killing needs. He might work in education or IT. It might have taken him a few visits to the shop to get up his nerve to buy the weapon. When they're going through the surveillance video, the techs should tag the men who show up more than once."

"Looks like Janice was engaged," Gavin said, pointing to the sapphire ring on her left hand. "Fiancé would know her schedule. Maybe something went wrong? Wedding planning got too stressful? He cheated? Or she did?"

"You can check out the fiancé, but I doubt it's him," Grace said. "We're looking for a guy who wanted to stay hidden. Maybe needed to stay hidden. If this was the fiancé's doing, he could've come right up to her without her suspecting anything. Shot her quickly with a handgun and run. It's faster, it's more efficient, and it doesn't involve expensive weaponry that's a pain to carry around. No, this guy . . . he likes the shadows."

"Professional resentment, maybe?" Gavin suggested.

"Possibly." Grace nodded. "We should see what she's been working on at the Department of Transportation. If she had any problems with people at the office."

She looked down at Janice again, trying to figure out what it was about the body that was niggling at her. But she couldn't place it. Was she just searching for a clue that wasn't there, or was she missing something? She hated this feeling, an uncertainty that had no place in her life. She took a deep breath. "I think that's all, for now, at least. Once we have more information, I can put together a better profile."

"Okay," Paul said. "Zooey, you need anything else from Grace or Gavin?"

Zooey shook her head. "I'll have everything in the lab by the morning. Brianne's headed there now to wait for the body."

"You can go home, then," Paul said to Grace. "You too, Gavin. Thanks for coming out. I'll see you both in the morning?"

"I'll bring the coffee," Gavin said.

"Good man," Paul said, smiling.

"Sinclair, you coming?" Gavin asked her.

She looked at him, assessing for a moment. "Yes," she said.

She followed Gavin into the SUV and got inside. "I could get an Uber," she said. "We do live on opposite ends of the city."

"I remember," he said, grinning, starting the engine.

"Is this the way it's going to be?" she asked as he pulled out of the parking lot and onto the street. "Are you just going to tease your way through my life?"

His smile widened. "You know what I think, Grace? I think you're secretly pleased to see me."

"Oh, really?" God, his cockiness was insufferable.

"We should go get a drink," Gavin said. "Catch up. You can explain why you never called."

Grace glanced over at him, suddenly calculating. "I know a place," she said. "Turn right."

She'd managed to surprise him, but he obeyed her directions over the next ten minutes, finally coming to a stop on the curb on a quiet street.

"Where's this bar again?" he asked, looking over his shoulder.

Grace reached over and plucked the keys out of the ignition. His hand lashed out, fast and precise, grabbing her wrist. Their eyes met and the air in the SUV immediately changed.

Suddenly, they weren't two agents. They weren't two people who slept with each other either.

No, suddenly, they were assessing each other like a predator scoping out prey.

"Grace," Gavin warned.

"You lied back there in the alley," she said, her gaze unmoving from his. "You weren't a sniper in the Army."

His lips twitched. "And how do you reckon that?"

Her heart pounded in her chest. Maybe she should've waited to confront him. But if her suspicions were true . . .

Well, she had to be sure. Especially after the CIA had meddled with Maggie's last case. The previous—and corrupt—director could've had moles remaining that the investigation hadn't found.

"If you'd been a sniper, there's no way they would've put you on bomb squad when you joined the force," Grace said. "You would've been assigned to SWAT."

"Not if I requested a change of pace."

His fingers slowly loosened around her wrist and she pulled the keys away from him, licking her suddenly dry lips.

Her eyes narrowed. Was he really trying to bullshit her? Now, of all times? Well, if he wanted to play that game, she was going to go for the jugular. "I've seen you naked, Walker," she said.

And there it was: his brown eyes darkened, the teasing snuffed out, seriousness spreading across his face.

"You have gunshot scars on your back," she continued. "And not the kind that were taken out and stitched up in a nice, clean hospital. You also have scarring on your feet. I bet you all the money in my bank account that if I pulled up your X-rays, your feet would be riddled with microfractures from being beaten with rubber tubing. And that's not even touching on the six-inch scar on your chest that's clearly a surgical scar over a much older, much cruder wound. Because when they catch spies, they torture them. And if you're a very good spy, they just keep on torturing you because a good spy never gives up their intel."

"A good spy never gets caught," he said.

"Well, consider yourself caught," Grace said.

"Oh, yeah?" There was a dangerous rumble to his voice, one that made Grace want to shiver. Instead her hand went for her gun.

"You were military intelligence," she said. "It makes sense, really. You're a little slippery, aren't you? And you're a charmer. A golden tongue, they call it. I bet you could just talk your targets into handing over intel, couldn't you?"

"I can neither confirm or deny," he said, and there it was again: that smile.

He kept trying to play her.

Her gun was out and on him in a second. His eyes widened.

"Christ, Grace, buy me dinner first," he drawled.

Anger sparked inside her. He was seriously joking? Now? "Who are you working for?" she demanded.

"I work for Harrison, just like you," Gavin said,

staring at her calmly, like she didn't have a gun on him.

"Bullshit," Grace said. "Do you think I'm stupid? Once a spy, always a spy. So tell me who you work for. CIA? One of the off-the-books collectives? Why are you here?"

"Grace." Gavin looked at her, his face somber. "I work for Harrison. I am not CIA. And I am not a spy."

She wanted to believe him. She truly did. But the CIA—under a crooked director—had been responsible for trying to stage a coup over Maggie's last case. They'd sent assassins after Jake. Paul could've died. The little girl Maggie had been trying to rescue could've died.

She was not going to risk her team.

"You don't get *out* of that kind of work," Grace said.

"You do when they consider you defective," Gavin ground out.

Grace frowned. "What are you talking about?"

Gavin sighed. "Can you point the gun elsewhere while I explain?"

She lowered her gun. Slightly.

"God, I should've known," he muttered. "I told Harrison he should clue you in. You're right," he said. "I was military intelligence. I was good, Grace. I was the *best*. I was four years into what was supposed to be a lifelong career—

even if that life might not be the longest, since it was dangerous work. I got stabbed, about three years in. It was bad, but I recovered. Or I thought I did." Even after all these years, the glint in his eyes was bitter. "I went back to work and it was fine for a while. But then it starts getting really hard to breathe. Like an elephant's sitting on my chest. Turns out there's a shitload of scar tissue built up in one of my heart valves. It's not the biggest deal, it's not gonna kill me or anything, but it means I'm no use to the United States Military. It means I'd be a liability in that kind of playing field. I can be a cop, I can be an FBI agent, but I can't be a spy. Not the kind I was trained to be. Because I'm reliant on meds so my goddamn heart works the way it's supposed to."

Grace knew every word he was saying was the truth—she could see it in his face, the openness, the hurt, the frustration. He wasn't a man who liked to limit himself. It must've been hell, especially when he first came back home. Was that where his sense of humor came from? Did he decide to just joke his way through the hurt? The loss?

"I gave up everything I'd ever worked for," Gavin continued. "I walked away from all of it. I came home and I tried to forget. I dedicated my life to my police work and it fulfilled me, to a point."

"But you needed more," Grace said in realization.

"I ran into Harrison and we got to talking. He knows my background. He offered me the job."

Grace took a deep breath, her cheeks turning pink. "I . . . may have overreacted," she said.

"You think?" Gavin asked. "You *really* don't like spies."

"I don't like outside agencies messing with FBI business," Grace said. "Last time the CIA got involved in one of our cases, my best friend nearly died. So no, I really don't like spies."

Gavin leveled her with a sincere look. "My loyalty is to the FBI, to my team, and to the people we're here to protect," Gavin said. "I promise."

Grace regarded him with new eyes. Now that she understood, now that she'd seen the missing piece of Gavin Walker. Not just a cop. Not just a son and brother. Not just a good man or a patriot.

He was sharp, naturally protective, and instinctively brave, with a self-sacrificing streak that would put a martyr to shame. In short, he had probably been a great spy. He had been a great detective. And she knew he'd make an even greater FBI agent. Because he was the kind of man who set his sights on something and did everything in his power to get it.

She understood that. Because she was like that too.

He tilted his head, taking her in as if she were a piece of art. It made her feel strange—almost cherished. She hated how much she liked the feeling, how it rushed through her like warm ocean waves.

"You're the damnedest woman," he said. "Mind like a laser. You just cut through all the bullshit."

It might have been the nicest compliment she'd ever received. It startled her, making her pause, her heart squeezing unexpectedly. She was used to being told she was beautiful. That she was intelligent. That she was a good FBI agent, a talented writer.

But no one had ever praised her bluntness before. Most people viewed it as a fault. Most men saw it that way.

Sometimes she saw it that way too.

There were times she wished she were softer. Easier to get along with. Less honest. More trusting. But she hadn't been built that way. To be those things, she would have to lose herself. She'd done that once. She'd never let it happen again.

But there he was, looking at her like Grace, the *real* Grace, was the hottest thing in the world.

His attention, his acceptance made something curious and tentative bloom inside her chest.

"I don't like bullshit." She shrugged, unwilling to examine this . . . this feeling she had.

She tossed him the keys and he started the engine, pulling back onto the street and heading toward her side of town. "Is that why you never called?" he asked.

"Gavin—" she started.

"I mean, come on, how could you ignore a guy like me?" He smiled, that sarcastic, self-deprecating smile chock-full of boyish charm. It had probably gotten him out of trouble since he was a kid. It certainly was one of the reasons she'd ended up in his bed—she was a sucker for a killer smile.

"It was quite the challenge," she said dryly. "But it was for the best."

"I wouldn't say that," he said softly.

"Gavin, it was one night," she said patiently, trying to ignore how her skin went hot at the memory. Okay, so it was one sizzling, memorable night that had occupied her dreams and thoughts for two years. But it didn't matter. She couldn't let it matter. She couldn't let him distract her. "You're a grown man. You've had one-night stands before. Don't act like you haven't."

"Maybe I wanted it to be more this time," he replied, his eyes going darker as he glanced over to her. "You're not exactly a typical woman, Grace."

She laughed shortly. "There's no such thing as a typical woman," she said. "We're all unique. And don't pull the 'you're not like other girls' crap on me. You're better than that."

He was. Her time spent with him hadn't been all sex. Though, God, that had sure been mind-blowing.

They fell into a silence—not an awkward or uncomfortable one—as he drove through the streets of DC and arrived at her door.

She unbuckled her seat belt.

"I'll see you tomorrow?" She meant it to just be polite, but it came out more tentative, almost hopeful.

"Tomorrow," he said.

She got out of the SUV and was about to close the door when he leaned forward.

"Grace?"

She turned back expectantly.

"The whole pulling-a-gun-on-me thing?" His wicked smile was back. "Way hotter than it should be."

She laughed, unable to stop herself. "Good night, Gavin."

He waited until she was inside her town house before driving away. As she dumped her purse and red trench coat in her hallway, she absentmindedly pulled the pins out of her braids as she made her way deeper into the house.

She would check with Paul in the morning about Gavin's military history, but she knew he wasn't lying to her—or spying on the team. His training from that time would likely prove to be an asset—it required a level of calm and thinking on your feet not everyone had.

As she got ready for bed, Grace turned her focus back to Janice Wacomb and the case that lay ahead. Once again, as she filtered through the facts in her mind, the images of the crime scene, that not-quite-right feeling she'd had niggled at her. She was missing something. What?

She closed her eyes, visualizing the body. The crime scene was burned in her brain, like they all were.

Hoodie. Worn leggings and shoes. Ponytail. No makeup.

She ran the images through her mind, checking them off on a mental list. Something wasn't right. Something was out of place.

The earrings.

She tensed up like lightning had just hit her. She remembered the flash of the diamond studs in the floodlights, half-hidden by the strands of hair that had come loose from Janice's ponytail.

Who wore diamond earrings on a run? Especially a woman as dressed down as Janice? They'd been large too—at least a carat each, set in yellow gold. Expensive jewelry for a practical woman—especially one who didn't like diamonds. The sapphire engagement ring on Janice's finger told Grace that she liked warmth, color. Not the status a diamond brought.

Grace frowned, getting into bed, making a mental note to ask Zooey about them in the morning.

Better be safe than sorry.

CHAPTER 6

When her alarm blared at 6:00 a.m., there was nothing Grace wanted to do more than throw it across the room. Or hit the snooze button a million times.

It had been past two by the time she got home. She took a good twenty minutes to untangle her hair, but she knew she'd regret it if she slept on the mess of braids. It took another ten minutes to remove her makeup before dragging herself into the shower. She almost nodded off a few times under the soothing beat of the hot water against her body but managed to drag herself out and collapse on her bed. She'd fallen asleep almost immediately, deep but not soundly. She kept dreaming of being chased, of diamond earrings and crushed roses.

She slapped the alarm off, launching herself out of her four-poster bed, leaving the rustic lavender linen duvet rumpled at the foot.

Her town house was built in the 1920s, with graceful Art Deco accents and curved alcoves set into the walls that held favorites from the art collection she'd inherited from her grandmother, as well as the pieces she'd purchased on her own. The small collection she'd started buying with her first book advance was nothing compared to what she'd inherited from Gran—Grace leased most of the pieces out to museums because she couldn't possibly justify keeping such historic beauty to herself. But a few select pieces—her favorites since childhood—she kept at home. A Calder mobile—one of the smaller, earlier ones—hung in her dining room, above the table. A series of sketches of ballerinas by Degas lined her hallway. Her guest room had a trio of Andy Warhol's early celebrity portraits. In the living room, an enormous Jackson Pollock—one of her Gran's favorites—dominated one wall, adding bold, abstract color to the otherwise all-white room.

She pressed a button on her stereo and made her way to the kitchen as the sweet sounds of Miles Davis filled the air. She pulled out a bottle of green juice from her fridge, along with a carton of eggs and some chives and red peppers. Humming along to the trumpet, she expertly cracked the eggs into a bowl and diced the veggies.

Reading the news on her iPad as she ate her omelet, she forced herself to drink the green juice without much of a grimace—why did that stuff have to be so good for you? It tasted horrible. She didn't care what the hipsters at Whole Foods said, it was like gulping down liquid grass.

Janice's murder had made the papers—just a few sentences in the crime blotter that said the police had no leads so far.

She checked her phone, but there were no messages. She'd be expected in the office by ten, where Paul would be waiting with Zooey's team to break down the forensic evidence.

Gavin would be there too. She tried to ignore the slight twist in her stomach at the thought, but it was getting harder the more it happened.

It wasn't as if she'd expected to never see him again. They both worked in law enforcement, so it was inevitable that their jobs and friends and social circles would overlap at some point. She'd heard his name many times before she'd ever met him, always spoken with admiration, often with a hint of jealousy, sometimes from men she dated. And when she met him, she finally understood why.

She first laid eyes on him at the Policeman's Ball, of all events. She was attending as a favor to an old friend, a retiring captain whose wife had fallen ill at the last minute. He ended up leaving the ball early, and Grace found herself alone, but not for long.

He didn't feed her some cheesy line or pull any slick crap, like so many men did. He merely held his hand out and said, "Care to dance?"

Then he smiled. She found herself placing her hand in his without a second thought, and then she was in his arms, spinning across the dance floor.

If she were a fairy-tale sort of woman, she would've thought the spark she felt when his eyes met hers was a portent of things to come. That a night full of magic would lead to a lifetime of it.

But she was a realist, through and through. And though that night with him was earthshattering, she was gone the next morning.

She wasn't one to leave a glass slipper—or the modern version of one—behind. So when he called, she didn't pick up. And being the respectful kind of man he was, he'd taken the hint.

Seeing him again reminded her that a part of her—a small, hidden part—had wished she'd picked up when he called. But that wasn't a thought she needed in her head, especially now that she had to work with him.

The alarm on her tablet went off. COUNSELING W/ DOROTHY 8:30 AM.

Grace checked the time, grateful for the escape from her memories. If she didn't hurry, she'd be late.

SHE'D BEEN VOLUNTEERING since boarding school—it looked good on a girl's college applications—but the kind of volunteer work her parents and boarding school teachers had approved of was nothing like what she did now. Counseling troubled, at-risk youth was difficult but even more rewarding. And it gave her an excuse to use another side of her psychology degree.

She ran group and one-on-one sessions, working with kids as young as ten. Many of them had seen too much, experienced too much, in their short lives. Sexual assault. Parental abandonment or imprisonment. Death. Addiction.

Every day she worked at the counseling center, the more she believed in the resilience of the human spirit. The kids—wary and burned by adults before—didn't always like her, but that didn't mean she couldn't help them.

The Herman Counseling Center was on the east side of DC. The squat little gray building didn't look like much, but it was a haven for the kids who had nowhere else to turn. Grace breezed in through the double doors at eight twenty, relieved that she'd made it in time.

Starting a one-on-one session late sent the wrong message to the kid—that they weren't important or worth her time. And the girl she was seeing today would have taken that awful feeling in her stomach and gotten hostile.

Sheila, the director, was speaking with Jessica, the receptionist, when Grace came in. Both women looked up, smiling.

"Grace, great to see you," said Sheila.

"I wasn't able to bring coffee today," Grace said, apologetic. She always liked to bring the staff something—they worked so hard. "I caught a case late last night, threw my entire schedule off."

"Didn't you have your awards dinner last night?" Jessica asked.

"Yes," Grace said. "Trust me, it was so crowded, no one noticed I left early."

Sheila laughed. "Grace! You were the guest of honor!"

"Okay, maybe a few people missed me," Grace admitted. "But there was so much champagne and food, I'm sure they forgot quickly."

Sheila shook her head, picking up a file on the desk and tucking it under her arm. "You're hilarious," she said. "Choosing crime scenes over cocktail parties."

"You know it," Grace replied with a grin.

"Dorothy's waiting for you in the teen area, if you want to head in."

"How's she doing?" Grace asked, lowering her voice so they wouldn't be overheard.

"So far, I think her mom's staying away from the abusive boyfriend," Sheila said. "When he's around, she spends a lot more of her evenings here."

"That's fantastic to hear," Grace said.

"But the grades are still a problem," Sheila explained. "She's still flunking math and history."

Grace sighed. "She's so smart."

"Tell me about it," Sheila said. "She scored off the charts on her tests. She just doesn't have any sense of self-worth. She says that only people who are going to college need to do well in school."

Grace shook her head. "I'm going to get that girl to college if it kills me," she vowed.

"I'm going to hold you to that." Sheila smiled. She checked her watch. "You should probably get in there."

"Thanks, Sheila," Grace called over her shoulder, hurrying down the hall to a room with tables and chairs and an unsteady foosball table that had a stack of books jammed under one leg. A tall dark-haired girl with a permanent scowl and at least six piercings in her ears was slumped on one of the faded couches, reading a thick book. Her jeans were tucked into her combat boots, the neon blue laces a stark contrast against the scuffed black leather. "Dorothy, hey."

Dorothy glanced up from her book, looking bored. "We doing this?" she asked.

"Right this way." Grace gestured down the hall, where a series of private rooms lined the corridor.

Once they had settled in the second room, Grace in one worn red armchair and Dorothy in the other, she pulled out the leather folder she kept her notes in. She'd already met with Dorothy a few times—the teen had grown up in an abusive household and was a repeat runaway. There had been an incident with drugs last year. Dorothy insisted that she wasn't using anymore, and she'd tested clean, so the center had given her a chance to turn things around.

"How have things been going?" Grace asked, uncapping her pen.

Dorothy shrugged. "Same old, same old. Sheila's riding my ass, as usual."

"Sheila cares about you," Grace said.

Dorothy snorted. "Yessirree," she drawled.

"Last time we talked, things with your mom were getting better. Is that still the case?"

The girl shrugged. "Things are okay, I guess."

"Has Randy come back?" Grace asked, naming her mom's (hopefully) ex-boyfriend.

"Not yet," Dorothy said. "But it's just a matter of time."

"You don't think they'll stay broken up?" Grace knew the answer to the question, but she was curious to see if Dorothy did.

"They never stay broken up," Dorothy said. "He'll be back. She'll take him back. She always takes him back, no matter what he does."

"And you don't want him back in your lives," Grace said.

"Would you want a woman-beating asshole in *your* life?" Dorothy asked, her eyes challenging, her mouth pressed together tight, like she was trying to keep all her feelings trapped inside.

"No, I wouldn't," Grace said.

"If he ever moves from hitting Mom to hitting Jamie, I'm gonna kill him," Dorothy muttered.

Jamie was her half brother. He was one of the few things that caused Dorothy to light up when she talked about him. Grace got the impression she'd done most of the child rearing, her mother too high or too beat up or just too tired to deal with another kid.

"Or you could call the cops," Grace suggested.

Dorothy laughed, a harsh sound that said everything about how she saw the world—how she'd been forced to see the world. "The cops don't care about people like us," she said.

"That's not true," Grace said. "I'm a cop. I care about you."

"You're not a real cop," Dorothy sneered. "You're, like, a fancy agent profiler. You don't go around arresting people for beating on their women."

"Sometimes I do," Grace said. "I've worked domestic violence cases before."

"You can't help someone who doesn't want help," Dorothy said in a monotone, like she was parroting it from something that was said or read to her. "My mom's her own worst enemy. She's in love. The kind of love that gets you beaten is fucking stupid, if you ask me."

"You already help your mom," Grace pointed out. "You take care of Jamie. You're staying in school, even though I know you don't want to, because you promised her you'd graduate. You could make a better life for yourself, Dorothy."

The teen snorted again, shifting in her seat, unable to meet Grace's eyes. "You know that from your weird profiling stuff?"

"I know that because I've talked to you," Grace said. "And because Sheila and I believe in you. And because it's clear you don't want to mess up the opportunities you've been given. If you did, you wouldn't show up for counseling."

"Don't get too big a head," Dorothy said. "I'm just here because it's better than at home."

Grace's heart twinged. Dorothy was such a smart girl. There was a part of Grace who looked at Dorothy and saw another angry, grieving girl. That girl Grace had been, leaving boarding school, starting college, ostracized by her parents, looking for any kind of comfort.

But where Grace had had wealth and opportunities, Dorothy had nothing. No one to value her intelligence, no one to encourage it—or her—no one to bolster her self-confidence.

That was why Grace dedicated so much time at the center. She'd been born into a privileged, if lonely, life and had all the prospects possible. Every door in the world had been opened to her and she knew how valuable that was. This was one of her ways of paying it forward. Because girls like Dorothy deserved all the chances Grace could give them.

"Where'd you learn all that stuff anyway?" Dorothy asked in that bored voice teens used when they really wanted to know something but didn't want the person they were asking to know that.

"The profiling?" Grace asked, seizing on her curiosity.

"Yeah, it's like, what, mind reading or something?"

Grace laughed. "I wish!" she said. "That would make my job a lot easier. I got my BA in psychology and criminology, and then I earned my master's in psychology while doing a doctorate in criminology."

"That's a lot of school." Dorothy shook her head.

"I always liked school," Grace said. "Between you and me, I was kind of a geek."

Dorothy's stormy face, usually so bored and apathetic, broke into a reluctant smile. "I can totally see that," she said. "I bet girls like me teased you."

Grace didn't want to tell her that there weren't any girls like her at the exclusive $100,000-a-year boarding school she'd attended. "There were a few," she said. "But I couldn't have landed my job by just studying hard," Grace explained. "When it comes to some of the special fields like profiling or hostage negotiation, for instance, you really need to have a knack for it. An instinct."

"How'd you know you had it?" Dorothy asked.

Though Grace usually hesitated to talk about herself, this was the first time Dorothy had shown real interest in anything other than weaseling out of their counseling session as soon as possible. It gave Grace a spark of hope—if the girl was intrigued by profiling, that might be a way to connect with her and encourage her.

Maybe that dream of getting her to college wasn't an impossible one.

"A lot of profiling is noticing details that other people don't see. We look beyond the surface, into the heart of people."

"Like into their souls?" Dorothy asked skeptically.

"More like into their minds," Grace said. "What do you see when you look at me?"

"Expensive clothes, long hair, you need a manicure."

Grace had to suppress a smile at the teen's bluntness. "Okay," Grace said. "Good start. But what do those things tell you about me?"

Dorothy frowned, thinking. "Fancy clothes mean you're probably rich, right? Maybe you keep your hair long because you're girly but you're not in a really girly job. So it's, like, your thing. To stay girly. To remind people that you're not just one of the guys. And I bet it trips some people up, that you're so pretty but you're so smart. People always think pretty girls aren't smart, like they don't have to be. And the manicure . . . You probably haven't had the time. You were almost late today, and you're never late. You've been busy. Probably with FBI stuff. Was there a murder or something?"

Grace was impressed but not terribly surprised. Dorothy was a survivor—her experience in an abusive household had taught her how to read people in order to stay safe and protect her little brother. "Those are excellent insights, Dorothy," she told her. "I am very girly, and I do like to keep my hair long because it makes me feel feminine in a career that's male dominated. Law enforcement is still a boys' club. That's why, as a woman, I want to bring as many talented women into the field as possible. And I've missed three mani-pedi appointments in the last month. You don't even want to see the state of my feet. It's a full-on lizard situation."

There it was—another rare grin flitting across the girl's somber face. Progress! Finally, something to connect with her on. Grace was overjoyed. So far, Dorothy had been a hard nut to crack.

"Do you think . . . I mean, I know it sounds stupid," Dorothy began. "But do you think I could do that? Do what you do?"

"Absolutely," Grace said, meaning it 100 percent. "Dorothy, you are a smart young woman. The only reason you're getting bad grades is because you're not applying yourself. And you're tough. If you study hard and get your degree, I will write you a recommendation when you apply to Quantico—that's the FBI school. I can't promise you'll get in, but if you do the right things, study the right stuff, and get good grades, I'd be surprised if they didn't want someone like you."

"They would? And you'd do that?" Dorothy asked, mistrust in her dark eyes. It was clear it'd been a long time since someone had offered her anything, no strings attached.

"As I said, I want as many smart, capable women working in law enforcement as possible," Grace said. "That helps all of us. You fit that bill to a *T*."

The girl looked at her warily. "I believe in your potential," Grace added. "We just need to get you to a place where you believe in yourself."

"That sounds like a Hallmark card," Dorothy scoffed, but there was a smile on her face.

Grace laughed. "It still applies," she said.

The timer signaling the end of their session beeped. Dorothy sighed, rising from the chair, her apathetic mask back on her face. She couldn't bear to get her hopes up too high, so she had to drag herself back down first, before someone else did. "Thanks for talking to me about this stuff. It sounds cool, I guess."

"I meant everything I said," Grace told her. "We'll talk more about it next session, okay?"

"Whatever," Dorothy said with a shrug. "Bye."

She shuffled out the door, and for a moment, Grace looked at her empty chair. This could be Dorothy's turning point. She just needed to build up the self-esteem that the abusive cycle that dominated her life had stolen from her. Coming to the center was the first step, and showing interest in the future was the second. The third step was the hardest, though: realizing that she could have that future, wading through the harmful rhetoric of her childhood, and breaking free.

So many people didn't make it to the third step, but Grace was determined Dorothy would get there. Even if that asshole abuser boyfriend of her mother's returned to wreak more havoc on her life.

"Good session?" Sheila asked as Grace headed toward the center's front doors.

"Yes," Grace said. "I think we had a little breakthrough."

Sheila's freckled face lit up. "That's fantastic! She's been interacting more with the other kids too. She doesn't spend as much time with the teens her age, but she's really good with the little ones. They love her."

"I think we might have another success story in the works," Grace said. Her phone buzzed in her purse, and she dug through her bag to grab it. "God, I can never find anything in this bag," she muttered, finally fishing it out from under her wallet. She saw it was Paul calling her. "Sheila, this is my boss. I've got to head out. I'll see you?"

"Bye, Grace. Thank you."

Grace waved, taking the call as she pushed her way through the double doors out into the sunlight. The day was warming up already, and she pulled her jacket off and tossed it over her arm. "Hey, Paul, I'm headed over now."

"Change of plans," he said. "I assume you're at the counseling center?"

Grace frowned. "Yes," she said.

"Agent Walker will be by in five minutes to get you. You're needed at a crime scene."

"Another one? But I haven't even started going through the Janice Wacomb case—" Grace started to say.

"We're going to have to juggle cases," Paul said. "I'm at the scene of a home invasion in Maryland. Grace, I need you to come."

The tight tone in his voice worried her. "Are you okay, Paul?" she asked. Just a few months before, he had been taken hostage by a man bent on revenge for his brother's death. Although Paul had been cleared by FBI psychologists for active duty, she still worried about him. One night when a group of them had gone out drinking, he'd admitted to her in confidence that he still had nightmares about the bomb vest he'd been forced to wear.

"I'm fine," Paul reassured her. "But this is a bad one. Fair warning."

"I understand," Grace said. A black SUV—the same one from last night—pulled up to the curb. "Agent Walker is here," she said into the phone. "I'll see you soon."

CHAPTER 7

Gavin rolled down the passenger window, smiling when he saw Grace. "Need a ride?" he asked.

"You didn't have to come pick me up, you know," she said, striding toward the SUV. Her hair was twisted up in a bun today. Long hair at a crime scene was a forensic liability, of course. She must always wear it up on the job. For some reason, that made the memories he had of her with it long and loose, falling down her shoulders, all the way to her naked hips, even more erotic. A part of her that not everyone saw.

"I was a cop for a long time," he said. "I'm used to having a partner."

"You'd think you'd be used to lone-wolfing it," she said casually, hopping up into the SUV and closing the door.

A flowery but crisp scent wafted through the

cab. Her perfume. It fit her, feminine with just a hint of bite.

Gavin sighed as he pulled onto the street. "Are you going to bring up the spy thing every time we talk now? 'Cause Harrison's technically the only one with enough clearance to know my military background."

She raised an eyebrow. "I don't know," she replied. "Are you going to stop being sneaky?"

"I wasn't being sneaky," he protested.

"You lied to my face last night," she said. "And to the rest of our team."

There was a seriousness to her voice that made the hairs on his neck rise. Honesty was important to Grace. She was too straightforward for anything else.

"Did I lie about something that would've affected our investigation?" Gavin asked.

Her delicate eyebrows drew together. "No," she said.

"Did I give any information regarding snipers that was incorrect?"

She twisted her mouth, cottoning on to his line of thinking. "No," she said between gritted teeth.

"Exactly. I told one fib about what I did in the military a million years ago. Because our team doesn't have the clearance to know the real story.

Because I know where the line is, Grace," he said. "Promise."

She let out a little huff of breath. "See?" she demanded. "*Sneaky.*"

It would take at least an hour in morning traffic to get to the address Harrison had texted him—an exclusive gated community outside of DC. "Did you have a good morning?" he asked, hoping she'd go with his change of subject.

"Yes, actually," she said, and the smile that flitted across her face was triumphant.

"What happened?"

"Oh, you'll think it's silly," she said, waving him off.

"Try me," he said, glancing over at her. He wanted to know. If he was being honest—which he knew she liked—he wanted to know everything about her. She'd haunted him for two years. Not just in his dreams, not just in the memory of her body pressed against his. It was *her*, the woman, everything about her. That was what tugged at him and he'd fought it, but now he wasn't sure he could resist the pull anymore. It was that unconventional, incisive mind of hers . . . Sure, it helped that such a fascinating woman was beautiful too. But her mind, her heart, her soul—that was what made him burn with curiosity.

"I do counseling at the center," Grace explained. "And I had a little bit of a breakthrough with one of my kids today."

"That's great," he said.

"She's so smart," Grace said. "And tough. I can't bullshit her, you know? I can't tell her that everything's going to be okay, because it's not. She's been beaten down by life and circumstances since she was born, and none of it's her fault, but it's her reality."

He could hear the emotion in her voice, see how much she cared in the way her hands fisted on her purse, like she was ready to pummel anyone who dared hurt one of her kids.

Mama bear, he thought, suppressing a smile.

"But you're part of her reality now too," Gavin pointed out as they hit the clogged highway out of the city and traffic slowed to a crawl. "And that could mean everything. You could change her entire life."

"I hope so," Grace said. "I've had kids at the center go on to do great things. Maria got a full ride to NYU. And Samuel opened his own barbershop and he does free haircuts for all the kids at the center. But others . . ." She trailed off. "You know how it is. You know this city. Abuse. Drugs. Poverty. Prostitution. Prison. Some of these kids are just eaten up by the system even before they age out."

"It's not fair," he agreed. He'd seen it too, as a

beat cop once upon a time and as a detective. The destruction that addiction and poverty wrought on families. The desperation that drove women to stay with abusers. The fear in a child's eyes when gunshots went off in the neighborhood. "But that's why we do this, right? So we can repair what's broken from the inside, make the world a safer place for everyone."

She didn't answer, and he glanced from the windshield to her, curious. "What?" he asked, because she was looking at him like she'd never quite seen him.

"Nothing," she said. "I just . . . You really care about this, don't you?"

"You're the one getting up at 6:00 a.m. so you can counsel at-risk kids before work. You could give me a run for my money."

She smiled. "Maybe," she said. The snarl of traffic they'd been caught in finally cleared, and Gavin kept focused on the road, while Grace picked up her phone and scrolled through her emails.

"Did Paul give you any information about the scene?" she asked as she paged through her messages. "I have about a million sad-face emojis from Zooey."

"That girl is a character," Gavin said.

"But she's not easily shaken," Grace pointed out. "I mean, she's a forensic expert. And she's the best. She started MIT when she was fifteen. Paul had to get a special dispensation from the director to hire her, because she's not officially old enough to work at the Bureau yet."

Gavin frowned. Zooey looked young, but he hadn't realized she was some sort of FBI version of Doogie Howser. "How old is she?"

"She just turned twenty-one," Grace said. "We had a party. We indulged in more than a few fruity cocktails, and I had to nurse her through her first hangover. It would've been adorable if there hadn't been so much puking."

"The sugary drinks will get you every time," Gavin said, changing lanes as they approached their exit.

"Harrison didn't give me the details," Gavin said. "Is that his MO? Wait until we get to the scene to break it down? I'm not criticizing," he added hastily. "I just want to get a feel for how things go here. I know working with a team is different."

"Sometimes," Grace said. "Usually he texts me the immediate details so I can start on victimology. But Paul's . . . He's been through a lot, the last few months."

"I'd heard he'd taken some leave," Gavin said tactfully. He'd heard more than that. Harrison's last case had landed him at the mercy of a kidnapper who had strapped a bomb to the man's chest. That would mess up anyone for a good while. Hell, he still had the occasional night-mare from his years spent in the bomb squad. There'd been a few close calls during that time, where he was just one breath away from becoming pink mist.

You didn't forget the close ones. But you got better at dealing with them.

Gavin exited the highway and after a few miles, took a right onto a street lined with tall maple trees. Everything around them screamed wealth, privilege, and security. As they pulled up to the wide iron gates, a security officer leaned out of his station. The lines around the man's mouth were tight, and Gavin felt a flash of sympathy for him. He and the rest of the security company must be sweating bullets, wondering if this was their fault.

"FBI," Gavin said, handing over his credentials.

The man glanced down at them and then handed them back. "It's the first right," he said, his voice hoarse.

"Thanks," Gavin said.

The gate rolled open, and they drove through.

"We're going to need schematics of the entire neighborhood," Gavin remarked as he took the first right. "All the entrances, guard schedules, patrols. Background checks on all security."

"Plus canvassing the neighbors," Grace said, dread in her voice.

"They're going to love that," Gavin said. Rich people bought into communities like this for privacy as much as security. They wouldn't like the FBI nosing in on them—and some of these folks worked for important people. Hell, some of these folks *were* important people. And important people didn't like following the rules.

Gavin pulled up to the house, an imposing Greek-style mansion with Corinthian columns, surrounded by an expansive lawn. Agency SUVs were parked all along the curb, and the forensic van had pulled into the driveway.

Gavin watched as an intern bolted out of the house, down the driveway, a gloved hand clutched over his mouth. He collapsed onto the lawn, vomiting into the grass.

Grace raised an eyebrow, looking over at him. "You ready?" she asked Gavin.

It was a clear challenge. Whatever it was that was waiting for them inside was sure to be horrific.

But he wasn't afraid of blood or death. He'd seen more murder than most people could ever dream of. Put more killers behind bars than almost anyone his age on the force.

It was time to show Grace Sinclair what he was made of.

"I'm ready," he said.

CHAPTER 8

Grace snapped blue sterile booties over her heels with the practice of a woman who'd done it hundreds of times. After handing Gavin a pair of gloves, she smoothed her hair back a few times to make sure nothing was loose before putting on her own pair.

The neighborhood was full of neat, manicured lawns, tastefully painted mansions—and nosy neighbors who were currently gathered outside the cordons, looking worried and nervous.

"You feeling better, Josh?" she asked the intern who'd thrown up all over the lawn.

He shook his head, looking miserable.

"First few crime scenes are always bad," she reassured him.

"You'll get used to it," Gavin added.

He was right, of course. Grace was used to it—desensitized more than most, able to detach in a way that others admired—but when she walked up to the mansion, she felt apprehension coiling in her stomach, ready to strike.

Then Gavin stepped behind her, and warmth washed over her back—the man ran as hot as he looked—and she didn't want to admit it, but it soothed her.

She opened the door carefully and entered the house.

The smell hit her first—a coppery stench she knew well. Blood. A lot of it.

"Do you want a mask?" Zooey asked to her right. "The smell . . ."

"I'll be okay," Grace said.

"Gavin?" Zooey asked.

He shook his head.

"Okay, just warning you," Zooey said. "Let's go."

They walked into the foyer and stepped around a large pool of blood.

"From the drag stains and how the bodies are positioned," Zooey began, "my working theory is that the killer rang the bell or knocked on the door. Mr. Anderson, the husband, answered it. Killer forced his way in—see the chunk of plaster missing right here, on the wall."

Zooey pointed to the wall behind the door, where it was dented from the doorknob swinging too hard into it. Gavin moved forward, examining it.

"You retrieve the bullet yet?" he asked.

".38 caliber," Zooey said. "It happened fast once our unsub was inside. He shot Mr. Anderson immediately, like, as soon as he got the door closed," she explained, pointing to the sheet-covered body to their right. "Do you want to see?"

Grace nodded. Zooey bent down, pulling the sheet back. Grace swallowed hard, suppressing the horror that jolted through her.

Mr. Anderson had been shot in the face.

"Close range, so it was a mess," Zooey explained bluntly.

"So I see," Grace said, breathing through her mouth. "Poor man."

"Pull it back a little more, Zooey," Gavin directed. The forensic tech did as he ordered.

"No defensive wounds on his hands," Gavin murmured. "Okay, thanks."

Zooey put the sheet back in its place. "I don't think he even had time to react or fight back. But that means it was quick, at least."

"Small mercy," Grace said soberly. It didn't matter how many times she was faced with the gore of a crime scene; it always hit her hard. But she couldn't let emotion take over. She had to set her feelings aside so she could focus on the science. On the psychology of the scene, of the space, of the kill. "Where was Mrs. Anderson?"

"Upstairs," Zooey said, leading them to the staircase.

"So he was downstairs already," Gavin said, turning to face the door for a second, pointing to it. "Doorbell rings. He answers. Our guy shoots him, and she comes running when she hears the gunshot."

"Easiest way to draw her out. It's shocking. Confusing. Either she comes running or she freezes and hides."

"She's either running right toward him or a sitting duck," Gavin said, looking back up the stairs. "She didn't have a chance," he said softly, almost to himself.

"She was brave," Grace said. "She went to face him."

"She was smart too," Zooey added. "She grabbed a phone." She pointed to the phone, lying halfway up the stairs. "I figure he got her midstairs. See?" She gestured to the blood spatter on the framed portraits lining the staircase wall. "She wasn't able to get away fast enough."

They hardly ever did. Not when it came to this kind of killer. Grace hated that. Hated standing in the center of a crime scene and knowing that no matter what the victims might have done, the end result would have been the same.

Gavin frowned, and Grace couldn't help but let her eyes linger on the way his brow furrowed. "Where is her body, if she was shot on the stairs?" he asked.

"Well, that's what's weird," Zooey said. "The killer moved Mr. Anderson a little bit, but it looks like it was just for access to the door, to get out of the house. Moving Mrs. Anderson makes no sense. I have no idea why he'd do it. Come on, I'll show you."

She led them through a beautifully decorated living room and dining room—the crystal was set on the table, as if they'd been preparing to celebrate—and into the kitchen.

Grace swallowed, breathing through her mouth as she carefully edged around the kitchen counter, to see the woman lying on her stomach, her long dark hair matted with blood.

"Christ," Gavin swore behind her. "Grace, careful."

Before she could react, his hand slid to her waist, pulling her to the side, away from the pool of blood she'd almost slipped into.

"Thanks," she said, shifting her attention back to the body, her mind turning over and over.

"I don't get it," Zooey was saying to her as Grace stepped back to take in the full scene. The husband hadn't been the priority for the killer.

No, the priority was the woman. Why?

"What don't you get?" she asked Zooey, moving back so two forensic techs who had finished taking photographs could get out of the way.

"Why drag her in here?" Zooey asked. "It

seems like a lot of work, and for what, exactly? It caused a lot more mess, took more time, created more risk. So far, I haven't found any footprints in the blood, but I haven't gone through everything yet."

Grace knew what she thought, but she looked over to Gavin.

She wanted to know what *he* thought. The man who'd left his dreams in the desert to become Metro's finest homicide detective. He was back playing with the big boys—and girls—now. Was he up to snuff?

"What do you think?" she asked him.

His eyes glittered. He knew she was testing him, and instead of annoyance flicking in his face, an impressed acceptance was there.

Amazing, but it seemed this guy didn't have the usual male ego. That meant he was really that good—or he was a moron.

She'd bet her life on the former.

"The husband's collateral damage," Gavin said. "He was in the killer's way. The real prize to our guy? Is her." He circled around the body, taking her in. There was an air of expertise as he bent down, pushing her hair back with a pen he took out of his pocket.

"Blunt trauma to the head before he shot her," he said. "I'd bet anything he didn't bash her head in just to get control of her."

"He was angry," Grace finished for him.

He looked up, his serious gaze meeting hers. "Oh, yeah," he said. "This is pure misogynistic rage."

"How do you reckon?" she asked, impressed that he'd use that word, and wondering if he'd noticed the thing she had the second she saw the body.

"The shoes," he said.

Something inside her leapt, because this feeling? This was a true meeting of the minds.

This was rare. Like lightning in a bottle.

"She's not wearing shoes," she said carefully.

"Exactly," Gavin said, straightening. "Barefoot? In the kitchen? This guy's sending us a very clear message about how he feels about women and their place in the world."

Zooey let out a low whistle. "I didn't even notice that," she said.

"I did," Grace said, unable to tear her eyes off Gavin's.

His mouth quirked. "I know you did," he said. "You don't miss anything."

"Apparently neither do you."

"I do my best," he said with a shrug.

Grace looked back down at the woman's body, frowning when she glimpsed something shining in the strands of hair that Gavin had carefully pushed back during his examination. Her stomach twisted, dread building inside it as she stepped forward.

"You see something else?" Gavin asked her.

But she didn't answer. She couldn't. Not until she knew for sure.

She crouched down, pushing the woman's hair away from her ears with her gloved hand.

And there they were, glimmering against the mess of blood and torn flesh: diamond earrings, sparkling in her ears.

A chill trickled down Grace's spine.

"What is it?" Gavin asked behind her. He bent down next to her, studying the woman's battered face.

"Are you two done in here yet?" Paul came striding in, phone in hand. He frowned when he saw both of them next to the body and Zooey standing near the counter, her arms folded and waiting. "What's up?"

"Grace was just about to tell us," Gavin said.

Grace glanced down at the earrings again. It could just be a coincidence. Janice Wacomb— the woman from last night's crime scene—her diamond earrings were out of place. But this woman had several diamond rings and a platinum tennis bracelet on her wrist.

But they're not bloody, a voice whispered inside her.

Grace glanced down at the rings. They were

stained with blood, and so was the bracelet. She'd tried to fight him off, so it made sense.

But despite the massive head wound, the earrings shone *against* the mess of blood, pristine and glittering, no trace of blood on them.

She hadn't been wearing them when he attacked her.

He'd put them in her ears himself. After he'd killed her. Grace was sure of it.

"The earrings," she said.

"What about the earrings?" Paul asked.

Grace reached over and grasped the woman's earlobe gently, exposing the back of the earring's stud.

No blood there either.

"Janice Wacomb had diamond earrings on," Gavin said, and Grace felt it again, that spark, that connection, that amazing feeling of being on the same wavelength as another agent.

"Okay . . . ," Paul said slowly, not getting it.

"You think they're the same ones?" Gavin asked.

"They were exactly like these," Grace said.

"Grace," Paul said, looking at her like she was crazy. "Lots of women have diamond earrings. *You* have diamond earrings."

"But these aren't bloody," Grace said. "Look. There's blood everywhere but not on the earrings."

"Good catch," he said, sounding impressed. "That suggests they were put on after she stopped bleeding."

Paul leaned down, frowning. "Okay, but what are we theorizing here?" he asked. "That our killer from last night is the same guy? That he's . . . putting diamond earrings on women after he kills them?"

"Why not?" Grace asked sharply, because the skepticism was dripping off him.

"Grace, it was two totally different MOs," Paul said. "This is a home invasion. A robbery, clearly. The safe upstairs is cleaned out. Last night was a sniper attack. And you think we've got a serial killer . . . based on some jewelry? That's a whole hell of a reach."

"It's a pretty apparent signature, though," Gavin said, straightening when Paul did. Grace continued to stare at the earrings. They were the same square-cut design as the ones Janice Wacomb had been wearing, at least a carat each, in a yellow gold setting.

That was another odd thing. The rest of Mrs. Anderson's jewelry was platinum and white gold.

"Both murders are a little off," Grace said firmly, finally getting to her feet. "Killing someone in that alley was less than ideal for an experienced sniper. This, the moving of the woman's body? That's just weird for a robbery, where speed's essential—but our killer takes his time to drag her body into the kitchen? For what reason, unless it's some sort of compulsion or way to send a message? There was no sexual assault, right?"

"No sign of sexual assault," Zooey confirmed, shaking her head.

"So he's a misogynist but not a rapist," Gavin said.

"He could be impotent," Grace suggested.

"And projecting his rage on women?" Gavin finished, nodding. "Possible. But why the earrings? What is he telling us with them?" He spun his hand in circles as he thought, like he was used to tossing something back and forth at his desk. He was a tactile man, used to touching, feeling, as he thought things through.

"A gift, maybe? A sign of remorse?" Gavin shook his head almost as soon as the words were out of his mouth. "Nah, this guy? He's not remorseful. He's calculating."

"If we follow the barefoot-in-the-kitchen message, he could be saying that women only want men for one thing: money."

"Okay, now we're getting somewhere," Gavin said, pointing at her.

Paul cleared his throat, breaking the two of them from their reverie. "Agent Walker, I appreciate you indulging her. But, Grace, come on.

I know you're always on the lookout for new book material, but a serial killer with a jewelry obsession? That's going over the top."

"But—"

"No," Paul insisted. "There's no connection between the cases. I need both of you to treat them separately. Okay?"

Grace resisted the urge to glare at him. As friendly as they were, he was her boss, after all. "Okay," she said, not meaning it for one second. The facts were there, the clues were there, and if Paul refused to see them, she'd just have to make him. "Send me all the crime scene photos. I'll give you a profile after I've examined them thoroughly."

"You can't just do it now?" Paul asked.

"No," she said sharply. "I can't. Walker, you coming?"

"I am," he drawled, clearly amused and knowing she had no intention of following Paul's orders.

Without another word to Paul, she turned and walked out of the house.

CHAPTER 9

I thought you said you and Harrison got along," Gavin commented as they made their way through traffic toward the freeway.

"We do," Grace said, but even she sounded a little skeptical.

Harrison hadn't respected her in the Andersons' house, and it rankled Gavin more than he'd like to admit. *She* was the profiler, the expert, and Harrison had dismissed her insights *and* put down her writing.

"It's been a bad few months," she said eventually, when Gavin didn't say anything. "He's being extra cautious lately."

"Can't say I blame him, what with the whole bomb-strapped-to-his-chest thing," Gavin said, flipping the turn signal and merging into the next lane. "And I don't want to start defying my boss on my first case, but, Grace, those earrings . . ."

"Are exactly the same kind Janice was wearing," Grace finished for him, holding out her phone. She'd pulled up a crime scene picture of Janice, zooming in on the earrings. He looked at it, seeing exactly what she saw: The earrings were exactly the same kind as the ones Mrs. Anderson had been wearing.

"Well, damn," Gavin said, shaking his head. "Defying the boss it is."

"Seriously?" she asked.

He glanced over at her. "I've got your back," he said. "No matter what."

"Just like that," she said.

"Just like that," he said. "I mean, it helps that I'm pretty sure you're onto something. But even if I wasn't sure"—he shrugged—"you are. That's enough for me."

Her brows knit together. "So the whole loyal thing isn't an act."

"No," he said. "I'm your partner. I'll take a bullet for you, if need be. Figuratively or literally."

That rendered her silent, though it really shouldn't have. FBI agents had each other's backs—or at least they should. But as much as she'd accused him of being a lone wolf that morning, he knew the truth: Grace was the real lone wolf here.

"So what's our next move?" he asked.

"Well, since you're on board . . ." she said, taking out her phone. She dialed a number and turned it on speaker.

"This is Zooey," said a voice.

"Hey, it's Grace," Grace said. "Your team was looking for the jeweler who made Janice Wacomb's earrings, right?"

"Yep," Zooey said. "We tracked them down this morning. A little family-run place called McCord's Jewelers."

"Excellent. Mind texting me the address?"

"Defying Paul, are we?" Zooey asked.

"Someone has to," Grace said, and Zooey laughed.

"Gavin in on this with you?"

"You know it," Gavin called into the phone.

"Already got him on your side . . . I'm impressed," Zooey said. "I texted the address to you. Don't come running to me when Paul finds out and gets pissed."

"He won't be pissed when it turns out I'm right," Grace said. "Thanks, Zooey."

"Anytime. Bye, you two."

Grace reached over and plugged the address Zooey had texted her into the SUV's GPS. "Want to take a road trip?" she asked.

Gavin grinned. "Let's go hunt down some diamonds."

McCORD'S JEWELERS WAS a tiny place, tucked in a nondescript brick building just outside of downtown DC. The gold-leaf letters on the door shone bright as Gavin pushed it open, and bells tinkled as they entered.

Gavin automatically glanced all around, taking in the two cameras situated in the room. Surveillance meant tapes. Maybe they'd be able to catch their guy buying the earrings. That'd make this an open-and-shut case, for sure.

An older man with gray hair and a sweater-vest looked up from his place at the counter, where he'd been examining a tray of loose diamonds. "Welcome," he said with a smile. "How can I help you? Wait." He held out his hand. "Let me guess. An engagement ring?"

Gavin could feel his cheeks heating up a little as he glanced over at Grace. But she just smiled, shaking her head, pulling out her badge. "I'm afraid we're here for business, not pleasure," she said. "I'm Special Agent Sinclair. This is Special Agent Walker."

"Oh, my," he said. "I'm Anthony McCord. I own this place with my wife. How can I help you?"

"We're investigating a murder," Gavin said. "We believe the victim in question was wearing earrings purchased from your shop."

Grace held out her phone, the screen showing

a picture of Janice Wacomb's earrings in an evidence bag. "Do these look familiar to you?"

Mr. McCord pulled on his glasses, leaning forward and looking at the phone. "Yes, those are definitely my work."

"Can you remember who you sold them to?"

"If you get me the serial number, yes," Mr. McCord said.

"Serial number?" Gavin asked.

"Each diamond that we sell has a serial number engraved on the stone. It's microscopic; you can't see it with the naked eye. It's done for insurance purposes—if a piece of jewelry gets stolen or lost, it can be traced that way. Isn't that how you found the store?"

"We're not forensics, but I'm sure that's how they found you," Grace said. "Just give me a moment; I'll get the serial number for you."

She stepped away and Gavin smiled at Mr. McCord. "While she's doing that, mind if I ask just a few more questions?"

"Anything I can do to help," Mr. McCord said.

"What's your surveillance like here? I see the cameras. Do you save your tapes?"

"We don't have the capacity for that, I'm afraid. We're just a mom-and-pop shop. We keep the tapes for only a week. Then they're erased and recorded over."

"Okay," Gavin said. Damn, unless their killer

had bought the earrings in the last week, they weren't going to get a video of him. They would have to rely on Mr. McCord's memory to discover if he'd been the one to sell the killer the earrings. "And how many employees do you have?"

"Just my wife and me," Mr. McCord said. "She does the books, I make the jewelry."

"Sounds like a good system," Gavin said.

"She's always had a better head for numbers than me."

"And what about your customers. Anyone stand out to you lately? Maybe he was nervous?"

Mr. McCord smiled. "I'm a jeweler, Agent Walker. That means most of the men coming in here are looking for engagement rings. And that's almost guaranteed to make a man nervous."

Gavin laughed. "Okay, fair enough," he said. "What about someone who put in a big order? Was there someone in the last few months who ordered multiple pairs of those earrings Agent Sinclair showed you?"

Mr. McCord frowned. "Actually, there was," he said. "I remember there was a gentleman who came in to buy a pair of earrings for his wife. And then about a week later, he came back in and put in an order for three more pairs. He said that his wife had loved them so much, she wanted their granddaughters to have matching pairs. It was very sweet."

"You remember when this was?"

"I'd say maybe two months ago?" Mr. McCord said.

"I've got those serial numbers for you." Grace pushed a piece of paper across the counter and Mr. McCord took it.

"Let me go look in my files," he said. "Just a moment."

He disappeared into the back room, and Grace leaned lightly against the counter, gazing at all the baubles surrounding her. Gavin couldn't help but think she shone the brightest, even surrounded by all these diamonds.

"You like this stuff, Sinclair?" he asked, gesturing to the dazzling array of bracelets in the glass case in front of him.

"Diamonds are a girl's best friend," she said, but there was a dry note of sarcasm in her voice that surprised him. He looked over to her questioningly, and she shrugged. "I'm more of an art collector," she said. "Most jewelry isn't exactly practical in our line of work. I have a few pieces, but they're mostly sentimental and inherited."

"From your grandmother," he said, remembering how she had mentioned her that night they'd spent together. She'd been wearing a necklace then; the sapphires had glittered darkly against her skin, making it seem luminous.

Something flickered in that extraordinary face of hers, her eyes widening in what looked like confusion . . . or maybe surprise. "You remembered," she said.

Gavin couldn't tear his eyes off her. He wanted nothing more than to reach out and touch her— any part of her, just to remind himself what it was like. "I remember everything about you," he said quietly.

Her tongue darted out, licking that lush lower lip, a nervous little tic that he found adorable.

The door to the back room swung open, disrupting the moment. "Here we are," Mr. McCord said. "I'm afraid it might not be much help. The serial numbers do match the first set of earrings I sold to the gentleman I mentioned," he said. "But he paid cash, both times. And it was two months ago, so I have no video of the sale. I'm so sorry."

"How many pairs did you sell him?" Grace asked.

"Four in total," Mr. McCord said. "I—Do you really think he killed a girl?" The old man looked very troubled.

"It's just one of the leads we're following," Grace said. "Do you remember anything about this man? Age? Height? Weight? Coloring?"

"He was white," Mr. McCord said. "Older. Not as old as me, but in his fifties, maybe? And he wore a hat—I remember because I said something to my wife about how men don't wear hats anymore."

"Like a cowboy hat or . . . ?" Gavin asked.

"No, one of those newsboy caps. He had it pulled down over his eyes. He . . ." Mr. McCord's frown deepened. "He was trying to hide his face from my cameras, wasn't he?"

Gavin sighed. "It's likely," he said.

"Oh, God," Mr. McCord said. "This is horrible."

"Do you think, if we brought you an FBI sketch artist, you could describe him?" Gavin asked.

"I can try," Mr. McCord said. "I don't know how helpful I'll be, but I will try my hardest."

"Here's my card," Gavin said. "We'll give you a call to set up an appointment with the artist."

Mr. McCord nodded. It was obvious the jeweler was shaken. "Why don't you call your wife," Gavin suggested. "Maybe close up early today. Spend some time at home."

"I think I'll do that," Mr. McCord said.

"You've been very helpful," Grace assured him. "We'll be in touch."

Grace and Gavin left the jeweler's shop, the cheerful sound of the tinkling bell following them out into the street. But their expressions were anything but cheerful.

"Four pairs," Grace said, voicing exactly the thing he was thinking. "That means . . ."

"He's got two more kills planned. At least," Gavin finished. "And who knows if this was the only jeweler he bought from?"

"He's escalating. He went from killing far away to face-to-face in just twelve hours. That fast of a kill cycle usually means the killer's devolving, but here . . ." She frowned, worrying at the edges of her silk cuffs as she thought. "I don't think he's devolving. He's not getting sloppy or panicking."

"He's getting more violent. More personal," Gavin said.

"He's got plans," Grace said, looking up at him, her face worried but determined. "We need to get in the way of those plans. Quickly. Or more people are going to die."

"We've got to convince Harrison," Gavin said.

"We're going to need more than an old man's recollections and a few serial numbers on diamonds," Grace said. "And if we do it from headquarters, Paul's gonna stick his head in to check on us and get pissed when he finds out I ignored him."

"So what's your suggestion?"

"You take Janice's case. I take the Andersons.

We comb through the evidence separately. We present our findings to Paul separately. But they'll be the same profile. The same guy. He won't be able to deny it when *all* the facts are in front of him in black and white. And he won't be able to say we're just feeding off each other's take on the cases."

"Good idea," Gavin said. "That means I should drop you off somewhere so we can get to work. Where to?"

"My place," Grace said. She punched in the address to the GPS.

"So you think Harrison's gonna be pissed?" Gavin asked as he made a right toward Logan Circle, where she lived.

"I think he'll get over it," Grace said. "This thing he's doing? The stubborn thing? It's not an ego thing. Paul isn't like that."

There was a softness in her voice that made him pay attention, dread building in his stomach. Were she and Harrison an item? He hadn't picked up on any heat between them, but maybe she was really good at keeping that away from the job.

"You two are close," he said, and he knew it was awkward, but he couldn't help it. Was she taken? He found himself hating the idea with a fierceness that shook him.

"He and my best friend used to be engaged,"

Grace said, and something like relief flooded him. Grace was *not* the type of woman who would date her best friend's ex-fiancé under any circumstances. "We've spent a lot of time together through the years."

"You're worried about him," Gavin said, realizing this was where all her softness came from: concern for Harrison's well-being.

"PTSD's a bitch," Grace said. "I see it in some of my kids at the center, and I've done work with vets and with agents who've suffered trauma or worked undercover. It can be a long road back. And there are always bumps in the road."

"Harrison's a good guy, and if he's got a support system with you in it, I wouldn't worry too much, Grace," he said.

She smiled, a grateful, sweet smile that he'd never seen on her face before, and it made his heart thump too hard in his chest, like it wanted to tear right out of his rib cage. "I hope you're right," she said.

"Arrived at your destination," the GPS chirped as Gavin pulled up to a well-kept brownstone. The place was beautiful, with a long flight of stairs leading up to the dark blue door.

"I guess I'll see you tomorrow," he said.

"Tomorrow," Grace agreed, getting out of the SUV, but then she turned back, hesitant. "Thank you," she said.

He frowned. "For what?"

"For having my back. For seeing what I did at the crime scene. For understanding about Paul." She shrugged, her cheeks reddening. "For being you."

Before he could say anything, she spun and hurried up the steps, then bent down to pick up a package on the porch before disappearing inside.

Gavin sat there for a moment, feeling both warm and dumbfounded. Grace Sinclair had a way of yanking the floor out from underneath him when he least expected it. He wanted nothing more than to march up those stairs, knock on her door, and kiss her the minute she opened it.

But it was too soon. There was too much work to be done.

She wasn't ready. And he wanted to make sure the next time she was in his bed, she was there for good.

He pulled away from the curb and was driving down the block when his phone began to ring. When he saw it was Grace, he frowned.

"You miss me already?" he said into the phone.

"I'm really counting on you being a sneaky, very prepared former spy right now," she said and everything inside him went cold, because her voice was shaking.

"Grace, what are you . . ." he started. He was already turning the SUV around, his fingers numb.

"Because I'm pretty sure someone sent me a bomb," Grace interrupted. "And I'm holding it."

CHAPTER 10

I want you to stay very still," Gavin said.

Grace licked her lips. They were dry, and she could feel her lipstick wearing off as she worried her lower lip with her teeth.

"This is really bad," she said, trying to keep her hands motionless. She was still holding the package she'd picked up from the porch, trying to keep it as level as possible.

"What tipped you off it was a bomb?" he asked, bending down to stare at the box in her hands.

"The corners on the paper," she said, her voice cracking as anxiety filled her. She bit down hard on the inside of her cheek, trying to clear her mind. She had to stay calm. She couldn't let the adrenaline take over. Her hands would shake.

Her hands couldn't shake.

"The corners were folded too neatly. And then the handwriting . . . as if he wrote it with a ruler under the letters. They were too straight. It was meticulous and deceptive . . . like him. I knew the second I glanced down at the address." She was babbling. She couldn't help it.

"You should go," she told him, her eyes darting around the room. "There's no cover here if it goes off. You'll—"

"Grace," Gavin cut her off softly. He didn't touch her—he couldn't—but his voice wrapped around her like a blanket. Comforting. Soothing. "Breathe. Nice and slow. I will get you out of this. I promise. I'm not going anywhere. Neither are you."

"But—"

"Grace," he said again. "I'm in charge now, okay?"

Her eyes fluttered shut. *Breathe, Grace,* she thought. *Trust him. You can trust him.*

"Okay," she said.

"Bomb squad's on their way," he reassured her. "They'll be here as soon as they can. But we need to get it out of your hands and into the blast container." He nodded at the bucket-like container he'd brought inside with him. "We don't know if it's pressure sensitive, so we need to do this carefully. Okay? You've gotta do everything I tell you, when I tell you."

She almost nodded but then forced herself

not to. No movement. "Okay," she said again as sweat trickled down her collarbone between her breasts. "So, do you travel with bomb disposal equipment in your SUV all the time?" she asked, a pathetic attempt at a joke. "Is that a retired-spy thing?"

"I'm known for my explosive humor," he said, deadpan, and it cheered her more than it should have as he grabbed the container and set it down at her feet. "Let's just say there's a story behind my bomb disposal kit. It involves unstable chemicals, chewing gum, ice cubes, and cheap dollar-store hair spray."

"Who do you think you are, MacGyver?" Her voice trembled and he looked up, his eyes serious and sympathetic to her panic.

"We're gonna do this nice and slow, Grace," he said. "You're gonna get as low as you can without moving your arms, and then you're gonna carefully lower it into the container, nice and level, and set it down as gently as you can. And then you're gonna scramble the hell away, as fast as you can. On my count, okay?"

"Wait," she said. "Um . . ." She let out a deep breath, trying frantically to think. It could blow in her arms. It could wipe her out. Wipe them both out. Pink mist. That's what bomb squad called it when there was nothing left of you.

"If you tell me to get out one more time, I'm gonna be pissed," Gavin said. "I'm not going anywhere. I am *not* leaving you."

"My art collection," she said.

"You want to talk about your art collection right now?" Gavin asked, gaping at her.

"It's worth a lot of money. It was my grandmother's legacy. I just—Please, make sure that it gets dispersed the way it's outlined in my will, okay? It's supposed to go to the counseling center after I'm gone. And the royalties from all my books. They go to the center too. A special college fund for the kids. My friend Maggie Kincaid is the executor of my estate. I need you to make sure—"

"Grace," he interrupted. "No," he said firmly, reaching out and then stopping himself before he made contact with her cheek. His hands fisted, like it was physically painful not to touch her. "No dying today. You are not finished. *We* are not finished."

"I just—" Grace didn't know what to say. If these were her last words, they should mean something. Shouldn't she be thinking about her parents? Her work? Her friends?

But all she could see was him. His eyes, reassuring and steady, his face somber and determined.

This was a man who would never let her fall. He would always catch her.

Trust him.

She licked her lips again. "All right," she said. "Let's do this. Get low. Then lower the box. Nice and steady. Set it down gently. Then scramble."

"You got it," he said. "On three. One. Two."

Grace took a deep breath.

"Three."

CHAPTER 11

He'd been through countless do-or-die scenarios. Four years in intelligence. Two years on bomb squad. Eight years in homicide. He'd been tortured. He'd been shot three times, stabbed twice, and he had the scars to prove it. Plus there was that one pesky failed poisoning incident during his Army years.

But he realized he'd never known true fear until he'd walked into Grace's home and seen her holding what was very likely a bomb.

It had taken all his training, all those years of dangerous days, to keep himself steady and calm as he talked her through getting the box into the blast container. When she lowered the bomb inside, he closed it and grabbed her by the arm. He picked her up off her feet in his haste and she leaned into him as he ran out of the building.

The bomb squad truck pulled up just as they got to the bottom of the stairs, and the agents streamed out, half of them marching into Grace's house, the other half scattering to alert the neighbors.

"Jeremy," Grace said as a burly guy with silver hair and a scar through his eyebrow trotted up to her.

"Grace, you okay?" he asked, grabbing her arm, looking worried.

"Agent Walker covered me," she said. "He talked me through it all. He has bomb squad experience."

Jeremy's eyes shifted to Gavin. "What's the situation?" he asked.

"I found the package on the porch. I was so stupid. I didn't think—I just picked it up," Grace said. "It's about the same size as the box the tea I buy from India comes in."

"She got inside, realized what it could be, and called me," Gavin finished. "We got it into the blast containment unit I keep in my rig. It doesn't seem to be pressure sensitive, which means it's probably on a timer."

"Or our bomber's around, with a detonator," Jeremy said.

Grace shivered, looking over her shoulder. "I want to go back inside," she said.

"No way," Gavin and Jeremy said at the same

time. The two men glanced at each other, sharing a rueful smile.

"Let me take care of it, scan it, and make sure it's totally contained," Jeremy said. "I'll come right out when I'm done."

"Be careful," Grace said. "Jessica will kill me if anything happens to you."

Jeremy smiled. "That she will," he agreed. "I'll be right back."

"His wife's a friend," Grace explained. She folded her arms across her chest, feeling unbearably cold. "God, this is surreal," she said. "Bomb squad milling around my rare books and antique couches."

"You have a nice place, by the way," Gavin said, trying to lighten the dark cloud on her face. "At least, what I could see of it before I started focusing on the bomb."

Her lips pressed together, like she was trying not to smile. "Thanks," she said dryly.

"It'll be okay," he said.

"I know," she said quickly. Too quickly. "It's just . . ." She looked up at the brownstone. "It's my home," she said.

This place was her sanctuary. The few glimpses that he'd gotten told him that in spades.

And someone had tried to violate that. Someone was very possibly trying to violate more than that. Gavin felt a burst of anger roar to life inside him as she let out a shaky breath, hugging herself. He wanted to take her in his arms. He wanted to track down the man who'd scared her so much and make the bastard pay.

He wanted to never let Grace out of his sight again.

"Who would do this?" she murmured, seemingly to herself.

Gavin couldn't help it any longer. He reached out and his hand settled in between her shoulder blades. She didn't tense or move away. Instead he felt the muscles underneath his fingers relax for the first time as she looked up at him.

"Gavin—" she started.

"Grace!" Footsteps pounded toward them as Harrison came running up, looking as if he'd gotten the shock of his life. Gavin's hand quickly fell away from Grace's shoulder, and he stepped back a little, just in case. "I heard over the radio—are you okay?"

"I'm fine, Paul," she said.

"Bomb squad's in there?" he asked, making a move toward the steps.

"Paul, *no!*" Grace said, her voice so sharp that even Gavin's head jerked toward her. "You are *not* going in there."

"But I—"

"No," she said firmly. "Do you want to trigger yourself?"

Gavin stared down at the ground, uncomfortable. This was a private conversation he had no right to be involved in. Grace was a psychologist. She understood this stuff better than he did. She was clearly worried about the PTSD that Harrison was dealing with after his last case, and he didn't blame her. Sending a guy with bomb-related PTSD into a building with a bomb was a terrible idea.

Harrison was keeping it together well enough, but everyone in their line of work had triggers—things, sometimes innocuous ones, that reminded them of the worst moments, of the trauma, of the death that they saw. Gavin couldn't stand the smell of oranges—they reminded him of his first homicide, where the father had murdered his entire family at the breakfast table. The orange juice had been knocked over, the smell rank and putrid by the time the bodies were discovered.

He'd remember that until his dying day. And every time someone offered him orange juice, he'd shake his head and he'd be back in that horror, just for a second.

"Give me a radio, then," Harrison said curtly. One of the agents who'd evacuated the neighbors handed him one. "Jeremy, it's Harrison. Where are we?" he asked.

"Looks like the box is lined with foil." Jeremy's

voice crackled over the radio. "We can't get a scan on it, so we're going manual. Stand by."

"Standing by," Paul said.

"We're hot, boss," Jeremy said a moment later. "The device is crude as hell. Explosives are blast dynamite. He got them from a construction site, my bet. Two lead wires. Very basic. He probably put it together from diagrams online. Cutting the wires now. Stand by."

A tense minute passed, and then: "All clear, boss. Bomb is defused. You'll want to come in here and see what we've got."

The three of them hurried up the steps and into the brownstone. The bomb squad was grouped around Jeremy, his back to them.

"What is it?" Grace asked.

He turned. "This was in there with the bomb," he explained, holding the book out to her.

Grace's latest book.

"Oh, no," she said.

All Gavin could think as she stepped forward were her first words when he first saw her holding the box, thinking it was a bomb: *This is really bad.*

"Someone give me some gloves," Grace said. She was handed a pair, which she snapped on. "Let me see it," she said.

Jeremy handed it to her. She removed the dust jacket and searched the dark blue cover. When she flipped it open, all the blood drained out of her face. Gavin stepped forward, alarmed, half-afraid she was going to keel over. But instead she began to read.

"'My dearest FBI,'" she said, her words halting. "'Is this the best you can do? If you want to put it all together, you're going to have to dig deeper. Good luck.'"

He watched as she began to leaf through the pages, his chest tightening as her face grew whiter and whiter. "There's a code," she said. "Passages are underlined, letters and words are circled. It looks random but . . ." She looked up, her eyes searching for and then finding his. "We need to crack it," she said.

CHAPTER 12

Grace's mind raced, jumping from possible scenarios to criminal profiles. Someone meticulous and intelligent who felt downtrodden and ignored. He had an ego, a sense of grandeur that people in his real life either dismissed or mocked. Obviously a perfectionist, he was a planner. He was probably in a job that made him feel undervalued and ignored.

"If it's coded, then we need to get it to the math guys at headquarters," Paul said, gently taking the book from her. "Walker, give her a ride to HQ."

"We're going to get out of your space as soon as we can," Jeremy said reassuringly. "We did an initial sweep of the house, but I want to do one more, inside and out, just to be safe. The device in the box was basic, but it would've gone off. I want to make sure he hasn't tucked any more around your house. I promise we won't break any of your pretty baubles," Jeremy said, waving his hand at the sculptures and paintings that were sprinkled across Grace's living room.

"Of course. Do whatever you think is best," Grace said. She was almost positive there wasn't a bomb in the house—her guy, whoever he was, wasn't a sophisticated bomb maker if the amateurish explosive he'd dropped on her doorstep was any indication. It didn't fit the profile that was beginning to take shape in her head. "Just make sure everything's locked up when you're done?"

"Will do," Jeremy said. He clapped his hands. "Boys, we're gonna sweep the house one more time. Michael and Luke, upstairs with me. The rest of you take the dining room and kitchen and basement."

Grace grabbed her red trench coat, pulled it on, and looked at Gavin. "Let's go."

She was quiet during the whole ride to headquarters, even when they got caught in a tangle of lunchtime traffic. But Gavin made no attempt to coax her into conversation. She was grateful for it—she needed to think.

They walked together through the maze that was the underground parking structure and took the elevator up in continued silence. As soon as the doors opened on the second floor, a flurry of activity and people greeted them.

"Agent Harrison is with the press liaison in his office," Paul's secretary said. "He'll let you know when he's available."

"Grace, are you okay?" Zooey asked, leaning in for a hug. "When I heard bomb squad was over at your house, I freaked."

"I'm fine," Grace reassured her. "Gavin got the bomb contained."

"Right on, cowboy," Zooey said.

Gavin smiled.

"I need you and your team to take a look at this, though." Grace held up the book she'd taken back from Paul before leaving her house.

"We're set up in the north conference room," Zooey told them. "Come this way."

They followed her into the room and took a seat at the huge oak table, Grace gripping the book tightly.

She wasn't going to let it out of her sight.

Zooey sat down next to her, snapping on a pair of gloves and spreading a sterile paper sheet across the table. Grace set the book on it.

"Okay, so what's the deal?" Zooey asked. "That's your latest book."

"It was in the package with the bomb," Grace said.

Zooey frowned. "Doesn't that kind of defeat the point?" she asked. "If it went off, the book would be in pieces."

"It was a test," Grace said. "Our unsub wanted to see if I'd pass. If I didn't, I'd get blown up. If I did, I got the next clue." She pointed to the book. "It's in code," she explained. "You can check it for fingerprints or DNA, but I can tell you now, whoever did this isn't leaving anything behind."

"He's too damn careful," Gavin said.

"Yep," Grace said, the *p* popping a little in her anger. She shook her shoulders, trying to get rid of the adrenaline that was still pumping through her.

"Well, you're in luck, because one of my hobbies is code-breaking," Zooey said. "The guys have me sit in sometimes. And speaking of the guys . . ." She nodded to the door, which opened, and a group of techs and code-breakers poured in.

"I'm Agent Sinclair, to those of you who don't know me," Grace said to the group. "This is Agent Walker." She held up the book. "And this is the evidence in question. We need to figure it out fast, people."

Grace handed over the book to the lead tech as the team set up their scanning station on the table.

"That'll take ten minutes at least," Zooey explained. "You don't exactly write short books."

Grace let out a burst of laughter that sounded a lot harsher than she had intended. She closed her eyes, breathing in deep. She could practically feel her nerves starting to fray, her calm unraveling, her control spinning free.

"I'm going to get you some coffee," Gavin told her.

"Oh, you don't need to," she said, even though a cup of coffee sounded like heaven right now.

"But I want to," he said. "Be right back."

"I think he's sweet on you," Zooey whispered as Gavin left the conference room.

"Oh, shush," Grace said.

"You're blushing." Zooey grinned. "I'm gonna let you alone to think." She reached down, hugging Grace lightly. "I'm really glad you didn't blow up," she said.

"Me too," Grace said.

Zooey patted her shoulder. "It's gonna be okay," she said.

"Of course," Grace responded automatically, but she didn't quite believe it.

As the techs scanned each page and transferred the information to the laptop, Grace sat and tried to puzzle it out the organic way: with her superior human brainpower.

It was her book on her doorstep. Whatever was inside it, whatever the coded message, it was meant for her.

He wanted her to feel small. Scared. That was the only reason to make her think the package was a bomb. He got off on fear . . . on feeling smarter than everyone else in the room.

And he liked tricks.

Grace sat up straight, insight hitting her hard. Breaking his code would mean they were smarter than he was—and that would enrage him. He wouldn't want to feel that.

No, he wanted to make them feel stupid.

"Zooey!" she called out.

"Yeah?" Zooey looked up from arguing with one of the techs about page numbers and algorithms.

"Where's the box the book came in?"

"Jeremy said he'd take it to my lab for me," Zooey said. "It should be there."

"I'll be right back," Grace said suddenly.

Before anyone could protest, she raced out of the room, almost slamming right into Gavin, who was carrying two cups of coffee.

"Where are you going in such a rush?" he asked.

"I've got an idea," she said, grabbing the mugs and putting them on a table. "Come with me." She took his hand and hurried down the hall toward Zooey's lab.

Like Zooey herself, the room was an odd mix of sterile science and colorful eccentricity. Her computer area was surrounded by vintage toys and a few random Legos. There was even a framed photo of Zooey performing as Janet in a shadow-theater version of *The Rocky Horror Picture Show,* complete with corset, blond wig, and platform heels.

Grace smiled at the picture and walked over to the stainless steel table. The box was sitting there, looking completely harmless.

"The unsub wants to feel smarter than us. Smarter than *me*," Grace explained to Gavin as she picked up the box, examining the outside from all angles. She traced her finger over the neat handwriting. He was obsessive, clearly. Fastidious. He'd put a lot of thought into presentation.

"So you think there's something in the box? That the book's just a red herring?" Gavin asked.

"I don't know," Grace said. "He designed the package just so. Perfect enough to make me pause if I was smart enough."

"It's a huge gamble," Gavin said. "What if you hadn't noticed? Or been unable to defuse his crappy bomb?"

"He wanted me to call the bomb squad," Grace mused. "He wanted me to get it all the way to HQ. Why?"

"Maybe he's getting off on the idea of playing us the fool? Fucking with the FBI?"

Grace picked up the box, tipped it upside down, and shook it gently, but nothing fell out.

With a pair of tweezers, Grace grabbed an edge of the foil lining and began to peel it back. Her eyes widened when she saw a strip of paper laid across another layer of foil. "Look," she said, pulling the foil back farther, revealing more strips of paper sandwiched between the sheets of foil.

"Shit," Gavin said. "More games."

He'd double-lined the package so the paper would be hidden from the X-ray. Tricky. Smart.

"This guy likes to be the smartest person in the room," Grace said, peeling back the first layer of foil. "When he's challenged, he probably throws a fit."

"And now he's challenging you," Gavin said.

"Lucky me," Grace said wryly. She lifted the strips of paper with the tweezers as they were revealed and placed them on the table.

By the time she was done, she had ten strips, all with random markings.

A puzzle for her to solve.

"Who the hell is this guy?" she asked under her breath as she began to arrange the strips, fitting them together.

"You need help?" Gavin asked.

She shook her head. "Let me try on my own first," she said.

It took her just a few minutes—she'd always been good at puzzles. Once she'd fit the longest

slashes with the shortest, what looked like ar-
bitrary lines on the strips of paper suddenly
morphed into a message:

117 Lincoln Blvd. #105
2:00 p.m.

Grace looked up at the clock in the lab. It was
almost three.

She swallowed, her throat suddenly dry.

"Shit, we're late," Gavin said.

"But what for?" Grace asked. "Who's waiting
for us at that address?"

Gavin looked at her soberly. "It's time to go
find out."

CHAPTER 13

My pretty girl,

I've waited. Patient, steadfast, for you to come to me. To atone for your behavior.

I had faith you would return. I'd hoped you would remember what you really were, how we were. Who you belonged to. I prayed the guilt would crush you into the woman you were truly meant to be.

Your sins, they're countless. Immeasurable. Yet instead of crumbling at my feet where you belong, you continue. You live and laugh and keep climbing.

So ambitious, always. Prepared to do anything. Fuck anyone.

You never knew your place.

It's high time I teach it to you.

Starting now.

CHAPTER 14

17 Lincoln Boulevard was a large brick apartment building favored by professionals—lawyers, doctors, lobbyists. Expensive and tasteful, and by 4:00 p.m., it was swarmed by SWAT and DC police.

"We're just waiting on the all clear from the advance team," Paul said.

"We're already late," Grace snapped, the tension seeping into her voice. Paul frowned at her, and she let out a long breath. "Sorry."

"We need to be careful," Gavin reminded her gently.

She softened for a moment. "I know, I—" She stopped, realizing that one of the cops stationed near them at the door was rolling his eyes at her impatience, and all that softness Gavin brought out in her dissipated.

"Hey, you!" she called. "Yes, you. Don't look at me like that. I'm not your mother."

The man's eyes went big. "What?"

Grace propped her hands on her hips. "You heard me. Don't take your problem with women in authority out on me just because your mother was a career woman."

He gaped at her. "Have we met?"

"No. Now go do your job and stop eavesdropping."

She turned back to Paul, who raised an eyebrow.

"What?" she demanded.

"You need to—"

"If you tell me I need to calm down, we're going to have a problem," Grace said, an edge to her voice. "I told you there was more to these cases. I told you there was a connection—and you dismissed me, Paul! You mocked me. Tell me the truth: If Gavin had come up with similar theories and taken them to you alone, would you have dismissed *his* ideas?"

"I—" Paul sighed. "I don't know," he said, in a way that told her that he *did* know—it just made him uncomfortable to think about. This time, she was the one rolling her eyes.

She'd chosen a male-dominated career, but sometimes she wished she didn't have to fight so damn hard to be taken seriously.

She was done. This case was grating at her, and he was being so stupid. "This is bullshit," she growled. "I'm not going to cater to your male ego when there are lives on the line!"

"Grace," Paul said, his voice sharp.

"I'm gonna give you two a few minutes to talk," Gavin said tactfully, stepping out of the way.

Paul grabbed Grace's arm, pulling her down the street, away from the throng of people. She went, but angrily. And as soon as they were out of earshot, she rounded on him. "You are being an *asshole*," she hissed. "What is going on with you?"

"You're crossing a line, Grace," Paul warned.

"It's one thing for you to dismiss my concern about your well-being when I come to you as a friend," she said. "But it's another to dismiss my theories as a psychologist and a profiler. This is my *job*. This is what I am *brilliant* at. I am the best there is, and I am on *your* team, which is barely being kept together right now because you're not leading it!"

"I'm doing my job," he said, his mouth a hard line of disapproval.

"You're hiding behind a desk because you're scared of making the wrong decision again," Grace said.

And there it was, out in the open. The truth. She could see it in his stricken face, in the way Paul's shoulders slumped all of a sudden, like all the fight had gone out of him.

"You dismissed Maggie's theories about the cabin during the Mancuso case," Grace continued, gentler now, knowing she was finally getting through to him. "She didn't want SWAT to go in that soon. But you overrode her. You thought you knew best and you made a choice and people died. And you got a bomb strapped to your chest. That would mess up anyone, Paul."

"I'm a goddamn FBI agent, Grace," he said, his voice low and tight, his eyes full of a pain he'd been hiding. "I am supervisory agent. I lead an elite team. I've worked in the field for fifteen years. I'm better than this."

"Oh, screw that," Grace said fiercely. "Trauma is trauma, Paul. We can't predict how we'll react until it happens. You can't be 'better' than PTSD. It's not weakness, and it's not mind over matter. But it's just going to get worse unless you learn coping mechanisms and how to deal with it."

"I *am* dealing with it," Paul gritted out.

"You're hurting yourself," she said. "You're worrying the people who work with you and care about you. And you're hampering my investigation. And we both know you *are* better than that."

The radio in Paul's hand crackled. "We're all clear here, boss," said a SWAT team member. "One body. Female. Late thirties. We're going to need forensics. And an ME. And that profiler of yours. This is a weird one."

Grace looked at Paul. "I'm going in there," she said. "And if there are diamond earrings on that corpse, you *are* going to give me the freedom to treat these cases as serial murders."

"And if I refuse?" he asked.

Grace's stomach twisted. "Then I'll go over your head," she said. "And they'll side with me over you, Paul. Not just because I'm right. But because I bring in a hell of a lot of good press for them."

"You would really do that?"

"I will do anything to catch this guy," Grace said, that fierce heat climbing inside her chest at the thought. "That's my job. You might want to remember it's yours too."

Without another word, she stalked down the sidewalk, Gavin falling into step with her as she entered the lobby.

"How'd it go?" he asked as she pressed the elevator button.

"Well, he didn't fire me. Yet," Grace said.

"You've got some nerves of steel, Grace," he said as the elevator doors shut behind them. "I like that in a woman."

"You like everything about me," she said sarcastically, grateful for the distraction of his teasing at a moment like this. She hated confronting

Paul almost as much as she hated what was happening to him.

"True," Gavin replied, and the unabashed honesty in his voice startled her into looking up at him, her eyes wide.

"Come on, it can't be a surprise," he said. "You're a hard woman to forget."

"Gavin, I—" she started, but then the elevator chimed and the doors opened into a hallway swarming with forensic techs and SWAT.

"Later," he said. "Let's go."

They made their way through the throng and arrived at the apartment, which had crime scene tape crossed over the door. After putting on booties and gloves, Grace slipped between the tapes into the apartment.

The decor was tasteful. Expensive. Nancy Bantam, the divorce lawyer who'd lived—and died—here clearly liked luxury. Grace took in the vintage Waterford crystal vase holding still-fragrant hothouse flowers that she knew must have been flown in from Hawaii, the honed Carrara marble counters in the kitchen but no pots or pans in sight. She could feel Gavin at her back, silent and watchful, as she got a sense of the space as she moved into the kitchen. She opened the fridge. Lots of fresh-pressed juice and meals from a high-end meal service, neatly packaged.

This was a woman who ran a well-organized life. Who didn't like fuss, clutter, or domestic work. Who knew what she wanted and had gotten it. Until . . .

"Nothing's out of place," Gavin observed as they made their way into the living room. The throw pillows on the delicate pink couches weren't even askew. "He tried to make the Andersons' place look like a robbery, but he didn't bother here."

"The ruse was up the second he sent me that package," Grace said. "He didn't want us to make the connections before. But now?"

"He's rubbing it in our faces," Gavin finished disgustedly, shaking his head. "Man, I do not like this guy."

"Ready for the bedroom?" she asked him.

He nodded.

They entered the bedroom and came to a stop. Grace could hear Gavin swear behind her, so quietly she knew she was the only one who'd heard.

She couldn't blame him. The scene was horrific.

Nancy was laid out on the bed, which was carefully made under her. Her body, entirely naked, and the chartreuse comforter were scattered with Polaroid pictures.

"God, this guy *hates* women," Gavin said as

Grace reached over and picked up one of the photos. It was of Nancy, already dead, reclining in a bathtub full of water. Grace looked over her shoulder—she could see the adjoining bathroom from here, and the claw-foot tub from the photo.

Gavin reached over her shoulder, taking the photo from her. "This is so fucked up," he said. He frowned as he and Grace looked at each other. "Maybe too fucked up?" he questioned.

"Like something out of a TV show," she agreed.

"It's kind of on the nose," he said. "Like he's trying to show us how bad he is."

"They're for us, not for him," she said. "If they were mementos, a way to relive the killing later on, to fetishize it, I'd understand. But this?" She turned in a slow circle, taking in the room. "He gets to humiliate her and taunt us at the same time."

Zooey glanced up from examining the woman's hands. "There was a struggle here, as you can see." She gestured to the large broken mirror on the opposite wall. "She fought him off, but you wouldn't know it from looking at her."

"He groomed her," Grace said, her eyes skating over Nancy's perfectly coiffed hair.

"He bathed her," Zooey said. "He put lotion on her. He did her nails. There's a little spilled polish right here, see?" She pointed to the pink smear near the pillow.

Grace could see it in her mind: the care the unsub took with Nancy's body. He'd even taken photos to document it. Were they proof? A signal? His twisted way of saying *I care about her*?

"He spent his time with her," Grace said. "Doing all this . . . it took time. He didn't take time with the others."

"He didn't humiliate the others like this either," Gavin said. "Shooting Janice was cold and removed, with no message. Killing Megan Anderson was rage fueled, complete with the sexist message of where he thinks women belong. But this?"

"It's calm. Orderly. She means something to him," Grace said, voicing the thing they were both thinking.

"Maybe they knew each other," Gavin suggested. "She's a divorce lawyer. Maybe a disgruntled client? Or a husband who thinks he got screwed over by her? What's the cause of death, Zooey?"

Zooey straightened, propping her hands on her hips. "I can't be sure until the ME gets here, but from the raw tissue around her mouth he wasn't able to cover with makeup, I'd say suffocation. Probably with one of the pillows." Zooey tugged at the edges of her gloves, looking troubled.

"This is . . . solicitous," Grace said. "Careful. He treated the body with care."

"But he left her naked," Zooey said, confused.

"Her clothes, they'll be folded up in the bathroom. Carefully, neatly. Precise," Grace said.

"She's right," called one of Zooey's cronies, a short man with horn-rimmed glasses, walking up from the hall. "The clothes are sitting on her vanity in there. He even scrubbed out the tub."

"No detail left unnoticed," Grace murmured, walking to the other side of the bed. "The grooming, the attention to her femininity—it isn't respect. Or remorse."

"I thought usually when they took care of the body after, it meant remorse," Zooey said.

Gavin shook his head. "This isn't remorse," he said. "This is all about shaming. Shaming her for her sexuality, reducing her to a pretty doll for him to play with. He's objectifying her in death, stripping her down to her femininity, banishing all traces of her brain, her work, her agency, because he thinks women are only good for serving men's desires."

"So he's the type who thinks women owe him everything," Zooey said.

"Definitely," Gavin said.

"Well, I know that type," Zooey said. "But at least the jerks on the dating sites just send dick pics—they don't kill you."

"He needs to disempower his victims to make himself feel superior," Gavin said. "He feels inadequate in his life and he's gone for the easy target that men and society have gone after for centuries: successful, independent women."

Zooey raised an eyebrow. "Someone paid attention in his women's studies classes," she said.

"Understanding how half the population lives and what they deal with is essential if you want to be a good cop," Gavin said.

"I wish every guy was such a good feminist ally," Zooey said dryly. "But, alas . . ."

"Where are the earrings?" Grace murmured, half to herself as she stared down at Nancy.

"What was that?" Zooey asked.

"The earrings," Grace said, brushing Nancy's hair back. "She's not wearing them."

Had he forgotten?

No. He wouldn't forget. The earrings meant something to him. They represented someone—his mother? An old girlfriend? A woman he never had a chance with?

There was a slight smudge of pink along Nancy's lower lip. Something horrible and dark swooped inside Grace's stomach. With gentle hands, she tilted Nancy's mouth open.

The diamond earrings glittered against her blue, swollen tongue.

Grace's stomach clenched when, for a second, it felt like the floor was dropping out from under her.

She'd been right. Dammit. There was a part of her that had hoped she was wrong.

She had a serial killer on her hands. One who seemed to have put his focus on her, if her theory was right.

He was playing a game, and he'd set it up for her to be his opponent. He'd waited to reach out to her—and she'd had to prove herself worthy to even get this far by solving his puzzle. And now he had delivered her another murder victim, displayed like a virgin sacrifice.

Why focus on her, though? That was the question. Was it just because she was more in the public eye than most of the FBI's profilers? That would be the simple answer.

But Grace had a feeling, a dreadful, chilling feeling, that none of the answers here were simple.

"Hey, Zooey!" called a tech from across the room. "Over here on this wall there's some discoloration. At first I thought it was just a bad paint job, but looking closer, I'm not sure. Will you check it out?"

The three turned to look. The blue wall did look slightly darker in the area he was pointing to—like paint or ink that hadn't quite dried.

"Shine a UV light on it," Zooey directed.

The tech grabbed one from his box of tools, switched it on, and passed the beam along the wall.

"Well, crap," Zooey said as the light revealed two painted words in the same neat block letters used in the inside cover of the book.

TOO LATE

Grace stared at them, her palms starting to sweat in the blue nitrile gloves she had snapped on earlier.

"Okay," Gavin said quietly, taking Grace's arm lightly. "Zooey, Agent Sinclair and I are going to discuss some things in the hall. Bag the earrings for us, please. And let us know if you find anything else unusual."

Grace let him steer her through the apartment, into the hallway, which had thankfully emptied of the throng of SWAT and techs from earlier. Now it was empty and quiet.

She looked up at him, and the horrible tightness in her chest eased a little when their eyes met. He hadn't dropped his hand from her arm, and she didn't want him to.

"Grace," he said. "Have you noticed what I've noticed about the three women's appearance?"

She swallowed, her throat terribly dry. She could play ignorant to him but not to herself.

"I could maybe look past the similar coloring," he continued. "But, Grace, they all have hair like yours. And most women don't keep their hair long like that."

She touched her pinned-up braids, her heart beating fast. "I know," she said. She had known since the second she'd realized the package contained a message.

This was about her.

Those women? Mr. Anderson?

They'd died because of her.

"He's performing," she said, finally. "He's staging all different kinds of kills. He's showing off." She gestured haltingly around her. "'Look what I can do. See how many ways I can kill. You're a fool for not catching me.' That's what he's saying—to me."

Gavin's mouth settled into a grim line. "So what are we thinking? A deranged fan? Do you have any stalkers? The popularity of your books must bring some delusional people out of the woodwork."

"I don't know," Grace said. "He has an ego—a big one. He wants recognition. Maybe from me specifically . . . but I feel like this is rooted in something bigger."

"If the women are surrogates for you, then that means you're in danger," Gavin said.

Grace could barely hear him, her mind was racing in so many directions as she tried to puzzle it out, as she tried to nail down the exact profile of this . . . this monster.

"Maybe I triggered something in him," she said "Or, God, maybe my books did." She pressed her hand against her mouth, trying to calm the panic rising inside her. Her skin felt too tight for her body, and a headache started to pound at her temples.

"Hey." Gavin's voice was a soft rumble and then he was stripping off his gloves and his palm was cupping the back of her neck, his fingers settling against the nape. It took a moment, but she finally met his eyes and instead of feeling lost and afraid, she felt as if she was suddenly found. Like she was being seen, truly, really, for the first time.

"This is not your fault," he said firmly. "And it's not your book's fault."

"I know," Grace said. And she did know. Intellectually. But emotionally . . .

That was harder. She loved writing. She loved the morality of the world she'd created, where the good guys always won and the bad guys ended up in prison. It was comforting.

But if her words had somehow led someone to do this . . .

No, she told herself sternly. She wasn't going there.

That was surely what the unsub wanted.

Gavin's thumb was making long, slow sweeps against the curve of her neck, and it sent little trickles of warmth spreading through her.

"Let's think about this. What does he want?"

"He wants me to think he's brilliant," Grace said immediately. "He wants admiration for what he's done. And he wants me to feel terrified. He wants me hopeless and useless against his brilliance." She pressed her lips together. "Well, he's going to be disappointed," she said, steel entering her voice. "Fear is motivating if you use it."

"That's my girl," he said, all affection and heat in his gaze. The moment the words were out of his mouth, he seemed to realize what he'd just said, and the high tilt of his cheekbones started to redden. "I mean—" he started.

"Nancy was a much tougher target than the two other victims," Grace interrupted smoothly, unable—not even unwilling, just plain *unable*—to examine the burst of emotion she'd experienced at his words. Now was not the time. "He had to get past the doorman and kill her quietly enough that her neighbors didn't even notice. Plus, the elaborate care he took in staging her body. He's evolving. The first kill removed him from the blood, from the intimacy of the act. The second, he got a little closer to what he wants. But with Nancy, it was the first time he got to be alone with the body for a long period of time."

"And he got performative and freaky," Gavin said.

"He's finding out what he likes," Grace explained, sick to her stomach. "And once he does, it'll be hard to stop him."

Gavin sighed. "You know we're going to have to take this to Harrison."

"I know," Grace said.

"And he's going to want to put you under a protective detail," Gavin added.

Grace's eyes flared. "I can take care of myself."

"Yeah, I don't think Harrison's gonna be very moved by that argument," he said.

CHAPTER 15

Predictably, Harrison was absolutely not moved by Grace's impassioned argument that she didn't need a security detail. He stood there next to Gavin, his arms crossed over his chest, his blue eyes glittering with a stern light as Grace clashed with him inside his office at headquarters.

"This is ridiculous!" she said. "Just an hour ago, you didn't believe me when I said there was a serial killer and now you want me to go to a *safe house* to avoid him?"

"Grace," Paul said. "You can't have it both ways. Either there's a serial killer and he's targeting you and sending you codes in your books and killing women who look a lot like you, or these are all unrelated murders with a few weird similarities. I thought you'd be happy I'm on board."

"Not if you assign me babysitters!" Grace

shouted. "I'm a better damn shot than most of the security detail team, and I've got the marksman trophies to prove it."

"Is that true?" Gavin asked Harrison under his breath.

"Yes, it is," Grace snapped.

"She's a better shot than half of the FBI," Paul said, looking cross. "It's incredibly annoying."

Gavin should probably not have found that such a turn-on, but he'd always been a little bit drawn to dangerous women. "Tell you what, Sinclair," he said. "If you can outshoot me, you don't need a security detail."

Grace stopped her pacing for a moment, looking at him, suddenly calculating. "And if I lose?" she asked, because she was too damn smart to walk into that one without knowing all the angles.

"Then you come and stay with me until this is over," Gavin said. "I'll have your back."

"This is absurd," Paul protested. "Completely against protocol."

"I've seen your place," Grace countered, completely ignoring Paul. "The front windows are perfect for an ambush. If I lose—and I won't—you'll come and stay with me at my brownstone."

"He knows where your brownstone is," Gavin protested. "He already sent you a bomb."

"It has fewer access points than your place," she shot back.

"Fine. Let's go down to the range right now," Gavin said.

"You two—" Paul started, but Grace had already dashed out the door.

Gavin clapped him on the back and winked. "Don't worry, boss. I've got this," he promised.

Grace was at the elevator leading to the basement level by the time he got to the hallway. He jogged down it and caught up with her just before the elevator doors closed.

"You're stressing Harrison out," he said, leaning against the elevator wall as he regarded her.

Grace's neat crown of braids was starting to come loose from the careful pins. There were smudges underneath her eyes, and her normally perfectly straight shoulders—she held herself like a queen—were slightly slumped.

She was exhausted. She needed to rest.

"I can convince Harrison to let it just be me watching over you," he coaxed. "You've got to have a guest room in that brownstone of yours. I am an excellent houseguest. Very clean. I even make breakfast."

"Oh, yeah?" she asked.

"Eggs, bacon, pancakes. The works," he said. "If you hadn't ditched me last time, you would know that already."

She shot him a look, a disapproving "don't talk about that" look. And God, it was the wrong kind of look to give him, because it made him want to do all sorts of things. To hit the stop button and press her against the wall, kissing her until she regretted leaving him that night. Until she remembered what she'd been missing. What they'd both been missing.

She brought the mischief out in him—all he wanted to do was tease and pull at her braids and lightly nip his way down her perfect stomach until she was gasping for it.

The elevator doors opened and Grace strode out toward the gun range and he followed. They had the range to themselves, and Grace immediately walked over to the middle row, pulled out her Glock, and set it on the counter in front of her.

He wasn't so full of himself that he was sure she couldn't beat him. He was a crack shot, but if she was as good as she—and Harrison—said, he'd have to be at his best.

But even if she won this little game of theirs, there was no way in hell he was letting her out of his sight. He was coming home with her and he was going to make sure she was safe.

This unsub, whoever he was, was the worst kind of murderer. He was exploring his urges, perfecting them.

Once he was satisfied with his skill set, he'd come for Grace.

Gavin gritted his teeth at the thought as Grace lined up the paper targets and pushed the button that sent them zipping to the back of the range.

"What do you say?" she asked. "Best out of three?"

"Sure," he said, taking the row next to her and pulling out his .42. The weight of it was familiar in his hands as he looked over to her. "Ladies first."

"Such a gentleman," she said, and he hated the tightness in her voice and face. He wanted to ease it.

But he knew better than that. Grace was a woman on a mission. She sought justice. Maybe it consumed her a little, like sometimes it did him. And this—this entire case—was personal.

She raised her Glock, all the tension fading from her in a split second as her stance settled, as she focused on the target, everything else falling away.

She fired off four shots in rapid succession, two in the target's head, dead between the eyes, and two neatly paired in the center of the chest.

"Maybe I should start calling you Annie Oakley," he said, taking his .42 in his right hand and leveling it. He breathed in, then out, then in, and in that crystalline point between breaths, his finger squeezed the trigger gently. One. Two. Three. Four.

Grace frowned as she brought the targets forward, examining his.

"You learn to shoot like this in the military?" she asked, switching out the used targets for new ones.

He laughed. "No," he said.

"Really?" She sent the targets back to the end of the rows.

"No. Texas, actually."

She looked over at him, one slim brow raised questioningly.

"My grandfather," he explained. "He was a Texas Ranger. He could hit a quarter in the air from fifty feet away. Damn fine shot. Finer man."

She tilted her head, a smile tugging at her lips. "You miss him."

He didn't even have to ask how she knew he'd passed away. She knew things like that. Intuited them or used that big brain to puzzle them out from his facial expressions or word patterns or whatever. "Every day."

There was a moment where she looked at him, soft and understanding, and he felt that jolt inside him, the same one he'd felt the night they'd met and she'd placed her hand in his when he'd asked her to dance. It was a rightness he'd never experienced before, a feeling that had echoed through him the last two years when he'd been with anyone else, because he finally knew what he'd been missing.

What he'd been looking for.

He'd never considered himself a terribly romantic man. He believed in love—valued it, understood that lasting love was rare, that sometimes it was work. But he'd never felt the earth shake or sworn he'd found a missing piece of himself or any of the things people talked about.

Then one night in November he went to the Policeman's Ball. Grace Sinclair entered his orbit. He'd been drawn to her as if by a gravitational pull, holding his hand out and asking her to dance before he even realized what he was doing. She'd burned her mark in his soul with one touch, one smile, one night of the most intense connection he'd ever had with another person.

And now they were here, partners, teammates. He knew she felt it: how well they worked in sync, how they didn't think the same but instead in conjunction. She approached things from the psychological and he from the emotional—and it was *working*. It was like fireworks being on a crime scene with her. Like a Roman candle sparking in his brain and gut as they moved through a scenario, every step they took in tandem. A dance they were never taught but seemed to know innately.

This was more than attraction. More than a meeting of two minds. And he wanted all of it.

All of her.

"I'd never picked up a gun until Quantico," Grace said, raising her Glock again. Her stance was just a bit too wide, he thought as she fired.

Sure enough, the bullet snagged the top of the dark circle in the middle of the target. Still a great shot, but by her standards, probably not.

She was hard on herself. The kind of driven that came from long-buried hurt. He didn't know the specifics, but he'd been around her enough to see it: some man had screwed with her, maybe when she was young, probably college, and whatever he'd done . . . it had left a wound. It had caused her to put up walls so thick not even the most determined, devoted man could get through. Not unless she let him.

God, he wanted her to let him. She was the most beautiful thing he'd ever seen, a gun in her hand, confidence and ease and strength in every inch of her body. A warrior queen, a fierce protector, a woman you wouldn't want to reckon with.

Grace let out a frustrated little breath and then adjusted her feet, slipping back into that perfect form. She waited, breathing for a few seconds, getting ahold of herself. His eyes were on her face instead of her hands as she fired, three perfect shots to the head. Her mouth quirked up triumphantly.

"So you're a natural," he commented, turning to his own target. He fired off his shots quickly, the muscle memory singing through him like an old friend.

"That's what my instructors told me," Grace explained primly, switching out the targets again. "Deciding round," she added.

Her shots were perfect. Clean, grouped tightly together, and hard to beat.

"I have a confession," Gavin said, and he couldn't resist the tug of his smile as she frowned, confused. He moved his gun to his left hand. "I'm not actually right-handed."

He barely glanced from her to the target before he fired, four rapid shots, the sound reverberating in his ears. He pushed the button to bring the target forward, and Grace stepped from her row to his to examine the paper.

There was just one hole, dead center in the target's head. Each bullet had gone through that hole, neat as a pin, barely disrupting the edges of the paper.

He'd won.

Grace's mouth twisted, disapproving, and God, she had to stop doing that or he was going to . . .

She propped her hands on her hips, facing him. "Sneaky," she said, and his mouth curved, because it was the first time she'd said that with approval—even if it was reluctant approval.

"So you tell me," he said.

"You play dirty," she said, and there was a timbre to her voice, a huskiness that made his stomach tighten and his fingers twitch, desperate to touch her.

He dipped his head down—she was tall for a woman, especially in those heels, but he was taller than most men. Her eyes flicked up to his and then down, lingering on his lips.

"You like it," he said.

He wanted so many things in that moment, he felt torn in a dozen different directions. He wanted to kiss her, hard and fast and deep. He wanted to take her home and put her in his bed with a shot of whiskey and tell her everything would be okay and then somehow make it that way. He wanted to fall to his knees and push up that skirt and show her exactly how dirty he could be.

"Maybe I do," she said, and she straightened slightly, so that her breasts brushed against his chest, just barely. She smiled when she heard him take in a quick breath at the touch. "What are you going to do about it?"

After a shocked second, he leaned forward, so close that he could feel her breath against his lips. Instead of drifting shut, her eyes stayed on him, and it was even hotter that she wouldn't break the gaze as she challenged him to take what they both wanted. He lifted his hand and curled it around her cheek, dragging his thumb across her lush lower lip, still stained red from her lipstick.

"I'm going to take you home," he said. "And I'm going to make sure you're safe. Because I won."

She let out a little huff of breath that was half a laugh. "Barely," she said, and he pulled back, his gut aching as he put space between them. He couldn't kiss her here. If he kissed her now, he wouldn't be able to stop. And every inch of this place had cameras. He wasn't going to mess with her reputation like that.

"You put too much weight on your left leg," he said, expecting her to protest or roll her eyes or deny it.

But instead she nodded. "I know," she said. "My second year on the job, I got shot. Right thigh. When I'm stressed, I shift my weight."

"You got shot?" It came out a lot more alarmed than he wanted. But the idea of someone marring her skin, hurting her, spilling her blood . . .

He wanted to kill them. Instantly. Intensely.

"It was years ago," she said, grabbing her gun and holstering it. "The unsub kind of kidnapped me."

"Grace, there's no way to 'kind of kidnap' someone."

"Fine—he got the drop on me," she said shortly as they walked out of the gun range. "Knocked me out. But Maggie got me through it before I bled out."

"That's your friend the hostage negotiator?"

Grace nodded as they entered the elevator.

"So," he said slowly, wondering if he should ask it, "when you said you have experience with PTSD . . ."

"I had a lot of trauma to deal with after that case," she said. "Hiding it, not talking about it? That doesn't help anyone. Stigmatizing something that so many of us go through isn't healthy—it's harmful. And we need to be healthy physically *and* mentally to protect the people who need it."

He wondered if she knew how brave she was, if she had any kind of inkling of what it took for some people to even admit they needed help—let alone ask for it or take their own experiences and use them to do good.

"You're looking at me strangely," she said, softly.

"You're beautiful," he said, because all he had

was honesty in the wake of her courage and passion. "I mean, you have to know that."

"I do," she said, and any other time, it would make him smile, her cool acknowledgment. She had heard it hundreds of times, he was sure. Men had been telling her she was beautiful her entire life, and she was smart enough to know what her beauty meant, how it changed people's perceptions, for better or worse.

"But here." He reached out and pressed his fingers against her collarbone, his palm on her breastbone, above her heart. His hand moved to her forehead, tracing over the elegant wing of her brow. "And here?" His fingers rested lightly on her temple. "Way more impressive."

And that's when Grace, true to form, surprised the hell out of him. Because instead of scoffing or pulling away or laughing him off, she tilted her head up and kissed him.

CHAPTER 16

She kissed him because it'd been forever since someone had pulled a fast one on her, and it'd been *years* since someone had beat her at shooting.

She kissed him because of the crinkles around his eyes and the teasing in his smile and the sensory memory of his callused hands catching in the most delicious ways against the softness of her skin.

She kissed him because, quite frankly, she was sick of fighting this feeling in her chest, the whisper of *maybe* and *what might happen.*

She wanted to know if it was as good as she remembered.

His hand slammed down on the stop button and she suddenly found her shoulders up against the wall of the elevator, the solid, warm weight of his body pressed against hers.

His hands were in her hair, buried in the neatly

wound braids, his palm cradling the back of her head, protecting her already.

It was like drinking water after days lost in the desert. She pressed closer to him as they kissed, long, languid kisses that seemed never ending. His hands fell to her hips, hoisting her up against him. She wrapped her legs around his waist, grateful for the kick pleat in her skirt. The hard planes of his chest pressed against the sweet curve of hers, making her gasp into his mouth. His lips moved from hers, tracing the sensitive line of her jaw, resting against her ear. He panted against her skin, and she couldn't stop the self-satisfied smile that curled her lips. She'd made him do that.

"You're killing me," he said, his breath tickling her ear, making her shiver as his lips brushed the silky skin. "We can't do this here."

He was right. The security team would be alerted soon about the elevator stoppage.

But the last thing she wanted to do was pull away.

His hands dragged down her sides, settling on the dip of her waist as he slowly lowered her to the floor. His forehead was still resting against hers, and for a moment, they just stood there, breathing in each other's presence.

"I have to get you home," he said.

"You don't need to—"

"You're not gonna go back on your word, now, are you?" he asked, and he leaned away from her to quirk his eyebrow questioningly.

"I can take care of myself," she insisted. How was she going to handle him in her house? She wouldn't be able to resist—and she needed to.

He was the worst kind of dangerous, because he was a straight shooter. He knew what he wanted and he didn't hide it. He'd tease, but he wouldn't play games.

All Grace did was play games. Games that were familiar. Games that kept her from getting hurt.

She could see into a person and know them after less than an hour of observation. She could recognize some of the deepest, hidden parts of people. It made her who she was. It made her great at what she did. It was a gift. It was a curse. It made her unable to trust. Slow to reveal. Hard to love.

But Gavin Walker . . .

He looked at her as if *he* were the profiler. As if he saw through her, to *her* deepest, hidden parts—and he didn't turn away. He didn't flinch.

He kept moving forward. Toward her. Always the straight shooter.

Everything inside her told her to run, like last time.

But that hidden part of her—the part she was sure he could see—urged her to stay.

"Fine," she sighed. "Take me home."

STRANGELY, THE DRIVE home wasn't horrible. She'd worried that it'd be long and drawn out, the tension simmering between them. But instead he coaxed her into a conversation about the merits of bebop jazz versus swing, and she was surprised to find him pulling up in front of her brownstone before she knew it. Still aflame from his touch, she marveled at all the parts of him that she had no clue about . . . but now longed to discover.

They walked up the stairs, both of them drawing their guns as they entered. Methodically, they cleared the downstairs and upstairs before meeting back in the living room.

The light was fading from the sky, the room darkening with each minute, so Grace turned on the lamps, casting the room in a golden glow as Gavin took in the surroundings.

"I didn't exactly get a good look at the place last time," he said with a grin. He pointed to the main wall, where an enormous Jackson Pollock dominated the room. "This part of your art collection?"

She nodded.

"A Pollock?" he said, looking up at the mess of

blues and greens. "But that would mean . . ." He frowned. "When you said your collection was worth a lot of money . . ."

"I meant a *lot* of money," Grace said, wondering if this would be the thing that would shake his ego. Some men were drawn to her because of her wealth. And others, it drove them away—it was too intimidating. She'd been worth tens of millions of dollars the day she turned eighteen and inherited Gran's collection. It had enabled her to walk away from the trust fund her father tried to use to control her, but it also made people who knew treat her differently.

"So you're an art heiress," he said.

"You could say that." She watched him closely, looking for any trace of intimidation or unease. But instead he picked up the bronze sculpture on her mantel, weighing the sphere in one hand, then the other. "I like this one," he said. "That one"—he nodded to the Pollock—"kinda reminds me of my niece's finger painting." He grinned, to show her he was teasing, and she tried to suppress a smile.

"Well, I can't take credit for the Pollock," Grace said. "My grandmother, she was good friends with Peggy Guggenheim and had a tremendous eye for art. She started collecting Pollocks before people even knew who he was. But that . . ." She took the sculpture from him, the solid weight in her hand cool and familiar. "It's an early Jonathan Wylder. I got it at a little gallery in Bath about six years ago when I was traveling. It's worth a small fortune now that he's blown up."

Gavin whistled as she put it back on the mantel. "Looks like your grandmother wasn't the only one with an artistic eye," he said.

She flushed at the compliment. She had no artistic talent of her own—she could barely draw a stick figure—but her grandmother's collection was her pride and joy. Not just for its beauty but for what it had done throughout the years. She'd kept a few sentimental pieces—the Pollock being one of them—in her home, but the bulk of the collection was leased to various museums, and all the money was donated to charity. She'd been able to fund a new wing of the center last year and give a substantial amount to pediatric cancer research.

"You've got a lot of old books too," he said, looking at her rare book collection in the glass cabinets. "I like old books."

"You do?" she asked.

"I've got a set of first-edition Hardy Boys," he said with a rueful grin. "I loved those books as a kid."

She couldn't help but be charmed by the idea of him as a little boy, curled up under the covers with a flashlight, reading deep into the night. And the idea of the man that boy grew up to be, carefully collecting first editions of the books he loved so as a child, that maybe even inspired him to become a detective . . .

It was sweet. It was caring.

It was just like him.

"I like the fact that old books have history," she said. "Once, I found a love letter from the 1940s pressed between the pages of a copy of *Pride and Prejudice* I picked up in London. It was like something out of a movie."

She watched him as he observed her space, wondering if he was cataloging the little touches, if they helped him figure her out the way spending time at his cabin had helped her understand him.

"You live a carefully curated life, don't you?" he asked, finally, turning to face her. "Everything's got a place. Everything's neat and tidy and beautiful. Like you."

"I guess you could say that," she said.

"But here"—he tapped the files and papers spread across her coffee table—"you get a little messy."

She looked down at the files, another reminder of the people she'd failed so terribly. "My kind of work is always messy," she said. "People are messy."

"See, I'd say people are simple," Gavin said. "There's good, there's bad, and there's really evil. And you spend a lot of time in the heads of the really evil. It's got to get to a person after a while."

He was looking at her like she was a puzzle he wanted to solve. It made her want to open like a flower. To let him see all of her. To step forward and kiss him again.

But she couldn't. She needed to focus. They both did.

"It's been a long day," she said. "Why don't you order some food? I'm going to take a shower. The room with the green door at the top of the stairs is the guest room. Make yourself at home."

Before he could say anything, she'd hurried out of the living room and up the stairs. Once she was in the safety of her bedroom, she leaned against her door, breathing deep.

She shouldn't have kissed him. That was stupid. She'd just been overtaken with the urge, helpless to resist it.

She needed a shower to clear her head. Grace closed her eyes, and all she could think about was his mouth against hers.

Maybe a cold shower.

Her bathroom was connected to the master bedroom, an opulent room with a giant cast-iron tub and soft green deco tile from the 1920s.

She stripped off her clothes as steam billowed through the room. Standing in front of the large oval mirror that had a border of delicate blossoms etched into the glass, she began to undo her hair from its many pins. By the time she'd untangled her braids and finger-combed her hair long and loose, the room had heated up. She stepped into the water, closing her eyes as she tilted her head back, letting the water soak through her long hair. If only her problems could swirl down the drain as easily as the water.

She knew if she started thinking about the case, she'd crumble. She needed a moment, a respite. Just for a second.

So her mind wandered. Right to Gavin Walker.

He was just down the hall. She couldn't stop thinking about it. She couldn't stop thinking about him.

About that night, two years ago.

He had been so charming. Every woman in the room had been drawn to him, but the second his eyes met hers, she knew he was going to end up leaving with her.

It was in his smile as she came forward from across the ballroom, his warm approval of her boldness.

It was what she liked most about him—that not one inch of Gavin Walker was intimidated by her. Not then, and not now. He respected her, liked her, admired her, even—if the glint in his eyes when they connected over a theory, tossing ideas back and forth rapid-fire, was any indication.

They'd danced together, that night, at the ball. She'd thought she knew, that she could predict the way it would be between them, as their bodies moved to the music.

Later on, when he tumbled her down into his sheets, his mouth insistent, maddening, so, so skilled, she'd realized she had completely underestimated him.

He'd been a talker—it surprised her, because she hadn't taken him for one before they fell into bed. And it hadn't been that typical porn-like dirty talk that so many men thought was hot. No, Gavin Walker made the woman he was with feel *cherished*. His words, muttered in short, awe-filled bursts, accompanied by that touch that burned her up, were all about *her*.

Now he was back in her life, and it scared her. Because she could feel herself falling. She could see herself loving those words of his, believing them, and those hands—that worshipful command of her body.

She finished her shower, towel-dried her hair, and pulled on a pair of bamboo-cloth yoga pants and a soft blue sweater that slipped off one shoulder. She kept her hair loose and damp down her back—she never had the patience to stand there for a half hour and blow-dry it. There was a little hurricane of nerves inside her stomach as she went back downstairs and found Gavin sitting on her couch, looking big and warm and so handsome.

"I found your takeout drawer," he said. "Ordered us Thai."

"Sounds good," she said, sitting down clear on the other end of the couch from him. She knew he noticed, because his eyes crinkled, amused.

"I also put a call in to Harrison. He's sending a sketch artist over to work with the jeweler tomorrow. Maybe we'll get a hit off facial recognition."

"Good idea," she said. "We need to go over the rest of the evidence. He didn't choose his victims by happenstance."

"You think there's more of a pattern than him finding women who look like you?"

"He might work in a job that puts him in contact with a lot of people," Grace suggested. "Or one that gives him access to personal information. Maybe some sort of administrator."

"He has to be stalking his victims," Gavin said thoughtfully. "He had their routines down, knew when Janice ran, knew when the Andersons were both home, knew when Nancy would be in her apartment. Did you look at her work schedule Zooey sent over? The woman practically lived at her office. That made her predictable but gave him a very small window when it came to targeting her."

"There must have been easier victims," Grace mused, opening her laptop and bringing up the files Zooey had sent both of them.

"Finding women who look like you is clearly his number one priority," Gavin said.

But Grace wasn't so sure. She felt like she was missing something, like there was a connection she wasn't seeing. She just couldn't figure out what it was. She reached over to her side table, where her reading glasses were. She'd taken her contacts out for her shower and hadn't bothered to put them back in. She slipped her glasses on, then clicked through the evidence files Zooey had put together on each victim's last few weeks.

"I'm guessing you think otherwise," Gavin said and Grace looked up guiltily, realizing she'd gone quiet and contemplative.

She flushed. "Sorry," she said.

"You don't need to apologize for getting in the zone," he said. "We all do it. You should see Sunday dinners at my parents' place when all their boys are working on different cases. My mama likes to say you can drive a freight train through the silences. What are you thinking?"

"The women who look like me—it's obvious," Grace explained. "And I would understand if it was a compulsion. Some serial murderers do have compulsive preferences when it comes to victim type. But if it *were* a compulsion, he'd be a purist about it. He wouldn't deviate from his type—ever. He wouldn't have killed Mr. Anderson. Our unsub could've easily waited until Mr. Anderson was out of the house—we know he stalks his victims. So why didn't he just wait until she was alone, if he's so obsessive about the women looking like me?"

"So it's another red herring?" Gavin asked.

"To keep us from digging deeper. There's another reason why he chose *these* people. We just have to find it."

The doorbell rang.

"That's our food," Gavin said. "Let me get it. We'll eat. And then we'll get to work."

CHAPTER 17

There was something incredibly intimate about being in Grace's home, eating with her on the enormous dove-gray linen couch that was way more comfortable than it looked.

She'd come downstairs with her still-wet hair pushed over her shoulder, damp strands dipping into her eyes as she leaned over the laptop. With her hair down and wet, her face free of all makeup, and those glasses perched on her nose like some sort of adorable librarian, she looked different. Young. Innocent. Vulnerable.

This was a version of her he'd never seen; gone was the FBI agent, gone was the crack shot, gone were the perfectly tailored clothes and bold slash of lipstick she wielded like weapons.

This was just her—relaxed, at home, comfortable.

She'd never been more beautiful.

Until she stole the last piece of chicken satay,

and then he had to declare her his sworn enemy as she laughed and snapped the skewer in half, then handed one piece over.

But eventually, the last delicious mouthful was gone, and they got to work. Gavin took the stack of files on the Andersons while Grace combed through Janice's and Nancy's lives. She preferred to sit on the floor, her legs crossed and the papers spread out in front of her in a pattern only she could understand.

"Where did Megan Anderson go to college?" she asked.

"Reed, in Oregon," Gavin answered.

"Damn, I was thinking maybe he was picking women from the Ivies—Nancy went to Yale and Janice went to Harvard . . ." She glanced down at the paper in front of her. "Janice was a sorority girl and everything."

"This . . . what we're doing," he said.

"Victimology," she supplied.

"Right." Of course she had a fancy word for it. "You really think it can tell us something we don't know about our unsub? It's not like this guy has been subtle."

"That's why I'm sure there's an answer in the victims," Grace explained. "What he's been doing? The different methodologies of killing, leaving the diamond earrings, sending us these misogynistic messages through his positioning of the corpses? That's all deliberate. It's a narrative he's trying tell us. He's in control of it. He's all about messages. There's a connection between his victims. He wants me to find it."

"Another piece of his puzzle," Gavin said, staring at the papers.

"Not just that," Grace said. "He thinks he's in total control, but they never are. Someone can be the coldest damn killer in the world, the most experienced, and they'll still be making choices they're sure aren't part of a behavior pattern, but they are. All it takes is the right profiler to see it. The right profiler sees all." She gestured at the sea of papers in front of her. "I *need* to see all."

He felt the urgency behind her words. It mirrored his own. "Well, I've got the Andersons' schedule narrowed down," he said. "They were on a green cruise—those big boats that look like pirate ships and are all wind powered—for a month. They'd been home for only two weeks when he killed them."

"That's our window," Grace said immediately. "So we need to cross-reference all their schedules and the GPS coordinates from their phones." She grabbed her laptop and typed furiously for a second. "He chose them and stalked them during those two weeks," she said. "Nancy was probably the easiest, because he could just tail her from her office."

"She pretty much went only from work to home," Gavin said, reaching over and scanning the hard copy of Nancy's GPS coordinates they'd pulled from her phone. It was the same two, over and over. "Except here," he said, tapping a date within their two-week window, where it deviated. "Where is this?" He pulled up his phone and typed the coordinates in. "Car wash," he said.

Grace's head snapped toward him. "Car wash?" she echoed. "Janice had a car wash receipt in her pocket."

"Was it Leckie's Motors?" Gavin asked.

"*Yes,*" Grace said, her eyes lighting up. She entered the coordinates into the app she had analyzing the GPS coordinates and then let out a triumphant laugh. "Got you!" she hissed at the computer, and then her cheeks turned red as she realized Gavin had witnessed her little moment of glee.

"Let me guess, the Andersons took their car to get washed at Leckie's too."

"A week before he killed them," Grace said, pointing at the screen. "He's using the car wash to find his victims."

It made sense, and Gavin said as much.

"High turnaround rate, people are waiting around as the employees clean the cars—he'd blend right in," Grace said.

"You think he's posing as a customer?"

Grace shook her head. "He's got to be an employee," she said. "It's so much easier to go unnoticed. Plus, it gives him access to the cars. One look at the registration in their glove compartment while he's vacuuming out the passenger seat, and he's got their address."

Damn, she was right. They'd made it easy for him. "And then he stalks them until he's got the rest of their routine down."

Grace glanced up at the Georgian clock on her mantelpiece. It was nearly midnight. "I'll leave a message for Paul," she said. "There'll be no one at the car wash this late. There's no use in going in now—we might tip him off."

"He could be working tomorrow," Gavin agreed, the wheels of his mind turning. "Best to just show up, use the shock factor. If he's working, he'll start getting really nervous once we talk to his boss and start going through employment records. Might make him easier to spot."

"Tomorrow, then," Grace said, getting up from her seat on the carpet, raising her arms to stretch. The movement lifted her loosely knit sweater, a tantalizing glimpse of curved waistline appearing. "I want to get this guy before he has a chance to use that fourth pair of earrings," she said.

"We will," Gavin said, even though he knew it was foolish to make that kind of promise. But he couldn't help it, not with her. Not when she had that look in her eyes—guilt mixed with worry.

She took on each victim as a burden and a responsibility—each case not only a puzzle to be solved but a personal mission of justice for each one. She walked through their lives, even lived them alongside their spirits in a way, so that she could bring their killers to justice. And at the same time, she was putting herself in their killers' heads, figuring out every single murderous, perverted urge, every move that brought them closer to another kill.

It was a heavy weight to carry. He admired the hell out of her for carrying it with such, well, *grace*.

God, she was turning him all sappy. He found himself not really caring, because she was here, and so was he.

The moment—where her eyes were on his, their bodies instinctually angled toward each other, even though they were standing feet apart—lingered a little too long, kicking up the tension in the room tenfold. Gavin shifted from foot to foot, waiting.

It had to be Grace who made the first move this time. He had to be sure she wanted this as much as he did.

"We should go to sleep," she said softly, unable to tear her gaze from him.

"You're right," he said, despite that being the last thing he wanted.

He wanted to keep her up all night. He wanted to spend hours in her bed, between her thighs, until she didn't know any words but *please* and his name. He wanted to fall asleep curled around her and wake up in the morning with her ridiculous fairy-tale-princess hair tangled all over his face.

She licked her lips, a tiny, innocent movement that shouldn't have been erotic, but God, it was. He shifted again—for different reasons this time.

"Let me know if you need anything," she said, turning and walking toward the stairs.

"I'll do one more door and window check," he said, even though he'd done one an hour ago.

As Grace's footsteps faded upstairs, he went through the downstairs of the house, checking all the windows and the front and the back door, which led down to a small greenbelt. He was grateful for the time, trying to gather himself, to calm his raging . . . need.

He made his way upstairs, about to turn toward the guest room when something down the hall caught his eye.

She was leaning against what had to be the door to her bedroom, her palms pressed against the wood, waiting.

Excitement surged through him, his blood going hot, his cock hardening as they just stared at each other from across the hall.

A silent challenge. She knew exactly what she was doing.

But he didn't want to play games.

He just wanted her—all of her. No hiding. No artifice.

And no waking up without her in the morning.

"Grace," he said.

She didn't say anything. That's probably how she wanted to play it, let the need consume them, gasps and moans the only sound. Words complicated things.

Feelings complicated things.

He closed the space between them, and his hands traced the curve of her jaw, his lips brushing just barely over hers.

"Is this what you want?" he asked, his hips pressing into hers so she could feel what she'd done to him. Her fingers fisted in his shirt, her gasp of breath feathering against his lips, making him even harder. "Invite me in, Grace," he rumbled against her cheek, his stubble scraping against her skin, eliciting a shiver, "and you get everything you want."

He knew it was a request she was helpless to deny.

CHAPTER 18

Grace expected him to fall on her like a starving man, to press her against the wall of her bedroom and ravish her. She'd been picturing something hungry and maybe a little rough, in the good way.

But instead he closed her bedroom door behind him and leaned against it, looking at her with those brown eyes.

"Come here," he said.

Normally, she would protest at the request. She'd roll her eyes. She'd make the man come to her.

But there was nothing normal about her and Gavin. Not then and not now.

He was her exception. And now he knew it, just as she did.

She went, not helpless to resist but instead *tired* of resisting. Tired of denying herself this, denying herself him.

The second she was in reach, his hands were on her hips, pulling her to him fast and hard, his lips capturing hers. She sank into him, her head spinning, her body lighting up everywhere he touched. His fingers skimmed underneath her sweater, traveling up to cup one of her breasts. When the pads of his fingers brushed teasingly against her nipple, her head tilted back, and she moaned as his lips trailed up the exposed length of her neck. He backed her up across the room, and the back of her knees hit her bed, making them come to a halt.

"Fuck, Grace," he rasped out, his voice deeper than she'd ever heard it.

"That's the general idea," she said and she could feel his smile press against her cheek in the darkness.

"Cracking jokes is my job," he whispered, tumbling her expertly down onto the mattress. She fell against the wide expanse of her bed, his hand cupping the back of her head as he lowered himself over her.

Kissing him was like a drug—one that she never wanted to quit. Her fingers—clumsy with desire—slipped the buttons of his shirt free, and then the expanse of his chest was exposed to her. Beautifully cut muscle, with a smattering of gold hair across his chest, narrowing into a tantalizing trail down his ripped stomach. Her fingers followed the trail down, flirting with the waistband of his pants.

He bent down and kissed her again, the hand that had been at her hips moving to her front, grabbing the hem of her sweater, and pulling it up and over her.

Grace's head rolled back against the mattress, desire building in her stomach. Her nipples tightened against the lace of her bra as he pulled back to study her, his gaze intense and heated. His finger traced the delicate edge of her lingerie, excruciatingly slow.

"What do you need, Grace?" he asked. "Do you need this?" He bent down, his tongue running along the sloping curve of her breast that was exposed by the demicup of her bra.

She moaned, her hips rising to meet his, desperate for friction, for more, for *anything*.

"All you have to do is ask," he said, and there was the tease in him again. That devil-may-care smile as his fingers stroked over her nipple through the lace, making her fingers clench into his shoulders.

"Please," she said.

"What was that?" he asked, kissing her neck as his hands wandered from her breasts to her stomach, then down her thighs, gripping her ass. He made a noise when he realized she wasn't wearing anything underneath the yoga pants, his hips pushing deliciously into hers for a second as he groaned.

Yes. Finally.

"Just tell me what you need," he whispered, his voice hoarser now. His fingers trailed up the inside of her thigh, making her squirm.

For some reason, his using the word *need* instead of *want* made her even more crazy. He was right. This wasn't just desire. This wasn't just lust.

She needed this. She needed him.

No one else would ever do.

His palm pressed against her through the soft, thin fabric of her yoga pants and she moaned, the delicious pressure sending waves of pleasure through her. She grabbed the back of his head, pulling him forward and bringing their mouths together with a desperate kind of hunger. She needed everything. His touch. His heart. His body. She was filled with need for him, frantic for the feel of his bare skin against hers.

"I need you," she gasped, her hands finding the button of his pants. All she could feel was the heat of his body against hers, the frissons of electricity that went off every time they kissed. She wanted more.

He grabbed the waist of her yoga pants and

she tilted her hips up, allowing him to pull them off her.

He pushed away, just for a moment, to deal with the condom and then she could feel him against her. She gasped, suddenly aware of how incredibly wet she was.

"You need this, Grace?" he asked, his eyes on hers. The moment was unbearably intimate, because she *did*. More than anything, she needed him.

She wrapped her legs tight around him, pushing forward with her hips, moaning as he slid into her.

"Oh, God," she said, just before his mouth came down on hers and he kissed her tenderly. He moved inside her, his lips still on hers, his hands roaming over her body as he spun her senses with his kisses.

She was so close, so fast. What they felt had been building for hours. For days.

Maybe even for years.

She wound her fingers through his hair, bringing him closer. She needed him closer.

"God, look at you," he groaned against her skin. "You feel so fucking perfect."

His hand traced the long line of her thigh, up to between her legs, his thumb dragging in slow circles against her clit.

Her fingers fisted in his hair and he kept the pressure on her clit as he thrust strongly into her at an angle that made her cry out. It was too much. It wasn't enough.

It was everything.

He was everything. She was ignorant to everything else but the sensation of his fingers rubbing in maddening circles around her clit, his cock moving inside her, hitting her G-spot, making her start to climb toward orgasm.

His breath quickened against her ear and just when she didn't think she could bear the pleasure any longer, Grace stiffened, her orgasm taking her by surprise. She pulsed around him, gasping through the bliss as it rushed through her in waves. He groaned as her body clenched around his, thrusting one more time before he came.

For long moments, they clung to each other, not wanting to part. Not wanting the moment to end.

Grace placed her head on his shoulder, her body still singing with endorphins and sensation. She closed her eyes, thinking she'd never felt so safe.

THE NEXT MORNING, she found herself in her kitchen, making breakfast for a man.

It was a situation she had never put herself in,

she mused as she finished cooking the eggs. But as she heard the telltale creak of her stairs, she realized she didn't have much time to freak out over the sudden change.

"I thought you ditched me again," Gavin said, coming to sit on one of the tall stools she had grouped along one side of the kitchen island.

She rolled her eyes, trying to hide her smile. "But here I am, making you breakfast instead," she said, trying to come off as nonchalant. She slid the plate down on the counter in front of him, along with a mug of coffee.

She sat across from him with her own plate, trying not to think of how comfortable this was as she picked at her eggs.

Gavin took a bite of bacon, his eyes fluttering shut in an almost pornographic way as he moaned. "Is there anything you don't do well?" he asked.

"I can cook," she said. "But if I try to bake anything, it tends to explode."

"Good thing I'm an excellent baker," he said, chomping down on the sourdough toast she'd made and slathered with Irish butter. "You know, you aren't going to be able to get rid of me if you keep cooking for me like this."

"A baker, huh?" she asked, trying not to imagine him in her kitchen every morning, sleepily affectionate, rumpled, just a little scruffy.

The idea was much too appealing.

"My mom was very big on us boys knowing our way around the kitchen," he said. "My sister didn't come along until my brothers and I were already out of the house. She had all boys for twenty years and then her little surprise, as she likes to call Sarah."

"So your little sister has four older brothers?" Grace asked.

"Who are all law enforcement," he said.

"Oh, God, poor girl."

He laughed. "Not that she really needs our help. My dad's been taking her hunting with him for years. I wouldn't be surprised if she became a cop too."

"Well, I guess it does run in the family," Grace said, getting up and clearing her plate. He snagged the final piece of bacon off his plate before she took his and dumped them both in the sink. He stood, pressing up against her back, his hands cupping her shoulders. She couldn't help but lean into the solid weight of him—he ran so *hot* it was like being next to a fire. She wanted to whirl around and kiss him. To hike herself up on the edge of the sink and have him step into the cradle of her thighs, where he belonged.

"Thank you for breakfast," he said. He was so close she could feel the words vibrate in his chest where it touched her. "Normally, I'd thank you in a better, more naked way, but we've got to meet Paul at the car wash."

She swallowed hard, squeezing her thighs together. "I'll go change," she said, but he didn't move away from her. "Gavin," she said, trying to make it sound like a warning, but it came out more like a plea.

She didn't have to be facing him to know he was smiling.

His right hand moved from her shoulder to her neck, where he gently brushed her hair off her nape, his lips grazing over the sensitive skin. She shivered at the light touch, remembering how talented those lips were last night.

"You play so dirty," she gasped out, twisting in his grip, ducking under his arm with a laugh. "Don't you dare chase me!"

His eyes darkened and her stomach jolted as she realized she'd inadvertently tapped into a desire that maybe he hadn't even realized until now. Suddenly, all she could think about was him playfully chasing her through the house, her laughter drifting behind her, teasing him until he caught her.

He stepped forward before she could bolt and put his mouth on hers, biting down just a little on her lower lip, making her body sing.

"Talk about playing dirty," he said when they parted.

LECKIE'S MOTORS WAS a large outfit, with car wash bays and a garage to change oil and whatnot. The place was already bustling and the early morning sun bounced off the car windows, making them glint.

Men and women in red polos and black pants with towels slung over their shoulders were hard at work cleaning cars in the wash bays. The office was set at the far end of the parking lot.

Grace got out of the car, pulling her red trench coat over her shoulders as she and Gavin walked across the lot. She waved when she saw Paul arrive and a group of agents get out of his SUV.

"You have a good night?" he asked.

"What?" Grace said, her cheeks turning red.

Paul shot her a confused look. "Everything was uneventful? No more surprise packages?"

"Oh. Right. Everything was fine."

"I'm glad you got her to agree to you staying over," Paul said to Gavin.

"Yeah, me too," Gavin said.

If possible, Grace turned even redder at the double meaning in his voice. The agents who had driven over with Paul were already spreading out, stopping the workers and asking them to step away from the cars.

"I'll go start the initial interviews, if you'd

like," Paul said. "That way you two can talk to the manager."

"Sounds good," Grace said. "Let's go."

As Paul headed over to the wash bays, Grace started to walk across the lot to the office, but Gavin reached out, his hand settling gently on her arm. She looked down; the heat of his skin seeped through the thin blue silk of her sleeve, but instead of warming her up, it made her shiver.

"Why don't you let me take the lead?" Gavin suggested, giving her arm a light squeeze before breaking the touch. "Mechanics, guys who work with cars . . . they tend to be pretty macho. He'll probably talk to me more than you. The whole bro-code bullshit."

"You think the bro code's bullshit?" Grace asked.

That twist of a smile was back, devilish and pleased that he had surprised her. "I think a lot of dudes underestimate the hell out of women like you," he said.

"Men underestimate all women," she said dryly.

He laughed. "Okay, fair enough," he said. "But I'm pretty sure it takes longer to get information out of them when they think you're an airhead."

"Depends," she said. "If they get distracted enough, the criminal ones tend to slip up."

"Fair enough," he said. "But let me run this one. I've been following your lead this whole time. Well, except for last night."

She glared at him, which made him smile even wider.

"You're impossible," she hissed, hating how pleased she felt, deep down.

He shoved playfully at her shoulder with his own and once again, that tantalizing image of him chasing her through the house flitted through her brain. It had been a long time since she'd been able to play with someone, since she'd been that much at ease with a man. Sex was wonderful. Fantastic. She loved sex.

But the last few years, everything had seemed terribly rote. Beautiful, successful men tumbled her into their beds for one night of intense, athletic sex, but it was all serious and so, so obvious they were trying to impress her.

Gavin didn't need to impress her, because he just innately *knew*. And not just her body, her mind and heart.

Her desires. He keyed into them like she keyed into a killer's mind, and the connection both scared and thrilled her.

"Fine," she said as they reached the office. "You can take the lead. But I'll jump in if I need to. And I'm still in charge."

"I wouldn't dare to think otherwise."

They walked into the office together. A short man with a bad comb-over was standing behind the desk, his thin eyebrows drawn together in irritation.

"Hey, man," Gavin said. He flipped open his badge and pushed it across the counter. The manager picked it up and examined it closely, as if he expected it to be fake.

"You're disrupting my workers' day," the man said, gesturing outside to where Paul and the officers had pulled all the employees from the wash bays. "Do you have a warrant? Because I'm losing money here by the minute."

"I'm really sorry about the disruption," Gavin said, leaning against the counter, loose-limbed and seemingly unaffected by the man's frustration. "I promise, we're gonna get out of your hair as soon as possible so all you hardworking folks can get back to your day. I'm Agent Walker." He nodded his head at Grace. "This is Agent Sinclair. She's my partner. She's got some questions, and I'm thinking you're the guy with the answers. You're in charge of this whole deal, right?" he asked, waving around the office and out the windows at the parking lot.

Something flickered in the manager's eyes at Gavin's casual confirmation of his power. "Yeah, that's right," he said, his shoulders relaxing.

"Then you're the man Agent Sinclair needs,"

Gavin said. "She's after a really bad guy. Some scary shit. And she's got this thing called a profile, you know, like a sketch of a person?"

"I know what a profile is; I watch TV," said the man.

"Of course," Gavin said. "I keep forgetting there's a dozen shows about people like her. Well, Agent Sinclair's the real deal, you know? You mind answering some of her questions?"

He glanced at Grace, calculating. "I guess not."

Grace smiled, her charming, grateful smile that had brought men to their knees, falling easily into the role that Gavin had so expertly set up. "I *really* appreciate it," she said. "So, what I want you to do is think about your employees," she said, her voice soft and soothing. "I'm looking for a man. Probably early forties. Maybe late thirties. Most likely white. He's physically fit but not overly jacked or obsessed with fitness. He's a loner but not the weird type. He's polite, on time, he gets his work done, and no one complains about him, but he keeps to himself. He's not the kind to go out for beers after a long shift, but he'd pick up extra shifts if asked. And he would've been working the last two weeks in June."

"That sounds like Raymond," the manager said. "But he's not in his forties."

"Age is often the hardest thing to pinpoint," Grace assured him. "Tell me about Raymond."

"He's a good worker, but he's really quiet. I thought he had a stutter or something, the first few months. But then I realized he just doesn't like to talk."

"Is he here today?" Grace asked, looking over her shoulder to scan the vicinity, where Paul and the rest of the agents were beginning to conduct the interviews.

"No, actually, he hasn't shown up for the past few days," the manager said. "And didn't even call in sick, which is kinda weird for him."

"Do you have a picture?" Grace asked.

The manager shook his head.

"What about a locker?" Gavin asked.

"Yeah, in the break room. I guess you want to see?"

"That'd be great," Grace said.

"You might want to step back, just for safety," Gavin told the manager as Grace snapped on a pair of gloves.

The manager whistled as Gavin pulled out a small mirror on the end of a silver stick and handed it to Grace. "What the hell do you think is in there?"

"You can never be too careful," Gavin said.

Grace, using the manager's key, opened the

padlock and cracked the locker door open wide enough to insert the mirror. She angled it, exploring the inside. Nothing but metal walls. She grabbed the door and swung it fully open.

"Nothing," she reported back. "It's empty."

"Guess he cleared it out," Gavin said. "You think this is our guy?"

"Could be," Grace replied. "Do you have an address for Raymond?" she asked the manager.

He shook his head, sweat crawling down his forehead.

"Didn't he fill out paperwork? Give you a résumé?"

The manager looked over at Gavin, his eyes desperate.

"You paying him under the table?" Gavin asked, clueing in.

"Look, times have been tough . . ." the man said nervously.

"No worries," Gavin interrupted casually, clapping him on the shoulder. "We're not interested in busting you for taxes, man. We've got a lot more important stuff to worry about than some cash under the table, trust me."

"I've always paid him in cash," the manager admitted. "I don't know where he lives, but I know he takes the thirty-six bus sometimes, so maybe he lives somewhere on that route."

"Thanks," Gavin said. "We're gonna need

to get some people in here to brush for finger-prints, okay? And then hopefully we can let you get on with your day."

"We should go check in with Paul," Grace said. "Thank you for your help," she told the manager.

She could hear Gavin following behind her, but until he reached out to open the door for her, she didn't look at him.

"You did good in there," she said as they walked out into the cooling air.

"I'm not just a pretty face either," he said, winking.

A smile tugged at the edges of her lips. "You joke about everything," she said.

He shrugged. "Defense mechanism. Maybe you make me nervous."

"You? Nervous?" she scoffed.

"I've got butterflies right now," he deadpanned.

Why was he so charming? It wasn't the smooth, suave sort of charm she was used to. She'd been romanced by all types of men—PhDs, neurosurgeons, politicians, even a few elite military types. But there was something about Gavin Walker's awareness, his humor, and the comforting ease he had not just with himself but with her that drew her in, even though she kept fighting it.

"You look tired, Grace," he said, the light in his eyes turning somber.

"Now, that's what *every* woman wants to

hear," she said. Now she was the one using humor as a defense mechanism. "And you were the one who kept me up."

He smiled ruefully, but then his mouth flattened, going serious. "This is wearing on you."

"I'm fine," she insisted, but she could see in his face he didn't believe her.

"No, you're not," he said. And for some reason, that soft, simple declaration made everything she'd been pushing down rise to the surface—the fear and regret and guilt about the hopeless puzzle that was closing in on her with each breath. It was staggering, the emotion that swamped her, enough to bring her to her knees, but she stood tall. There was no other choice.

"No, I'm not," she said, hushed and honest. She was so worried that she was already too late—that their killer had already found a woman to "give" the final pair of earrings to. Maybe this was the end of the road—maybe all paths led to Raymond and they'd bring him in and it would be neat and tidy.

But life—and death—rarely was neat or tidy.

"I can help," Gavin said, his eyes earnest. He meant every word, and she believed him.

But she wasn't sure if she could open herself up to that. Not again.

She took a deep breath.

Maybe it was time to try.

CHAPTER 19

My pretty girl,

It's getting so easy to do this.

I thought it would be hard. But my God, it sings through me, this rush of adrenaline and dopamine. Killing is the greatest drug imaginable. Addictive, heady, a thrill impossible to deny.

Who would want to?

Who was the first person you killed, pretty girl? Does it haunt you? Did you cry?

Or maybe, just maybe, a part of you liked it.

Because once you have the power of looking into a person's eyes the moment they realize it's over, as they understand all they'll never be able to accomplish, just because of you . . .

Well, there's nothing else like it.

When they surrender to my power it's a beautiful thing. Everything reaches this crystalline point, sharp as a knifepoint, clear as glass.

And then she's gone. Now merely a husk of a pitiful slut no one will really miss.

I'm doing the world a favor. Just like I did with the others. Ridding the earth of its detritus.

I'm practicing, pretty girl. Perfecting.

For you.

Soon, I'll be close to you again.

Just the thought of you fills me. Flitting across my skin like a cool breeze. Soon, you will have no choice but to see . . . see what I've become. See what you've made me do.

This is all just a means to an end, after all.

I've pulled you into my game. Clever girl, you've figured some of it out. But you're not even close to solving the puzzle. I'm too quick for you, miles ahead when you're just getting started in the labyrinth of death I've chosen to play in.

I'll show you, outsmart you, and then I'll look into those pretty eyes—and finally hurt you the way you've hurt me.

I can't wait for you to make the next step. You've always been too confident for your own good, even back at school. And now I'm exploiting that.

I'll always be five steps ahead because I know you. I know you better than anyone.

I love you more than anyone.

Not that you deserve it, you bitch. Leaving

me behind. Writing those fucking books. Swanning around like you got those promotions on your own merit instead of on your back, like the slut you are.

You tried to run from me. You thought you succeeded, but you'll soon learn you didn't. That you'll never.

You're mine. You'll never stop being mine.

I just need to remind you of that. Starting with your next present.

I still have so much work to do. But it will be worth it.

Soon, it'll just be you and me. The two of us, and those wide, wide eyes of yours, full of tears and terror the moment you realize that you've lost.

And I've won.

CHAPTER 20

It took forensics thirty minutes to run the prints pulled from the locker. Grace paced in tight circles around the parking lot as they waited for the team to come back with the results. Gavin herded everyone away from her, keeping his distance as well, which was good because she didn't want to talk to anyone. She wanted to think.

But even that was hard. The heat of the day was starting to get to her, the humidity making her shirt stick to her back uncomfortably.

A voice in the back of her head was whispering that the car wash was too menial of a job for the unsub. She stopped pacing, looking up at the car wash, contemplating it.

Maybe the menial job played into it, she thought. If he felt denied the proper education he deserved, two things could happen: a lot of resentment could build through the years. And a lot of ego. If he felt like he was the smartest person in the room and was stuck for years in a dead-end job because he never had the opportunities education provided, that could feed into his narcissism.

And Grace knew for sure she was dealing with the worst kind of narcissist here. He'd taken his feelings of superiority to a deadly level, no longer content with whatever power he'd managed to wrest from "inferior" hands.

She wiped a trickle of sweat off her forehead, plucking at the front of her shirt, trying to get some air between the fabric and her skin. She thought fondly of the Swiss chalet where she'd spent last Christmas. The mounds of fluffy white snow, so crisp and cool.

"Grace, I've got Zooey on the line."

Grace turned to see Gavin holding a phone out to her, already switched to speaker.

"I'm here, Zooey," Grace said, stepping close enough to Gavin so the phone would pick her up. "It's hot as hell. You're lucky you're in an air-conditioned office."

"I am a lucky girl," Zooey chirped through the line. "Okay, so like I was telling Gavin, the prints on the locker belong to Raymond Nugent. He's white, thirty years old, originally from Virginia, but he's lived in Maryland for a decade."

"What about priors?" Paul asked.

"He's got some," Zooey confirmed. "But it's petty juvenile stuff that got sealed. Disorderly conduct, shoplifting, public indecency. Other than a few traffic tickets, this guy's been living clean since he turned eighteen."

"Is he married?" Grace asked.

"No, never been married."

"Single mother?"

"Um . . . let me see. Just a sec," Zooey said. Grace could hear the faint clicking of her keyboard.

"Because of his problems with women?" Gavin asked, seamlessly clueing into her line of thinking.

Grace nodded.

"And give a prize to the lady," Zooey said. "Raymond Nugent's father's parental rights were taken away from him before Raymond was even born. He was abusive. He threw Raymond's mother down the stairs when she was four months pregnant with him."

"Jesus," Gavin swore, his face twisting in disgust.

Grace bit her lip, piecing together the facts in her head. "Zooey, is his mother still alive?"

"Checking now," Zooey said.

"You think that her death might be the inciting incident that set this all off?" Gavin asked.

"Could be," Grace said.

"Sheila Nugent is alive," Zooey said. "But . . . oh . . . she was put in a nursing home last year. She has dementia."

And there it was: an inciting incident, a trigger that could break a psychopath on the brink.

"Okay," Grace said. "Zooey, send Raymond's address to Gavin's GPS. We're going to head out there and have a talk with him."

"ALL OF HIS juvenile records were sealed on his eighteenth birthday," Grace said as she scrolled through the file Zooey had sent to her tablet. "He's had one speeding ticket in the last ten years. If this is our guy, his escalation from shoplifting as a teen to serial killing is pretty speedy."

"Did Zooey dig up anything else?" Gavin asked as they drove down the freeway, heading toward southeast DC.

"According to Web records, he runs an amateur porn site on the side," Grace said. "Oh, gross," she said, making a face. "It's for 'hot housewives who want a one-night stand.'"

"Well, that could definitely fit into the hating-women facet," Gavin said. He signaled a lane change and merged behind a station wagon. "And at his most recent kill, he left photographs. Another form of visual documentation."

"True," Grace said.

"We still going with the impotent theory?" Gavin asked. "But if this is about sex, why no sign of sexual assault? Even with Nancy Bantam, who he spent the most time with. Who he bathed and touched and ritualized."

"If he is, I'd expect stabbing to show up in the killing methodology by now," Grace said. "It's a way of penetrating without actually . . ." She trailed off, catching sight of Gavin's disgusted expression out of the corner of her eye. "I know it's horrible."

"It is," he said. "But it's our job. I just . . . I haven't ever had a serial case like this. I gotta admit, I kind of hope it's my last."

"It won't be," Grace said softly.

Gavin turned onto Fifth Street and drove for a few miles. The houses and buildings grew progressively shabbier until they reached a busted neon sign for the Sleepy Rest Trailer Park.

"Let's go see if Raymond's our guy," Grace said, intensely aware of the troubled expression on his face.

They pulled up to a rickety fifth wheel that had seen better days and brighter paint jobs. It was painted black, with paint that was clearly not meant for steel, since it was peeling off in big chunks around the windows.

Grace drew her gun, taking Gavin's six without his having to ask as they approached the trailer. Gavin rapped hard and swift on the trailer door. "Raymond Nugent? FBI! Open the door!"

It was a tense moment because it was always a tense moment. A moment when you wonder if it's going to go south. If the unsub is going to come out shooting. It didn't matter how long she did this: Every time, for that infinitely short and impossibly long moment, she wondered. She tensed. And she prepared.

She would be ready for anything.

But this time, silence greeted them instead of the haze of gunfire. Gavin knocked again and then nodded, signaling her to go around back.

She moved in a half crouch, her pistol raised, making her way swift and smooth down the shaky trailer stairs and around the yard, then back to the windows. She peered inside, but she couldn't see any movement.

"Clear," she called, quickly coming back to the front of the trailer.

"Let's go in," Gavin said.

The door was unlocked—always a bad sign. No one who lived in a trailer park left their door open—it was an invitation to get your stuff jacked. Gavin went in first, Grace close behind him. But as soon as she was inside the trailer, which stank of mold and cigarettes, she lowered her gun.

"Shit," Gavin said, staring down at the floor in front of them.

A man with a necklace of black-and-blue bruises—cause of death: strangulation, her mind supplied numbly—was lying on his back in the middle of the small living room space. Stripped of all his clothes, he had a giant velvet Christmas bow wrapped around his waist. His blank eyes stared up at the trailer ceiling, his arms spread in a crucifixion pose.

Grace's stomach sank. It had been another red herring. The unsub had cherry-picked Raymond, letting his past lead her down the rabbit hole of *what if*. Once again, she'd been played for a fool.

Once again, whoever was doing this was steps ahead of her.

Grace moved forward, careful to not contaminate any evidence. She bent down, pulling a flashlight out of her pocket, and pointed it at the ribbon.

In the center of the bow, a pair of diamond earrings shone.

A HALF HOUR later, the trailer park was abuzz with FBI. Grace had stepped outside when the medical examiner arrived—it was getting crowded inside the trailer. She tried to distract herself—check her phone, go through the facts of the case—but it was hard not to let the creepy sensation of being watched and the crushing guilt crawl under her skin.

All around her, agents were canvassing, asking the neighbors questions, but Grace knew that they'd get nowhere.

He was too careful to leave any witnesses.

"Hey, you doing okay?"

Grace looked over her shoulder up at a blue blur that she recognized as Zooey's hair, realizing she'd folded her arms tight around herself as if she needed comfort. She relaxed, stretching, and smiled at Zooey. "Just thinking," she said.

"I cleared out so the ME could do her thing," Zooey explained, veering around a stack of rotting wooden lawn chairs to stand next to Grace.

"You find anything?" Grace asked.

Zooey's mouth pursed in frustration as she let out a gusty sigh. "No prints. No hair. No blood spatter. No footprints. No DNA at all. He's good."

"Yes, he is," Grace said. And he wanted her to know it. He wanted to rub it in her face.

"So, can I ask you something?"

Grace nodded.

"At the last crime scene, you said you thought this was all about the killer's hatred of women and their success. But this one . . . this one's a dude."

"I know," Grace replied, unable to keep the worry out of her voice. It'd been bothering her ever since they'd discovered the body. Mr. Anderson's murder could be considered collateral damage—but this? The unsub had chosen Raymond for a reason.

What was she missing? Was there something else the victims had in common that she hadn't noticed?

Was the initial misogyny in his previous kills just another red herring? A ruse to distract her?

Could she trust *anything* when it came to this guy? He was cycling through victims and killing scenarios like he had ADD. Was it all part of the game?

Was it less about the victims and the way he killed them and more about the game?

Grace straightened, her shoulders tensing up.

Was it *all* about the game? Was this even about an urge to kill? Or was he killing people just because the surefire way to get her attention, to get her to play, was to go on a murder spree?

Was that his sole motivation? It was a chilling thought. Only a true psychopath could achieve such detachment and viciousness. It spoke to a level of obsession that terrified her. How long had he been watching her, planning this? Months?

Years?

Her first book came out when she was twenty-four. If her novels were what put her on his radar, that gave a four-year window for his obsession to grow, for his plan to deepen into something real and complex.

"Grace?"

She jerked, realizing with embarrassment that she had totally spaced out on Zooey as she thought. "Sorry," she said. "Long day."

"Grace." Gavin ducked his head out of the trailer door, looking somber. "They found something you'll want to see."

Grace snapped on a fresh pair of gloves and climbed the rickety trailer stairs. The forensic team had been hard at work inside the trailer as Gavin observed, but the body was still uncovered. Grace tried to not let it affect her, but her stomach churned as if she were on a boat. This man—all of the victims—had very likely died because of her.

No, don't think like that, she ordered herself.

That was just what he wanted.

"What is it?" she asked Rebecca, the ME, who was crouched next to Raymond's body.

"I untied the ribbon to get him ready for transport," Rebecca explained. "And I found this. It's addressed to you." With a pair of long tweezers, she held out a creased piece of paper. Grace took it from her, bringing it closer, and read the letter out in a halting voice.

My pretty girl,
  I know how much you like gifts. Almost as much as I enjoy puzzles.
  Have you figured it out yet? Or is your delicate brain still trying to process what I've done? What I plan on doing?
  Don't worry. I'll explain everything.
  Soon.

The trailer was horribly, suffocatingly silent with the weight of the words. Grace had to tense the muscles in her arm to keep her hand from shaking. Her throat went dry; she was afraid to speak, afraid she'd sputter and cough, showing her fear.

She breathed in and out slowly, trying to gain some control. She needed . . .

God, she had no idea what she needed. The walls of the trailer seemed impossibly small all of the sudden. She wanted to get out of there. She wanted fresh air.

But then he'd be getting just what he wanted— to destroy her. She couldn't let him. Wouldn't let him.

Maybe it wasn't successful women in general that the unsub hated. Maybe it was just *one* successful woman: her.

He wanted to get to her. He wanted her emotion. Grace was beginning to think that was what all this was about. Her feelings and how he was trying to manipulate them.

He wanted a trembling, helpless woman— and she wasn't going to give him that.

"Can I see?" Zooey asked from over Grace's shoulder.

Grace showed her the note.

"Well, that's incredibly creepy," Zooey declared.

"I agree," said Rebecca, the ME. "Talk about a twisted love letter."

"He can't stop himself from putting you down," Gavin said, his voice tight with anger. "Delicate brain? Give me a break. You're brilliant."

Normally, his outrage would elicit a smile, but she couldn't summon one at the moment.

"Can you bag this for me?" Grace asked Zooey, carefully handing her the tweezers holding the note. "Gavin, come with me?"

He followed her outside. "Are you okay?" he asked, his brown eyes concerned.

"The victimology is all wrong here," she said.

"Does that matter, now that he's communicating directly?" Gavin asked. "He's reaching out. The inscription in the book was one thing—it was another puzzle."

"But this is a threat," Grace murmured.

"A pretty clear one," Gavin said grimly.

A car horn honked in the distance, and Grace looked over her shoulder to see news vans pulling up behind the line of SUVs that blocked the road.

"Who called the press?" Gavin asked, frowning.

Grace's eyes widened. "Oh, God," she said as an idea struck her. She whirled around and dashed back into the trailer.

"Grace, what are you—" Zooey started.

But Grace ignored her, peering up at the ceilings and corners of the room. Where was it? He had to have put it somewhere.

"He called the media," Grace explained, stepping up onto the sagging mattress, running her fingers along the edges of the trailer ceiling. "This is his version of a public flogging. He needs an audience. It isn't enough for him to think he's smarter than I am—he needs everyone else to think so too." She found nothing in the bedroom. She hopped off the bed and strode back into the main area of the trailer, her gaze narrowing in on the smoke detector.

She wrenched it off the wall and twisted it apart. Inside, nestled among the battery and wires, was a small camera.

"There we go," she said, holding out the pieces to Zooey.

"That's a webcam," the forensic tech exclaimed. "Short-range transmission. Which means . . ."

"He's close by," Gavin said.

Grace took the smoke detector, raising it so she could stare dead center at the camera. She refused to be afraid. Rejected the horror clawing inside her. It would do no good. It wouldn't help her. It would just help him.

She knew he'd be gone before the agents even dispersed to check the neighborhood. But right now, she knew he was watching.

"I'm coming for you," she said, a deadly promise in her words. "You'd better get ready."

CHAPTER 21

By the time they finally wrapped up the crime scene at the trailer park and processed all the evidence, it was getting dark outside.

"Go home," Paul said when he found the two of them sitting in a conference room with Zooey, going over the victims' schedules for the fifth time, trying to find a connection. "Get some rest and come at it fresh tomorrow. Until this guy makes another move, we're dead in the water."

Grace wanted to protest, but she knew he was right. This unsub was too careful to have left any traceable evidence. Until he decided to make contact or kill again, they were stuck.

She hated the waiting the most. In this case, she knew it wouldn't take long. This killer had unlocked a vicious need inside himself that couldn't be quenched. He'd make a move, and soon.

But that meant more victims. More death.

"What's going on in that head of yours?" Gavin asked as he pulled up to her town house.

"I just hate being stuck," she said, getting out of the SUV. He followed her inside, and they swept the house before meeting back in the kitchen.

She felt restless, her skin buzzing angrily with stress and guilt. There was a part of her that said she was missing something, that it was right in front of her, but she couldn't *see* it. The feeling was maddening.

She needed to do something. Anything.

She yanked her fridge open a little too hard, the bottles stored in the door rattling at the movement. "Do you want something to eat?" she asked.

"You don't need to cook for me," he said.

"I'm not. I'm cooking for us," she said absently, grabbing cream and Parmesan cheese, along with a stick of butter. "Does Alfredo sound good?"

"Sounds perfect," he said. "What can I do to help?"

"Sit there and look pretty," she said.

He laughed. "I knew you were only keeping me around for my looks."

"That is absolutely the only reason," Grace said, shooting him a wink over her shoulder. She couldn't miss the flash of heat in his eyes, the way he shifted in his chair. She set water to boil for pasta and diced a few cloves of garlic before measuring out the ingredients for the Alfredo.

"Who taught you to cook?" he asked.

"Oh, I picked it up here and there," Grace said. "Living in this city, you can survive on takeout. But there's something about a home-cooked meal."

"Purest form of love," he said casually.

Her gaze met his across the island, and they were *anything* but casual.

It should have scared her, what he wanted from her. The curse of the profiler was that she often figured out people's desires even before they did. And Gavin? He was the kind of man who went all in.

She wondered if he'd ever been in love. There was a part of her that doubted it, because she had a feeling that once he loved someone, that was it.

He was a forever sort of man. And she was a never-stay sort of woman.

It was a recipe for a disaster. It was one of the worst ideas she'd ever had.

And she just couldn't bring herself to care anymore. Because he made her want *more*.

She expertly put together the sauce in the time it took for the pasta to boil. After slicing a baguette in half, she spread it lightly with herb butter and toasted it under the broiler for a few minutes. She tried to ignore his admiring, watchful eyes as she moved around her kitchen, but her skin burned as if it were on fire, as if every second he was there and not touching her was agony.

"Let's eat in the living room," she suggested. There was something about her dining room that seemed terribly formal and unfit for someone as at ease as he was.

She liked him in her house, she thought as she took their bowls of pasta to the couch and pulled the coffee table closer to rest the food on. Gavin followed, with two glasses of white wine that she had poured earlier. Grace curled her legs underneath her, twirling pasta on her fork as he settled next to her, his thigh warm against her hip. For a moment, she had the urge to rest her legs in his lap, but she forced herself to resist.

"I'm really starting to think there's nothing you can't do," Gavin said, his eyes closing for a moment as he savored the rich sauce.

"I can't seem to catch this damn killer," Grace said and then sighed. "Sorry."

"You don't need to apologize," he said. "This has been a tough one. And it escalates each time. I want to catch him too."

"This is the problem with serial cases," Grace

said, taking a bracing sip of her wine. "If you can't catch them on forensic evidence or narrow it down through the profile, you're pretty much treading water until they kill again. I *hate* waiting for the next victim."

"The jeweler said he bought only four pairs of earrings," Gavin reminded her. "That's been the one consistency of these kills: that he leaves the earrings. He's used all the pairs."

"He could've bought more earrings from another jeweler," Grace said miserably.

"Or he could be moving on to the next phase," Gavin said.

But Grace knew what the next phase entailed: her. Her pain. Her suffering.

Her murder.

She suddenly felt exhausted and hopeless. She slumped against the couch, knowing it had to show in her face, because he put his arm around her, bringing her snug against him. She went willingly, leaning into him.

"Okay," Gavin said firmly. "That's enough. We're going to take a break. Thinking about this 24–7 won't do any good. So I'm going to take this"—he grabbed her wineglass and set it on the table next to the files—"and clear these all away." He picked up the plates and disappeared into the kitchen for a moment. She could hear the water running as he rinsed the dishes and left them to soak before he came back into the living room.

"Now you're gonna come with me." He pulled her to her feet, then settled his hands on her hips. "We're going to get your mind off this. You want to watch a movie?"

She smiled, reaching out and tracing the curve of his cheek with her finger. His skin was warm and just a little scratchy—he hadn't shaved today.

"No, I don't want to watch a movie," she said. "I want you to take me upstairs to bed. And I want you to make love to me until I forget."

His hand squeezed her hips, a reflexive, almost involuntary reaction to her words. "You once told me you didn't make love," he said, his voice gruff with an emotion she couldn't quite identify.

She kissed him, sinking into him. His arms came around her, holding her close. The feeling of safety, of contentment, made her head spin.

"Maybe I changed my mind," she said.

Maybe he changed it for her.

WHEN SHE WOKE, it was still dark outside. Gavin was fast asleep. He was a stealth cuddler: He started out on the other side of the bed, but during the night, he'd slowly gravitate to her side, wrapping himself around her.

She glanced at the clock; it was nearly 3:00 a.m.

She knew she wouldn't be getting back to sleep, so she carefully extricated herself from Gavin's arms and grabbed her robe and phone. She padded downstairs and turned just one lamp on in the living room before she began to methodically spread the victims' files out on the rug for what felt like the tenth time.

She was missing something; she was sure of it. So she was going to go old-school. She pulled out a pad of paper and a pen, then wrote each victim's name down and divided the paper into four columns. And then she began making lists. Of everything. Their education. Their hobbies. Their schedules. Their favorite restaurants, where they got their coffee, what charities they donated to, what organizations they belonged to.

"There has to be a connection," she muttered as she ran out of room on the fourth page of the notebook. She flipped the paper over, starting on the other side as her phone began to buzz.

It was a text from Zooey. She swiped on the screen to open it.

Artist sent over his sketch from his consult with the jeweler. Ran it through all the databases. No match. Here it is.

Grace scrolled down, but the photo Zooey had sent had only partially loaded. She turned her attention back to the list. Maybe there was some sort of event all five of the victims had attended?

She glanced back at her phone and froze. Her vision began to tunnel, her ears roaring as she grabbed the phone with suddenly shaking hands, staring at the sketch that had finally loaded.

No.

It *couldn't* be.

Oh, God.

Her breath began to come too quick, panic spiraling inside her.

It was a mistake. It had to be.

This couldn't be.

But it was. He was staring up at her in pen and ink.

He'd done this. All of this.

Because of her.

CHAPTER 22

Gavin stirred awake, reaching for Grace, still groggy. When he found her side of the bed was empty, he pulled on a t-shirt and went looking for her.

He expected to find her downstairs drinking coffee or maybe going through files. But instead he found her on the floor of her living room, her knees drawn up to her chest, papers spread across the Moroccan rug in a haphazard sea of files.

"Grace?"

She sniffed, brushing underneath her eyes.

She'd been crying.

Something horrible and dark was clawing at his gut as she glanced up at him, her eyes swollen and her face full of guilt.

"What's wrong?" he asked.

She gestured to the papers strewn all around her. "I figured it out," she said in a shaky voice.

"You know who he is?" But surely that was good news. The look on her face told him it was the worst kind of news.

"I know who he is," she said, her words clogged and choked, like she could barely say them. "And I know why he's doing this." Tears shimmered in her eyes. "This is my fault," she whispered. "This is all my fault."

GAVIN SET TWO cups on the floor, sitting down next to her. "Drink this," he said gently.

She obeyed, taking a long sip of the mint tea he'd brewed, closing her eyes as the soothing taste drifted through her.

"Now start from the beginning," he said.

"It's a long story," she sighed.

"I have time." The worry was hot and heavy in his chest: She'd totally withdrawn into herself, defeat written on every line of her body.

Grace wrapped her arms around her knees tighter. "I was never close to my parents," she said slowly. "My mother wanted a daughter to play the society game, and my father just didn't really bother with me at all. I got sent to boarding school after elementary school and I never looked back. I came home to visit my grandmother, and I saw my parents, but it was always just . . . formal. And I was fine with that, I really was."

Her fingers, clasped together around her knees, flexed nervously as she tried to figure out how to continue. "Gran and I were so close," she said. "She understood me. Encouraged me, even though my parents were horrified at the idea of me studying the criminal mind. She died three weeks before my eighteenth birthday."

"I'm so sorry," Gavin murmured.

"Before she died, she made some changes to her will," Grace continued.

Gavin's eyes widened in realization. "The art collection."

She nodded. "My father was wealthy, of course. He'd inherited my grandfather's company years before. But he expected to control the art collection someday, because he expected to control everything. That's his way. The rest of her estate was impressive, but it was *nothing* compared to the art collection."

"And she gave it to you instead of him."

"The day I turned eighteen, it became mine," Grace said. "My father was furious. He had plans to lease all the artwork to various museums. The income some of the pieces would generate . . . It was an enormous loss to him, not just monetarily but status-wise. He could've made some very valuable business connections in the art world with the collection. He tried everything he could think of—legally and emotionally—to discredit my claim. But my gran was a smart woman."

"I don't think your father and I would get along," Gavin said darkly.

Grace let out a watery little laugh. "No, you certainly would not," she said. "My father disowned me," she continued. "Took away my trust fund and banned my mother from speaking to me. So when I got to college . . ." Grace pressed her lips together, her fingers twisting and rubbing against each other ". . . I felt very alone," she said quietly. "I'd lost the one person I felt had ever truly been on my side, and both my parents were being so hateful, over money, of all things . . ."

Gavin didn't know where she was going with this. His lawman's mind was racing down the multiple avenues, examining the evidence, the facts as she gave them to him, but there were too many possibilities, too many variables still.

"I threw myself into my studies," Grace said. "I'd taken accelerated courses in high school, so I was able to take upper-level classes if I convinced the professor to consider me. I'd specifically chosen University of Maryland because they had one professor who I wanted to work with desperately. His name was Henry Carthage."

Something sick began to churn in Gavin's

stomach as the possibilities started to narrow in his mind.

"I'd read all of Carthage's papers and respected him to no end," Grace said. "He had a way of approaching the science—of putting himself inside the criminal mind—that seemed brilliant to me. I wanted to learn from him, so I did everything I could to get his attention. He liked my enthusiasm. Offered to be my faculty adviser. Started teaching me in a private seminar, because he said I was too good for his basic criminology classes already."

And there it was. Confirmation. Gavin's hand wanted to shake with anger when he pictured her, barely eighteen and vulnerable, still grieving and finding her footing, and this bastard . . .

"I should've known better," Grace said softly. "I was smart. I should've seen it coming and stayed away. He was a married man. I was eighteen, but I wasn't oblivious. But when I met him, I felt like someone understood me again. I was in the thick of it before I realized I'd crossed the line."

"He took advantage of you," Gavin said.

"No," Grace protested. "I really should've known better."

"Grace," he said, moving forward so he was kneeling in front of her. He took both of her hands, folding them between his own. "You were a teenager. You were his student and he was your professor. He was in a position of power over you. That shit is *predatory*."

Her eyes shone with unshed tears as her hands tightened in his.

"It only happened a handful of times before I came to my senses and realized the damage I could cause," Grace said. "I tried to break it off. I told him I didn't want to see him anymore. But he wouldn't take no for an answer. When I started looking for a new faculty adviser, he went off the rails emotionally, calling me twenty times a day. Showing up outside my classes, outside my apartment. Telling me he couldn't live without me."

"Oh, God," Gavin said. He couldn't even begin to imagine how hard that must've been for her to deal with, all alone, with no support system.

"I didn't know what to do," Grace explained. "I'd had romantic experience only with boys my age—never a man who could damage my future if I stayed. I didn't feel like I could go above him and report it. I didn't want to ruin his life or mine, and I knew that both our reputations would be ruined if the affair came to light. So I decided the only way to make him stop was to get away. I applied to transfer to Georgetown. And that was the nail in the coffin. Right before

I left, he put a present on my doorstep. A pair of diamond earrings."

Gavin went cold as the connection hit him. Carthage tried to court her back then with diamonds.

And he was trying to court her now, with diamonds *and* murder.

"So he's wooing you with bodies," Gavin said.

"Or showing me what's waiting for me," Grace said bleakly. "I don't know how he got from slightly unhinged to . . . *this*." She pulled her hands from his, indicating all the papers around her. "But I figured it out," she said.

"Figured out what?" Gavin asked gently, because her voice was trembling again.

"How he was choosing his victims. He made it so only I could figure out the connection, because they're all tied to that first year at college. Janice was part of the Alpha Chi Omega sorority. So was my freshman roommate, who was the *only* person who knew about us and encouraged me to leave him. Mr. and Mrs. Anderson belonged to the same country club my parents have for thirty years. Nancy Bantam was Carthage's wife's divorce lawyer when she left him—because she found out about me."

"And Raymond Nugent?" Gavin asked.

"He looks exactly like Carthage's teaching assistant," Grace said. "His TA was a friend of a friend. He was the one who introduced me to Carthage. He was doing me a favor. Until I had all the pieces laid out, I couldn't see the patterns. But then Zooey sent me the sketch our artist did with the jeweler, and it fell together."

"So he's killed the surrogate for your roommate," Gavin said. "The surrogate for your parents. The lawyer who he probably thinks destroyed his marriage. And the surrogate for a teaching assistant who introduced you."

Grace nodded, her lips pressed together like she might be sick. He felt the same way. Now that the path was clear, the motives, the *man* . . . it was horrific. It was terrifying.

He couldn't ask the question he knew he should, but once again, Grace voiced the hard truth with her typical fearlessness.

"The question is, are there more surrogates?" She looked over to him, her gray eyes like liquid silver. "Or am I next on his list?"

CHAPTER 23

I n a way, telling Paul was harder than telling Gavin. The pressure was different. The relationship was different. Paul was her boss, her friend, her leader.

And Gavin . . .

She didn't know what Gavin was. He was *more*. More than anything she'd ever had in her life. More than she'd ever let herself have. It was terrifying, but she kept coming back, flirting with the flame, daring it to burn her.

But what if it doesn't? that traitorous voice inside her asked. *What if he's the one thing in your life that endures?*

There was an acceptance with Gavin, a hurtful kind of healing as she told her story, revealed herself piece by raw piece. He'd held her; he'd trusted her.

He'd heard her.

But Paul . . . Her fingers twisted together nervously in her lap as she waited for him to say something. Gavin had wanted to come with her, but she'd insisted she tell him alone.

He was quiet for a long time after she finished, staring not at her but at the stack of files on his desk.

"Paul," she prompted quietly.

His eyes finally lifted to hers, his face all concern. "Oh, Grace," he said. "I am so sorry."

Relief flooded her like a dam breaking.

"This is not your fault," Paul continued.

No matter how many people said that, she couldn't quite make herself believe it. She hated herself for the feeling. It was wrong. It was victim-blaming. She'd never allow anyone on her team to think like this about anyone.

But when it was her? Her adolescent, angry choices? The mistakes she made?

Apparently she was her own harshest critic. Her therapist was going to have a great time examining that revelation next session.

"I've dispatched agents to Carthage's apartment and his office at the university," Paul said.

"They won't find him," Grace said. She doubted he'd been at either place for weeks. How long had he been planning this? Months? Years?

Her stomach swooped sickeningly and she swallowed hard.

"We need to figure out how to approach this," Paul started to say, but stopped when there was a knock at the door and his assistant, Amanda, peeked her head in.

"Agent Harrison, you have a call from upstairs. They said you asked them to flag any calls regarding Agent Sinclair? Well, they have one."

Grace got to her feet. "It's him," she said. She was sure of it.

He'd waited until now, until he'd left her the final corpse, the final set of earrings. He gave her all the clues, all the steps in the game, and now he was calling to explain the rules.

Her face hardened, her lips forming a line. "Have them transfer the call to the north conference room," she told Amanda. "And please have someone let Agent Walker and Zooey know they're needed."

Amanda hesitated, looking at Paul questioningly. He nodded his head.

"Do what she says," he said.

Grace took a deep breath, trying to center herself as she and Paul walked toward the conference room.

"I can call in Maggie," Paul said.

Grace shook her head. "He won't talk to her. This is about me and him."

"Which is why you shouldn't be the one negotiating with him," Paul said. "You're one of the victims here, Grace. You're a target."

"I know how he works," Grace said, opening the conference room door. Zooey was already inside, a computer to trace the call set up on the far end of the table.

"He's been on hold for five minutes," she said. "So far, I haven't been able to pinpoint his location. He's using some sort of bouncing algorithm. Unfortunately, there are hackers who whip up this sort of thing for the right price. It's going to take me a while to get even one cell tower, let alone enough for a good triangulation."

Gavin came jogging into the room. "I just heard," he said. "He's on the phone?"

"Grace is going to talk to him," Paul said.

Gavin frowned. "Is that a good idea?"

"Yes," Grace said pointedly. "Look, the longer we argue about this, the longer he's on hold and the more likely he'll get spooked and hang up. So, Gavin, Paul, quiet. Zooey, keep tracing. I can do this."

Grace was anything but good to go, but she knew she had no choice. It was the moment of truth.

Be calm. Stay in control. Direct the conversation. She could hear Maggie's tips for proper negotiation in her head, and they bolstered her.

Grace reached for the phone with a shaking hand, turning it on speaker. But when she spoke, her voice was steady, even though her heart was ramming against her rib cage like a drum. "Hello?"

"Hello, Clarice," said a voice. Then a chuckle that sent icy daggers down her spine. "Just kidding."

"Carthage," she said, deliberately not calling him Doctor. She wasn't going to play to his narcissism. Not yet. Not until she had a feel for this sick game he was playing. It was hard to hide the revulsion in her voice, but she knew she had to remain as neutral as possible. The second she got emotional, he had control.

"Oh, good," he said, drawling the words out. "You do know. I was starting to think I overestimated your intelligence, Grace. That maybe you had peaked when you were my student. I was afraid you wouldn't figure it out."

She gritted her teeth at his mocking. "Well, I did," she said.

"Did you like my presents? I wrapped the last one specially, just for you."

Her stomach clenched, the image of Raymond Nugent's pale, dead face flashing through her mind. She steeled herself.

"We both know none of that was for me," Grace said. "All of this is for *you*."

There was a sigh, a classic professorial expression of disappointment. "*All* of this is for you, Grace. All of this is *because* of you."

Grace swallowed, her throat scratchy. She needed water. "I never asked you to murder five people," she said.

"You never asked for anything!" he shouted. The sudden shift in volume made her jump. Everyone in the room stared at her in surprise, and she gripped the edges of the table hard, her palm sweating. "You just took and took and took, Grace. Heedless of the consequences. Heedless of *my* needs. You must be punished for that. You left me."

"I was eighteen years old," Grace said calmly, feeling anything but. She could still remember that pit in her stomach from the day she broke it off. How he'd reached for her over the restaurant table, how she'd fled, leaving him behind with a bouquet of dying roses and a bottle of expensive wine. "You were almost twenty years older. You were my professor. *You* were the one who had the power. You knew better, Carthage. But that didn't stop you."

"It didn't stop you either," he hissed. "You little slut, you were gagging for it."

Grace bit her tongue. She wanted so badly to yell. To scream. To accuse. To hang up. But when it came to crisis negotiation, she'd been trained by the best, and she wouldn't put Maggie's lessons to shame. Or endanger the case. She had to catch him, to stop this madness.

Zooey mouthed, *The signal's still bouncing,* at her. Grace nodded. She would need to keep him on the line longer so they could pin it down.

She had to be the one in control.

"You left devastation in your wake," Carthage muttered. "Hurricane Grace. Tearing through my life, turning everything upside down, making me crazy for you. Making me want you. Making Joann leave me."

"I didn't break up your marriage, Carthage," Grace said. "You pursued me. Just like you pursued the girls before me and, I'm sure, the girls after me. I was just the final straw for Joann. She knew about the others."

"I didn't love the others!" he shouted.

Grace glanced at Gavin, who held up a pad of paper with the words *He's losing control* scribbled on it.

Grace nodded. *I have a plan,* she mouthed back.

"But you loved me," Grace said, and it was a statement, rather than a question. A sickening fact she knew Carthage believed 100 percent. His version of love was impossible for a normal person to contemplate . . . where mutilated bodies served as courting gifts and her fear was his idea of foreplay.

"You deserted me," Carthage spat back. "You left me here to rot while you soared like some sort of avenging angel of justice. And I've had to watch it all. Your commendations. Your promotions. Your fucking *bestsellers*!"

The books. The books were the trigger. That's all she could think as he breathed hard into the phone, his fury radiating through the line. They'd propelled her to celebrity status, so countless people knew her name. He couldn't stand it. It made her less his, in his twisted, violent mind. It made him question his ownership of her. And that would've shaken his worldview to the core.

It would be enough to set him off on this sick game he was playing.

"I waited, Grace," Carthage continued ranting. "I kept waiting for you to call, for you to *acknowledge*. But that call never came. And then I saw that you dedicated your new book to someone else—you called *her* your mentor. Your *inspiration*. How dare you do that to me?"

"You think *you* deserve that title?" Grace asked, and she couldn't stop the disgusted skepticism in her voice. She winced, realizing it'd make him escalate further.

"I *made* you," Carthage hissed. "I took one look at you, and I saw it—the raw potential. I molded you like a sculptor molds clay. You were almost perfect. With my continued influence, you *would've* been perfect. But you rejected me. You ran away like a little girl scared of love. Scared of a *real* man. We were so close, my pretty girl. So close to perfection. And you threw it all away.

"You're not perfect now, bitch. You've undone all my hard work, stomped on the ashes. You need to acknowledge my hand in making you. You're *mine.*"

Fear and anger, twined tightly together, rose inside her at his last words. She had spent her life being told what to do by her distant father, only to have him turn his back on her the first time she ever defied him. She'd grown up with lectures about the Sinclair name, holding it up, being an example. She'd been raised to be an idea of a person, her free will bent to the will of the Sinclair family. She was supposed to exist only to better the name.

She had left that behind. Her life was hers and only hers.

"I belong to no one," Grace said, her voice ringing out clear and determined. "Especially not you."

He laughed, an unhinged cackle that made goose bumps prickle across her skin in waves. "You're always someone's bitch, Grace. You were mine once, you'll be mine again."

"We'll see," she said.

"Yes, we will," Carthage said, the dark promise heavy in his words. "Tell me, sweet Grace, what is that little profiler mind of yours thinking? Is it busy putting together pieces of me, assembling a bunch of psych-speak to explain me? Profile me, sweetheart. Right now."

Grace's eyes narrowed. Oh, he wanted to play that game, did he? She bit back her vicious words, practically hearing Maggie's voice begging her to stay calm and in control.

She had to be strong. Because she knew deep down that Carthage's weakness was his greatest insecurity. She was going to exploit that.

She went in for the kill: "You think you're a genius," Grace said, her voice flat, almost professorial. "You got involved in academia because you thought your intelligence would be appreciated. Valued. But it didn't quite work out that way, did it?"

Carthage let out a little huff of breath, loud enough for her to hear. She smiled triumphantly. She was getting into the cracks in his armor.

"No, it didn't work out that way," she repeated, starting to pace around the room. Filled with a frenetic sort of energy, she needed to burn it off as she revealed him to himself, layer by layer, digging down into that insecure core. "Suddenly, you were swimming with the big guys and you didn't quite measure up the way you'd planned, did you? Instead of your colleagues bowing to your superiority, you found yourself surrounded by people who were more intelligent than you. More accomplished. Better published. Higher climbing. And you just got left behind, again and again. It made you bitter."

"I am a brilliant scholar," he said, but she could hear just the barest doubt in his voice, lurking there, hidden to everyone but her.

"You're complacent," Grace said, making another circle around the room. Zooey still hadn't gotten a trace. Carthage must've spent a lot of money to scramble his signal like this. "You wanted things handed to you because you happened to be smarter than the nearest yokel in whatever podunk pond where you were the biggest fish. Since you couldn't get your colleagues' respect or admiration, you turned to your students. They became your proxies for success because you have so little of your own."

"Teaching is a passion," Carthage hissed back. "An honored and respected profession."

"You know what they say about those who teach," Grace sneered.

Zooey clapped her hand over her mouth, trying to suppress a laugh. Paul pressed his finger to his lips, shooting her a stern look.

Gavin didn't take his eyes off Grace, his stance

tense and protective. He was having a hell of a hard time holding his tongue, she could tell. She appreciated his restraint, though. One wrong move, and this went south.

"You're an angry man, Carthage," Grace said. "But it's not just your failure that makes you angry. No, what makes you really furious is the anonymity. More than anything, you hate that no one sees you. No one knows you. No one cares to. But I see you now, Henry. I see you crystal clear."

"And what do you see, Grace?" There was a disturbing ache in his words, like he was some earnest schoolboy, eager for instruction. It made her stomach flip over violently, and she leaned against the conference room table, her legs quivering.

But there was no sign of wavering in her voice as she answered his question. "I see a man past his prime who can't even seduce naive freshmen into his bed anymore. They're too sophisticated for you now, those girls you want so desperately to look at you like you've got all the answers. So you decided to focus on me. The one who got away."

"You're the one who caused the most damage," Carthage seethed. "You ruined my marriage."

"I didn't tell your wife," Grace said. "You did."

It was a guess, but now she was sure of the answer. He had told Joann himself. The question was why . . .

"Because I was going to leave her for you!"

Grace's disgust was palpable in the room. Next to her, she could feel Zooey shuddering in womanly commiseration.

"You keep telling yourself that," Grace said, knowing she sounded strong and sure, though feeling anything but. God, was he this delusional? That he willingly broke apart his marriage and then a decade later started killing people he deemed harmful to the institution? The hypocrisy was mind-boggling.

"I know what's true," Carthage said. "I know what's right. What's fair. You weren't fair, Grace. Your entire life—I should've been there. At your side."

"Reaping the rewards of what . . . being my sidepiece?" Grace said.

It was a calculated blow, meant to shatter the fantasy he'd obviously built in his head.

"Get real, Carthage," she added.

Zooey pumped her fist in the air in a "You go, girl!" gesture. It was oddly cheering in such a tense situation.

"Real?" Carthage thundered. "Do you want to hear something *real*? How about *I* profile *you*? Would you like that, Grace?"

"Not really," Grace said, trying to sound disinterested. Her stomach wound in knots, she looked over to the tech, who gestured at her to keep him talking. Were they ever going to get the trace, or was this fruitless? "But why don't you give it a try?" she asked.

Carthage chuckled. "Soon, my love," he said. "You know, I think back to those days . . . You were such a pretty girl. You had so much potential. You were so sweet, so trusting. And look at you now: bitter, loveless—I know *all* about your string of men, Grace. You never let them stay the night. You never see them more than once. You just use them and discard them. You're like those insects that eat their mates. Deadly, dangerous. You need to be stopped."

She wanted to reach through the phone and slug him. "I'm not the one who's killed five people in three days, Carthage," Grace said. "You are."

He sighed. "You need to be taught a lesson, pretty girl. It's really a shame it's come to this."

"Wait—"

But he'd hung up.

Grace looked at Zooey, who shook her head. "I couldn't triangulate the signal," she said.

"Dammit!" Grace threw the phone across the room, where it hit a wall and shattered. Zooey stared at her with wide eyes, and Gavin strode over to her, grasped her arm, and pulled her toward the door.

"Come on," he said. "You need to cool down."

Silent but still fuming, Grace let him steer her out of the room.

She didn't need to cool down.

She needed to get angry.

It was the only way she could win.

CHAPTER 24

My pretty girl,

I'm grinning like a boy who's seen his first naked woman right now.

How I've missed talking to you. It's been a long ten years. Lonely. You burned brightly, my Grace. You burned hot, searing into my skin, marking me forever.

At first, I tried to ignore it. The persistent ache that plagued me. I immersed myself in my work, my students—the loyal ones, not ungrateful little bitches like you. But as the years passed, as your achievements grew, I found myself unable to enjoy the things I once did.

There has always been something about you that set you apart. The other dalliances, they were easily dismissed. Girls who went on to achieve little, much to my disappointment.

But you soared . . . even though you made all

the wrong choices. You left when I didn't want you to.

I wasn't finished with you, and you left.

How dare you? When I loved you so? When I did everything to keep us together?

I deserve more than that from you. I deserve everything—your very soul.

I taught you your value, and instead of being grateful, you took what I unveiled, what I molded, and used it to get whatever you wanted. I can't imagine the number of beds you had to hop in to get where you are today. There's no way you got there on your own merit. You're talented, but you're devious. That pretty face of yours hides a vicious heart.

I love you for it.

I'll destroy you because of it.

I've forced you into a corner. You have to listen to me now. You have no way out. Not unless I let you. A pretty little girl in a clever trap you have no hope of escaping.

Perfection.

I have you where I want you. You talk a big game, spinning your stories like you do, and your idiotic theories, but I see through all that bravado.

I know you.

You're hurting. Weak. Emotional. Questioning. Angry.

I love it when you're angry. It's a pure, beautiful thing, pulsing off you like pleasure pulses off other women.

Anger means guilt. Guilt means blame.

You are to blame, you bitch. All the blood I've spilled is on your hands. You made me do it. If you'd just stayed, if you'd just submitted . . .

You've forced my hand.

You need to be put in your place. Below me. Under my control.

And I'm going to make it happen.

It's time to up the stakes, pretty girl.

Are you ready?

—C

CHAPTER 25

Grace stared at the Colonial-style house across the street. The rose garden up front was beautifully cared for, the blooms splashing color and fragrance across the yard.

She didn't want to go anywhere near the place. Gavin had offered to go with her, but she knew he'd be of more use raiding Carthage's office as soon as he secured a warrant.

Joann was her problem.

She was expecting her. Grace had called ahead, giving her a brief rundown of the situation. Partly, this was practical: She needed Joann focused when she spoke to her, and breaking the news that her ex was a serial killer over the phone gave her a good forty minutes to absorb the information before Grace arrived.

Partly, though, it was personal: Every time Grace thought about showing up at Joann's door with no warning, a sour, heavy feeling settled in her stomach like lead.

She couldn't do that to her. So she'd gritted her teeth and made the call. Then she'd gotten in her BMW and drove.

And now she was sitting there, drumming her fingers nervously on the dashboard, wishing she were anywhere else. She couldn't stop the dread from building inside her whole body. As she got out of the car and walked across the street, she felt like she was struggling through drying cement.

The dark blue door had a stained glass window set in it. Grace traced her fingers along the bright colored glass as she pressed the doorbell.

A few moments, and the door opened. And she was face-to-face with the woman whose marriage she'd helped to ruin.

Joann Taylor—she'd gone back to her maiden name—stood there, regarding Grace calmly. She was a statuesque woman with short auburn hair and delicate features, dressed in flowing batik pants and a sleeveless silk shell that showed off her toned arms. She wore no makeup, no jewelry, and it suited the raw, natural beauty of her face.

"Hello, Agent Sinclair," she said, stepping back to let Grace into her home.

"I appreciate you taking the time to see me,"

Grace said as Joann led her into a small living room. Pots of succulents were scattered across floor, tables and shelves, and large windows on the north wall allowed light to stream into the room, giving it an airy conservatory feel.

This was a woman who valued nature. Life. She was probably a vegetarian. Grace would bet her art collection that she did yoga. A tea drinker, instead of coffee. She'd traveled extensively, preferring Asia to Europe. Most likely an only child. She'd never remarried, and it was unlikely she ever would.

Grace couldn't fault her there.

"Sit, please," Joann said, settling herself on a sage-green fainting couch, folding her hands together. She looked at Grace, and her eyes softened as she smiled.

"Ms. Taylor, I know this is awkward—" Grace started.

But the older woman waved her off. "It's in the past. I've moved on."

"Still," Grace said, little frissons of shock going off under her skin at how casual Joann was acting. "I am sorry about what happened. I never meant to be the cause of a marriage ending."

"Honestly, back then, I thought you did me a favor," Joann said. "And now, if what I was told on the phone is true, I know you did."

Grace looked down, not sure how to respond to such magnanimity, class, and, well, *grace*.

"He was never a good husband," Joann continued. "I always sensed . . . something in him. A darkness, I suppose you could call it. He never yelled or belittled me, but I always felt very secondary in his life. He was so focused on his studies and then his students. Their admiration and respect were always much more important than mine."

Inside her purse, Grace's phone began to ring.

"Do you need to get that?" Joann asked.

Grace shook her head. "Please, continue," she said.

"Well, I'm sure you know you weren't the first of his . . . wanderings," Joann said. "But I could tell something had changed when you left for Georgetown. He locked himself up in his study for days, and when he finally came out, almost everything in the room was broken. He began to drink heavily. And one night, I came home to find him in a rage. Ranting about appreciation and fate and star-crossed lovers. About showing 'her' what he was made of. He was throwing things, tearing books off the shelf. I tried to stop him. And he backhanded me."

"So you left," Grace said.

"I was raised in a world where women were encouraged to ignore infidelity," Joann said.

"But a man hits me once, and only once," she added grimly. "I filed for divorce the next week."

"Did you have much contact with him after the divorce?" Grace asked.

Joann shook her head. "I ran into Henry once, at a restaurant, shortly after our divorce was finalized. He was polite but curt. I haven't heard from him or seen him since. That must have been nine years ago."

"You haven't received any calls from unknown numbers? Hang-ups, maybe? Noticed any strange cars on your block? Or mysterious packages on your doorstep?"

"Nothing," Joann said. "Agent Sinclair, am I to understand he's committed these horrible murders and you can't find him?"

"At the moment, his whereabouts are unknown," Grace said carefully. On her way to the house, Zooey had called her to let her know Carthage had given up his apartment a month ago. His office at the university was their only starting point, so Paul and Gavin were already en route.

Grace knew they wouldn't find Carthage there. It was too obvious.

He needed his twists and turns so he would feel clever . . . better than her.

"You know, we met once," Joann said.

Grace frowned. "We did? I'm sorry, I don't—"

"I doubt you'd remember," Joann said. "It was at your first book's launch a few years back. A friend of mine's in publishing and invited me to go. I must admit, I couldn't help myself. I was curious. You had done so well for yourself. I wanted to see what kind of woman you'd grown up to be."

Grace searched her memory of the night, but so much of it was an excited, anxiety-filled blur that she couldn't place Joann in it.

"I watched you that night. You sparkled. You had every person's focus. They were enraptured. You were so young and beautiful and talented, and I should've resented you or hated you. But then I noticed something: Whenever you didn't think anyone was looking, this shadow would fall over your face. And I realized you were a lonely girl in a crowd of people who thought they knew you but didn't even scrape the surface. Even though you knew them, maybe even better than they knew themselves. That's your job, after all."

Joann looked at her, sympathy written in the gentle lines of her face. "It's a bit of a curse, isn't it?"

"Sometimes," Grace said, prompted to honesty by this woman who *should* have resented her but who instead chose to see the bigger picture for the greater good.

"You were young, Grace," Joann said. "He took advantage of that. I lived with the man for fifteen years. He's a manipulator. But even I couldn't imagine he'd turn into this kind of monster." She shook her head, the horror in her eyes saying it all. "I wish I could help you more," she said.

"I will find him," Grace promised, the vow echoing through the room. "And I will end this."

"See that you do," Joann said. "Because you might be the only one who can."

AFTER SHE LEFT Joann Taylor's house, it took several minutes for Grace to gather herself together. Her palms were sweating as if she were sixteen and in debate class again. Her clothes felt too tight, restrictive. The air inside the car felt impossibly hot.

She needed to breathe. Focus on something else.

Her phone. She reached inside her purse, grabbing it. Her eyebrows drew together when she saw she had a missed call and voicemail from Dorothy, the teen from the Herman Center. She entered her passcode and raised her phone to her ear.

"Hello, pretty girl." His voice filled her senses, making each of them want to revolt, to flee. "I'm at the park, thinking of you. Thinking of us. Do you remember when I was your mentor, Grace? How you took that away from me?" There was a pause. "I'm going to teach you how it feels to lose your protégé. Poor little Dorothy, she can't just click her heels and say 'No place like home,' can she?" He laughed. "See you soon."

Then the line went dead.

The phone fell out of Grace's numb hands. She scrambled for it and dialed the number back, her breath caught in her throat. But it just rang and rang, before going dead.

Not Dorothy. *Please*, not Dorothy!

She shoved her keys into the ignition and screeched into the street, gunning the gas so hard she was afraid the car would stall.

She punched the center button on her phone. "Call Gavin," she directed as she took a sharp right, heading out of the cozy neighborhood and flooring it toward the freeway. Gavin's phone rang a few times before he picked up.

"Hey, Grace," Gavin said. "We're at Carthage's office. It's a bust. I'm—"

"Gavin, listen to me," she ordered. "Carthage is somewhere in Gusset Park. He's taken one of my teenagers from the counseling center. Dorothy O'Brian. You need to get over there. You're closer. I've just left Joann Taylor's, so I'm not going to make it in time. Call SWAT, call DC police, call the fucking National Guard—I don't care who. Just get someone there. *Now!*"

"Oh, God," Gavin said.

"Get there," Grace begged. "He's going to kill her!"

He hung up with no goodbye.

Grace raced onto the highway, veering around slow-moving cars, changing lanes like a mad-woman. She got caught behind a semitruck for a few minutes, forcing her to slow down, trap-ping her with her thoughts and the adrenaline pumping through her veins.

She'd ignored the call. She'd ignored Dorothy, and now . . .

"Dammit!" Grace swore, hitting the steering wheel with her palm.

Dorothy wasn't going to die, she told herself firmly as she finally passed the semi, zooming ahead of it. Gavin would get there in time. She knew he would.

Gavin would save her. He had to.

But the ball of dread in her stomach grew with each minute she spent careening down the highway, her heart in her throat, guilt pounding down on her.

If only she hadn't ignored the call . . .

CHAPTER 26

"Turn here, turn here," Gavin said as Harrison sped down the street, gripping the steering wheel so hard his knuckles turned white. Harrison screeched to a stop at the edge of the park, where a street fair was being held. They both leapt out of the SUV.

"You take the north side," Harrison directed him, "I'll take the south. Backup's on its way."

Gavin gave a quick nod and headed out. On the way over, Zooey had texted them a picture of Dorothy O'Brian, so he knew who he was looking for.

He moved swiftly through the crowd, his eyes sweeping the area with a tense but practiced gaze. This was the kind of work he was made for and he could feel his senses focusing, homing in as he scanned the area. *Find the asset. Remove the threat. Extract the asset.*

He didn't want to draw his gun and cause a

panic—or worse, tip off Carthage that they'd arrived. He couldn't know if Carthage had grabbed Dorothy yet—there had been no reports of disturbances from dispatch, but Carthage was tricky. He could've lured her away from the crowd before . . .

All Gavin could think of was his little sister as he made his way through the crowd and past the colorful booths hawking woven baskets and handmade soaps. Dorothy was her age. If someone like Carthage even got within a foot of her, he'd lose his mind.

Grace's plea echoed in his ears as he reached the end of the aisle of booths, peering over the sea of people moving toward the stage, where live music was playing. Even though he towered over most of the crowd, it was no use—he couldn't see a damn thing.

Okay. He needed a new plan. There was no way he was going to spot either of them—together or apart—in this crush.

He had to stop thinking like a cop.

And he needed to start thinking like Grace.

Where would he go? He'd need to lure her from the crowd. Dorothy wasn't some pampered, naive kid from a private school. She was a streetwise teen who'd probably seen way too much shit in her life already.

She'd be distrustful of strangers approaching

her, Gavin realized as he moved toward the out-
skirts of the fair, pushing his way through the
excited, murmuring crowd. Some old guy coming up to her, maybe trying to hit on her? She'd
know how to shut that down—fast. Her creep
radar would be well-tuned by now.

Which meant Carthage would need to either
gain her trust somehow—or take her by force.

Dorothy would scream her head off if he tried
to grab her. She would fight back.

So that meant the trust route. Gavin dashed
past the lemonade booth, heading behind the
stage, where a group of tall trees obscured one
of the park exits. What would make Dorothy
trust him? Who did Dorothy trust?

It hit him in a sickening wave as he sped past
the stage, the beat of the drum circle rising in
the air.

Grace.

Dorothy trusted Grace. If someone flashed her
a real-enough-looking FBI badge and told her
Grace needed to see her, she'd go.

Gavin pelted down the pathway through the
trees, his stomach tightening with dread with
each step. The crowd had thinned, and he could
see directly down the path, toward the park
gates.

Right in front of the gate, two figures were sitting on a bench, locked in serious conversation.

The man got up, gesturing toward the gate. The girl with him—her face was turned away from Gavin—looked toward the gate, then back toward Carthage.

"*Dorothy!*" he yelled, increasing his speed, running full out, pulling his gun. "Get away from him! Run!"

Carthage grabbed her, lightning fast, before she could even react. Gavin's gun was up and on him in a second as he finally closed the space between them.

"Not another move," Carthage said, looking meaningfully at the knife held to Dorothy's throat.

"It's gonna be okay, Dorothy," Gavin told her as Carthage began to retreat toward the gate, dragging the girl with him. Gavin touched his radio in his ear. "I need backup on the north entrance," he said. "You've got nowhere to go, Carthage," he warned.

"One of Grace's lapdogs, I see," Carthage sneered, his knife pressing hard against Dorothy's throat. She whimpered, her kohl-lined eyes widening in horror. "I don't recognize you from before. You must be new."

Gavin's mouth flattened. Of course he'd been stalking Grace's team too. God, how long had he been planning this?

"Let the girl go," Gavin ordered. They were

out of the park now, close to the curb, where a van was parked.

"I'll slit her throat if you come any closer," Carthage threatened, a manic gleam shining in his eyes.

"Please," Dorothy begged. "My little brother needs me."

"It's okay," Gavin told her again, even though it was anything but. What could he do? Let Carthage take her, hoping he'd keep her alive long enough so he could use her to hurt Grace? He couldn't be sure Carthage wouldn't just murder her as soon as he could.

Gavin's hands tightened on his Glock, his mind racing as Carthage reached for the van door.

Gavin leapt, his body reacting before his mind could process anything. It was all protective instinct, a feral urge that roared through him as he launched himself at Carthage. The man cried out, pushing Dorothy into the van and whipping around to Gavin, slashing at his face.

The knife sliced through his skin, and he felt his forehead split as Carthage dragged the blade down across his eyebrow, toward his eye. Gavin jerked back, blood slicking down his face in sheets. Shit. The bastard had got him good.

Carthage vaulted into the van and shut the door. Gavin lunged forward, scrambling for the door handle, the blood in his eyes making it impossible to find. "Dorothy!" he shouted, his fingers clasping the handle just as Carthage hit the gas. Gavin held on, his feet dragging against the pavement as Carthage sped away. He could smell burned rubber and blood. Carthage wove the van back and forth, trying to shake him off like a dog with a flea, but Gavin hung on.

Then Carthage hit the brakes, and Gavin was propelled forward by the abrupt stop. He managed to hit the ground rolling, his hands protecting his head as his right side scraped against the asphalt. He forced himself to his feet, chasing after the van, but it sped away, making a right and disappearing.

Gavin hit his radio. "Harrison," he panted. "Suspect is in a white van. Headed north on State Street. He got the girl."

Blood was still pouring down his face. He tried to wipe it away with his sleeve, but his cuff links scraped against the open wound, making him flinch. As the adrenaline was absorbed by his body, he became aware of just how hard he'd hit the asphalt. His entire side was raw, his button-up shredded from the impact. It ached dully, but he knew it'd hurt like hell soon.

"Gavin! Oh, my God."

He turned, and the horror on Grace's face was something he never wanted to see again.

"I'm okay—" he started to say but she didn't let him finish. She closed the space between them in two steps, her hands hovering for a second over his face before her lips pressed urgently against his. He knew he had to taste like hell—like blood and fear and anger—but she was like a cool drink of water after a week in the desert.

"What did he do?" she asked when they pulled apart. Behind her, he could see agents pulling up, Harrison jogging forward. Grace pulled off her sweater, pressing what was probably five hundred dollars' worth of cashmere against his wound like it was nothing. "We need a medic!" she called over her shoulder.

"He got Dorothy, Grace," Gavin said miserably. He stumbled a little. The leg he'd fallen on was shaking. "I tried to hold on to the van, but I couldn't get the door open. He braked and I went flying."

"He could've killed you," she said. "You are not allowed to do that!"

"What, die?" he asked. He would've raised an eyebrow, but that was a little hard right now.

"Yes!" she snapped, heedless of the irrationality of her statement. "You aren't a spy anymore," she said, lowering her voice. "You have a team now. You have me . . ." She stopped herself before she could say more. "No more pulling a James Bond," she ordered.

Normally, he'd make a quip about martinis or Aston Martins, but instead he met her worried eyes. He smiled at her, trying to be reassuring, because he could tell she was genuinely shaken. And because it warmed him more than it should, her worry over his well-being. "Promise," he said, and watched as the tension eased from her body.

She was learning he kept his promises, and he was glad, because he wanted to make all sorts of promises to her.

"Shit, Walker," Harrison said, finally catching up to them. "You need to go to the hospital."

Gavin shook his head. No way was he wasting that much time. "I just need someone to stitch me up," he said. "This isn't over. We've got to get Dorothy back."

Grace pressed her sweater harder against his forehead. It smelled like her, and it was the one good thing in his life right that second, so he breathed it in.

"We're going to get her back," he told Grace, because she looked like she desperately needed to hear it.

It was a vow.

And he intended to keep it.

CHAPTER 27

"Walk me through it again," Maggie said.

Grace looked up at her friend, her eyes burning with exhaustion. It had been twelve hours since Carthage had taken Dorothy, and there'd been no call, no contact of any kind. Now that this was a kidnapping case, Paul had brought Maggie in to advise. They'd set up in the north conference room, but so far, they were dead in the water.

"He's obsessive. Meticulous. But this is out of character for him."

"He kills people—he doesn't take them," Maggie summed up.

"We've got thirty-six hours, tops, to get her back," Gavin said from his spot in the back of the room. The massive cut on his forehead had been seen to, twenty stitches arching through his eyebrow. The road rash from his fall from the van was bad—she still couldn't believe he had hung on to a moving vehicle for that long. The forensic techs who had examined the scene had said he must've held on for at least a hundred feet, going at least sixty miles per hour. He could've been killed. It was amazing he didn't have a concussion or broken arms or ribs or a fractured skull. When she told him as much, he'd shrugged and said, "You have enough older brothers, you learn how to fall."

He'd been unable to meet her eyes since she'd come in with Maggie, and she knew why: He was blaming himself for not getting to Dorothy fast enough.

God, Carthage could've taken his *eye*. Any other person would've flinched—the instinct was rooted deep in the human psyche to protect your sight. But Gavin had forged ahead, ignoring the danger and pain and blood, desperate to get to her.

He'd done all he could. She knew that.

There was a dark part of her that was grateful that Dorothy got to see someone fight for her before . . .

Don't go there, Grace, she ordered herself. *Dorothy's alive, and you're going to get her back.*

"The call that comes next is important," Maggie told Grace. "Kidnapping isn't Carthage's modus operandi. He's not a professional, and he's not after money."

"He's after *me*," Grace said.

"He's not going to get you," Gavin growled.

Maggie raised a delicate eyebrow at the possessive rumble in his voice. Grace shook her head slightly when her friend shot her a questioning look.

"He's more liable to mess up here than anywhere else," Maggie said. "He's going to be spooked but trying hard not to show it. Taking a live victim, keeping her quiet and restrained—that's a huge stressor. He's going to need you to guide him to the right conclusion."

"Which is what, exactly?" Grace asked. She valued Maggie's insight more than anyone, but she wasn't sure where she was going with this.

"Your suffering is his version of ransom," Maggie explained. "He took Dorothy for one reason: to hurt you."

She was right. Grace wrapped her arms around herself, feeling very cold all of a sudden.

"The killing's not enough anymore," Gavin said grimly. "It's over too quickly for him."

Grace frowned. There was a bleakness to his face that she'd never seen. "What aren't you telling me?" she asked.

He hesitated. "He took her to torture her, Grace," he finally said. "And because he's not experienced, he's going to end up killing her, even if he doesn't want to right away."

Grace swallowed, a horrible lump rising in her throat at his words. There was something in his face that told her he understood torture. She thought about the thin, obviously old scars on his feet—the ones she'd noticed their first night together. They'd used rubber tubing to beat him, leaving those marks. They'd caused microfractures in the bones of the feet that hurt more than anything, but they wouldn't leave much of a mark on the surface unless the torturer got sloppy.

"I need to find him," she said.

"He *will* call," Maggie reassured her. "There is no way he'll be able to resist. He needs to experience your suffering."

There was a knock on the conference room door and Paul looked in. "Grace, I need to talk to you," he said.

Grace took one look at him and knew what was coming before she even got to her feet and followed him to his office. It was in his face, in the tense line of his shoulders, in the way he refused to meet her eyes.

She didn't even bother to sit down before saying, "You want to take me off the case."

Paul sighed, sitting down behind his desk. Grace took a seat across from it, folding her arms in front of her stubbornly.

"The press is going crazy, Grace," he said.

"They love this story. And it puts a magnifying glass on this case. If there are any screwups . . ."

Irritation prickled across her skin. "Have I screwed up?" Grace demanded. "Because as I remember it, I'm the one who realized the murders were serial, I figured out how they were connected, and I handed you your killer."

"Because you used to date him!" Paul said. "I've talked to Special Agent Cortes. He's willing to step in."

"Cortes?" Grace said incredulously. "You've got to be kidding me."

"Cortes is a fine agent," Paul said. "And an excellent profiler."

"Cortes is very good," Grace admitted. "If this was a human trafficking case, he'd be your guy. But his specialty is sex crimes. He's never worked a serial case, has he?"

Paul's silence said it all.

"I've handled over a dozen serial cases since I joined the Bureau," Grace said. "On more than half, I was lead profiler. And all but *one* ended up with the perp in prison. And you're telling me you're going to bring in a less specialized profiler and it's going to be fine?"

Paul's lips flattened in a hard line, disapproval radiating from him. "You have a personal connection to this case. I should pull you off just for that."

"That's the exact reason why you *shouldn't* pull me off," Grace explained. "Carthage's obsession is with *me*. You heard him on the phone. He loves me."

"You mean he *thinks* he loves you," Paul said.

Grace shook her head. "It would be stupid of me to dismiss his feelings," she said. She wasn't going to be stupid when it came to this. Not after he took Dorothy. She had to consider every angle, every word Carthage said to her, every action he'd taken so far. Everything had meaning, and something was going to lead her to him. Some small detail that seemed insignificant—until it didn't.

Paul blinked, baffled. "He's a serial killer; how can he even love?"

"It's not our version of love, clearly," Grace said, getting up from the chair. She needed to move around. The crawling feeling, like phantom bugs walking across her skin, was back. It was easier to ignore when she was moving. "But to him? It's real. For him, love is ownership. He sees himself as Pygmalion. In his mind, I'm his creation who's gone rogue. If you take me out of the equation now, he'll stop engaging with law enforcement. We'll have no hope to get Dorothy back safe. He'll kill her and dump her body."

She placed her hands on Paul's desk and leaned over, meeting his eyes dead on. "He would disappear, Paul. You could spend years chasing your tail, trying to find him, while he's off killing whoever suits his sick fantasies. Think about that before you pull me off this case. Think about the kind of damage he could cause for *years* before he's caught."

She couldn't let that happen. Deep down, it terrified her, the idea that Paul would pull her off. Because deep down, she knew if that happened, they wouldn't lose just Dorothy.

They'd lose any chance to get Carthage.

And she would have to make a choice.

She knew herself. She could deny many things, but the part of her that understood the darkness in people, that saw the most violent and vile parts of human beings, knew there really was no choice.

She would have to go rogue and hunt him down on her own. And if she did that, she wouldn't be bringing him back in cuffs.

He'd be in a body bag.

"Please, Paul," she said, softening. She knew the exhaustion was showing on her face, in her messy braid and tired eyes. "We've worked together for years. I've been right so far. Have some faith in me."

He sighed, rubbing at his mouth, avoiding her gaze for a moment. "I don't want you getting hurt," he admitted quietly.

Her heart squeezed. "This is reminding you of the Thebes case," she said. How could she have missed it? She'd been so wrapped up in her own chaos, she'd completely forgotten to factor in Paul's issues.

"Two of my team got overpowered on my watch," Paul said. "I got tied to a chair with enough C4 to blow me to kingdom come strapped to my chest. That I could deal with. But that little girl was right there next to me, dying, all because that bastard wouldn't give her insulin. And even *that* I could deal with. At least when it happened, it'd be quick. She wouldn't hurt. But then . . ." His voice faded. He knotted his hands together in front of him, his head hanging.

"Then Maggie walked into that cabin," Grace finished for him. "And she made him put *her* in the vest."

"My goddamn life flashed before my eyes, Grace," Paul said, his face haunted. "I'd made my peace with it—how she and I ended—but how could I accept being the cause of her death?"

"She didn't die," Grace reminded him gently. "And I'm not going to either."

"You said it yourself, Grace: He thinks he owns you," Paul insisted. "And if growing up with four sisters taught me anything, it's that when a typical man thinks that way, it's dangerous. Hell, it can be deadly. When a serial killer thinks it? It's both."

Grace was about to argue when there was a knock on Paul's office door. Gavin was waiting on the other side when she opened it. "He's on the phone."

"Grace—" Paul started, but she ignored him, racing down the hall and back to the conference room, the two men following behind her. Zooey had arrived, already trying to trace the call as Maggie hurried over to her.

"Grace, I'm not so sure this is a good idea," Paul said. "Maybe Maggie should—"

"Maybe Maggie shouldn't," Maggie said, shooting Paul a quelling look. "She's the only one he's going to engage with, Paul. She's the anchor here."

Paul folded his arms across his chest, looking torn. "Fine. Let's see if we can get an actual trace this time, Zooey?"

"It's hard, with the signal bouncing all over, boss," Zooey explained as Maggie pulled Grace aside.

"Okay, remember what I said," Maggie directed. "He's out of his depth here. He needs to be dealt with delicately. Don't show your anger."

Grace nodded, her heart hammering in her chest. Dorothy's life was on the line. She couldn't screw this up.

"You can do this," Gavin said behind her.

She took a deep, steadying breath and hit the speaker button on the phone.

"Carthage," she said.

"Once again, someone's got hurt because you're too caught up in your world to notice anything or anyone else," he spat, his anger dripping off his voice like bitter molasses.

"Have you hurt Dorothy?" Grace asked, trying as hard as she could to keep the rage out of her words.

"I was talking about that agent of yours," Carthage sneered. "Walker, was it?" He tutted. "He got in my way. He was *quite* determined. Very noble. I hope I didn't mess up his face too much. But maybe he'll get a pity fuck out of you, if he's a good boy."

Grace bit the inside of her lip, refusing to glance over at Gavin, even though she wanted to.

"Is Dorothy okay?" she asked.

"She's a screamer," Carthage said, and there was a delighted, sickening double entendre to his words.

Grace's stomach clenched, her fingers curling into fists. "If you've raped her—" she started, only to be cut off with his cruel laughter. The sound curled around Grace like a tentacle. She could barely stand it, the feeling of being trapped, of the world tightening around her, no room to breathe or run.

She'd lost control already. He'd pushed the right buttons and now he knew it.

"I'm not a rapist, Grace," he scoffed. "What do you take me for? We're just having a little fun with knives, Dorothy and I."

If you leave one mark on her . . . Grace thought, wanting nothing more than to reach through the phone and strangle the life out of him.

"I want proof of life," she said, unable to keep her voice from shaking.

"And I want the years you stole from me back," Carthage said. "Unfortunately, pretty girl, we can't always have what we want. I've given you all the clues you need. You have forty-eight hours to find us. Then Dorothy goes into the Potomac."

"Wait—" Grace said.

But the line was dead.

"Dammit!" she yelled, grabbing the phone and chucking it across the room.

She paced around the room, running her hands through her hair, clutching the base of her neck as she tried to clear her mind. She needed to think.

Everyone in the room was silent, watching, waiting for her to speak.

But she didn't know what to say. She didn't know where he was.

She didn't know what to *do*.

What was he expecting? For her to try to puzzle out whatever clues he was talking about. For her to come out swinging. That's what he wanted, and that's what she'd been giving him. Her acknowledgment of him as an adversary bolstered him—she was playing the game he'd devised.

A thought struck her, stopping her in her tracks. She looked up, meeting Gavin's eyes.

"What?" he asked.

"We need to change the dynamic," she told him. "I'm not chasing after him anymore. I'm bringing him to me."

"Okay," he said. "But how?"

"We're going to do what Paul wants," she said, looking over to her boss, who frowned, not understanding. "Paul, you're going to fire me."

CHAPTER 28

Are you sure it's a good idea for me to be doing this?" Gavin asked, adjusting his tie nervously and running a hand through his hair. The movement caused the thick locks to dip across his forehead. He let out a frustrated sigh. He needed a haircut.

"Stop that," Grace said, reaching out and smoothing his hair back absently. She froze when she realized what she was doing and snatched her hand away, but not before Gavin shot her an amused smile. "He's made a connection with you," she said, folding her arms across her chest like she was trying to keep herself from touching him more. He couldn't help but get a masculine sort of thrill at the thought.

"You're the only team member who's been face-to-face with him," she explained. "He thinks you're lesser than him. He thinks he won your last encounter."

Gavin's chest ached as he thought of how close he'd been to Dorothy. If he'd been able to reach out a few more inches, maybe . . .

He'd been so focused on her—on getting her out, on keeping her safe—that he hadn't been looking close enough at the knife before it slashed toward him.

He hadn't just failed the girl—he'd failed Grace.

"He *did* win," Gavin said. "If I'd just been a little quicker—"

"Stop," Grace said softly, grabbing his hand. She looked over her shoulder to make sure no one was in the hallway with them before reaching out and gently tracing the skin above the arc of stitches on his forehead. "You fought like hell for her. You risked yourself. You did everything you could."

"But it wasn't enough," Gavin said, the anger and self-blame audible in his voice.

"Sometimes it isn't," she said.

That was the hard truth of this work. They couldn't win them all.

But the sick game Carthage had embroiled her in? She *would* win. He knew it, even if he sensed that she was unsure herself.

Dorothy's kidnapping had hit her hard, made her doubt herself. But she was better than Carthage. Smarter. She would outwit him.

More than most people, Gavin could see how

this was wearing on her. Grace was good with her masks, with acting the way people wanted her to instead of how she actually felt. She'd done a fantastic job at keeping it together, but he'd caught a glimpse of her stress during the last phone call with Carthage. Her eyes had gotten that hopeless look that he remembered from the night she'd figured out Carthage was their unsub. She was starting to crack at the seams—and he couldn't blame her. Frankly, he was amazed at how well she'd dealt with all of this so far.

"I've never given a press conference before," he admitted, the nervousness mounting inside him. This had to go exactly as planned, or they wouldn't be able to draw him out. He could tell Agent Kincaid was concerned about Carthage's lack of experience when it came to kidnapping, and he had the same worries. Even if Carthage gave them forty-eight hours, that did not mean they actually had that much time.

Drawing him out was the only way to resolve this swiftly and safely for everyone.

"You'll be fine," she assured him. "Just follow the script Maggie and I came up with. Make sure you come off as dismissive of my contributions to the case. We want him confident, even a little cocky. Praise him. Talk about his skill as a killer. He'll be so puffed up he'll take the bait."

"Agent Walker, the team's assembled," the press liaison told him. Gavin fiddled with his tie again, glancing into the press room that had been set up for the occasion. Zooey and the rest of the team, along with Paul, were already up on the small platform. Chairs were spread across the front of the room, some journalists choosing to sit, others standing, their microphones and notebooks at the ready. The camera crew members were already focused like laser beams on his team.

Just like Grace wanted.

"They're ready for you," his press liaison reminded him.

Gavin nodded, making sure his tie was straight one final time.

"Wish me luck," he said, trying for a cavalier smile but failing, and then headed up to the podium. "Good afternoon," he said. "I am Special Agent Gavin Walker. I'm here today to discuss the recent murders in the area, as well as the kidnapping of a minor, one Dorothy O'Brian. The FBI's investigation has led us to this man . . ." He pressed a button, Carthage's face appearing on the screen behind him. "Dr. Henry Carthage, age forty-eight, is a criminology professor at the University of Maryland. He is considered armed and very dangerous."

A murmur broke out among the journalists.

"Is this our serial killer?" called out a reporter from the *Post*.

"Yes," Gavin said, looking directly in the camera, remembering Grace's gentle instructions. "Dr. Carthage is the man responsible for the recent serial murders in the greater DC area, as well as the kidnapping of Dorothy O'Brian. We have evidence Dr. Carthage has embarked on this killing spree as a personal vendetta against one of our profilers, Special Agent Grace Sinclair. He targeted Ms. O'Brian because of her connection to Agent Sinclair, who is a friend of her family."

"Grace Sinclair, the bestselling author?" one of the journalists shouted.

"That is correct," Gavin said.

The buzz in the room grew louder. Gavin kept his face impassive. *Call him Doctor*, Grace had directed. *Show respect. He needs to feel good.*

"Why is Carthage going after Sinclair?" asked a blonde reporter from the *Times*.

Gavin took a deep breath. He knew he had to do it, but the words were like sand in his mouth. He hated putting Grace's business out for the world to consume like this, but he had to. She'd *told* him to.

"When Special Agent Sinclair was in her first

year of undergrad, Dr. Carthage was her mentor," he said. "The two of them had an intimate relationship."

The room went wild. Questions flew from all sides.

"Are you saying he's killing people to get back at an old girlfriend?"

"It's well-known that Agent Sinclair finished school in record time. Was she of legal age when this relationship took place?"

"What about Dr. Carthage's wife? According to my sources, he was married during that time."

Gavin raised his hands, silencing the room. "I am not going to speculate on the personal life of Agent Sinclair," he said. "Dr. Carthage is the immediate concern here. He is a highly intelligent and very dangerous man, and the public is warned to *not engage* if they see him. Instead, get to a safe place and call our hotline or 911 as soon as possible. As far as we know, Dorothy O'Brian is still alive. Her picture is being circulated, and we encourage anyone to call our hotline if they think they see her. And I want to assure you that even though Dr. Carthage has eluded capture so far, the FBI and local law enforcement are using every resource to bring him in. My team and I"—he gestured behind him— "are working tirelessly to get justice for Dr. Carthage's victims."

"What about Agent Sinclair?" asked the blonde from the *Times* . . . Stella something. Gavin remembered her from when she was on the police beats. She was sharp, and he knew for a fact she could knock back whiskey like a cowboy, but she was the worst kind of dogged.

"Agent Sinclair has been taken off this case and put on temporary leave," Gavin said. "It was a clear conflict of interest, and she will not be involved any further. I will be taking the lead on this case."

"But what about—"

"Is Agent Sinclair going to write a memoir about how her ex-lover became a serial killer?"

"If Dr. Carthage has eluded you so far, what makes you think you can find him now?"

Gavin glanced over at Paul, who nodded his head firmly. It was time to cut this short.

Paul moved forward to the podium, smiling in a practiced manner. "We won't be taking any more questions at this time," Paul said. "Again, the public is warned to not engage if they see Henry Carthage. Get to a safe place and call the police immediately. Thank you, everyone."

Taking his cue, the team marched off the platform, and Gavin and Paul brought up the rear.

"Good job, guys," Paul said as they headed out of the press room and back to the building's private areas, where Grace was waiting for them.

"How was that?" Gavin asked.

"It was great," she said. "Time to start phase two. Zooey, you ready?"

Zooey smiled nervously. "As I'll ever be," she said.

CHAPTER 29

My pretty girl,

* You fucking bitch.*

* Who the hell do you think you are? Fuck you, fuck you, fuck you. You can't just quit. It's not allowed.*

* It's against my rules.*

* This is our game to play. I created it for us. A deadly jaunt of cat and mouse, where you never truly had a chance, even though I let you think you did.*

* You're mine. You're the only one remotely in my league. Those idiots you work for can't hold a candle to my brilliance. Those buffoons won't be able to find me. Only you will be able to figure it out. You have to know that.*

* You have to know this is for you and you alone.*

* Do those bumbling doughnut chasers think they can get to me? A manhunt? What a joke.*

They have no idea who they're up against. Morons. They think they'll get me on something easy. Some uniform will pull me over for speeding or on a parking ticket, and they'll crow in delight, revel in their success.

I think not. I'd rather go down in a spray of bullets than debase myself that way.

This will end with just the two of us, pretty girl. I can see it so clearly. I can feel the softness of your skin against mine, a sense memory that haunts me, day and night.

This isn't about the cops. And it's not about the people I've killed—they served their purpose.

To bring me closer to you.

This has always been about just the two of us. No one can compete. No one is on my level—not even you. But it's so sweet, so good, so satisfying, to see you try. To see you struggle to climb to meet me, to catch me, to enact the kind of biblical justice I know you want. An eye for an eye—that's my pretty girl, deep down.

And now you just want to throw that away? Throw me away? Again?

Never.

What kind of woman have you devolved into, that she'd throw this away? That isn't the girl I knew.

It's so much better when they're girls. Young. Fresh. Untainted.

They listen when they're girls, they admire, they follow a man's lead.

But then womanhood ruins them. Every time. They start thinking, they start demanding, getting independent.

Disgusting. Heartbreaking.

How could you do this? You are stronger than this. Walking away wasn't in you. It wasn't how I taught you.

Unless . . .

Oh. Oh.

Are you playing a game of your own?

Putting on a lovely little show? Look over here, while you creep up behind me.

Oh, my pretty girl. Trying to distract me. Trying to beat me at my own game.

Trying to piss me off enough to make me fumble.

It won't work, of course. But for a second, you almost had me. And now . . .

Now you've given me more hope than I could ever dream of. You've given me the kind of strength you should fear—for good reason.

You're finally playing the game. Fully engaged, no holds barred. You've embraced it, the idea of me as your adversary. As your competitor. Finally, finally, we are on the same page. Playing the same game.

Just like I wanted. Just like I need.

You'll never top me—that's just foolish thinking—but you're trying. Oh, how you're trying.

I love to watch you try. To struggle. To sink under the weight of your responsibility.

Taking the girl hurt you much more than I'd estimated. I should've known; you've always been drawn to strays, motivated to help, to share those gifts of yours.

Instead of giving credit where credit was due.

I read it, you know. The dedication in your new book.

The second I saw it, I knew what I had to do. I couldn't ignore such a grave insult. You were rewriting history—yours and ours—and I couldn't stand for it. I couldn't let you tell the world I was nothing to you. I had to remind you. To make you see you would be nothing without me.

You've always been so beautiful. The courtly, pure kind of beauty from the days of old. It has taken you further than your limited intelligence alone ever could, even though you would never acknowledge the part your looks played in your success.

But I know men better than you do. I know what they think when they hire someone like you. The kind of doors that open when a woman like that spreads her legs.

Whore.

Still, I wanted you, despite being damaged goods. Despite everything you've done to me.

I would kill a hundred people to get you. A thousand.

But maybe it won't take a thousand deaths for you to finally break.

Maybe it'll take just a few. A special few.

A targeted few.

The best way to break someone is to destroy everything she loves.

Or everyone.

—C

CHAPTER 30

Every muscle in Grace's body was tense. Sitting in the van parked across the street from the movie theater, she stared, riveted, at the camera feed. They couldn't move in until Zooey gave the word.

She knew he was inside. She'd given him something he couldn't resist, even with the added pressure of taking Dorothy hostage.

Killing Zooey, a slip of a girl who looked so fragile, would entrance him just as much as Grace quitting the case enraged him. It was a heady combination, designed to spin his head, cloud his mind. She knew he'd latch on to Zooey. She had practically focused a spotlight on the girl, and he was too angry to realize it . . . too wrapped up in his obsession to destroy Grace.

In just a few minutes, she would prove to him exactly how wrong he was.

Grace had had Zooey seed her social media

with mentions of the movie, and as much as she hated to, she ordered all agents to hang back as she made her way to the theater. Gavin had wanted to be in there with her, but they couldn't risk Carthage recognizing him.

Zooey shrugged nonchalantly when Grace proposed the plan, stressing that the forensic tech didn't have to do this.

"You'll be unguarded, unprotected. I'm almost positive he'll follow you to the theater; it'll appeal to his sense of the dramatic. But if he grabs you before—"

Zooey grinned, pulling out a palm-sized flashlight, flicking a button at the base of the handle. It sparked violently. "A girl's best friend is her Taser," she said. "Don't worry, Grace. I'm happy to play bait. We need to find Dorothy."

She'd been so confident, and Grace had hidden her concern, pushing it down to the place where her dark worries lived. But Dorothy's time was running out.

"You okay?" Gavin asked.

Grace nodded, her eyes glued on the feed.

Her radio clicked on. "Alpha, we're in position. Theater is surrounded. Omega Team is ready to enter the lobby."

"Omega Team, copy that," Paul said. "Wait for my go. Remember, suspect must be captured *alive*. We've got a girl's life on the line here, guys. We can't screw this up."

Minutes ticked by, but as the silence on Zooey's end grew longer and longer, fear began to build inside Grace's stomach.

Had she been wrong? Had Carthage not shown up?

Or was he lying in wait?

Or, she thought, as her chest went hollow with fear, had he gotten Zooey before she could radio them?

"Something's wrong," Gavin said, his voice tight.

"We should go in," Grace told Paul.

He looked at her, then at the feed, then nodded. "Omega Team, entry is a go. I repeat, entry is a go."

As soon as Paul gave the word, Grace burst out of the van and ran across the street, Gavin close at her heels.

"FBI," she said, flashing her badge at the bewildered ticket taker as she rushed by. They banged through the theater doors and into the lobby, where the Omega Team was positioned. "Carter!" Gavin shouted. "Where?"

One of Paul's tactical team members pointed to the theater on the left.

Grace plunged into the darkness, drawing her

Glock as she galloped down the center aisle. Gavin began clearing out the rows of people in the back as the Omega Team surged down the aisle.

Light from the film—some French thing in black and white with subtitles—flickered across the theater, casting gaping shadows.

She caught sight of two figures in the middle of one of the center rows. Neither of them had turned their heads as Omega Team entered and people began to flee.

"Paul, I need lights," she said into her radio, aiming her pistol at the two figures.

She moved swiftly as the man on the screen whispered sweet nothings in French into his lover's ear and they embraced. She was almost there . . .

The lights flicked on, flooding the theater, now nearly empty. Grace blinked, her eyes tearing up a little bit at the sudden glare.

Carthage was sitting next to Zooey, one arm around her shoulders—the other holding a gun to her head.

"Hello, pretty girl," he said, looking up at Grace with a wide smile. "Miss me?"

Grace's hand tightened on her Glock. "Drop the gun, Carthage," she said. "And back away from the girl."

His fingers dug into Zooey's shoulder. She bit her lip, trying to muffle a gasp of pain.

"Grace, I'm sorry. He got my radio—" she started, breaking off with a swift breath as he jabbed the gun roughly against her temple. Her eyes got big, tears pooling, her entire body rigid with fear.

"*Silence,*" Carthage hissed. "The grown-ups are talking."

Grace met Zooey's eyes, trying to beg her silently to stay calm. Oh, God, what had she gotten her into? This was a stupid plan. Desperate. Reckless.

Damn him.

Gavin came swiftly down the aisle, his gun pointed at the back of Carthage's head. Grace widened her eyes at him, and he came to a halt three rows behind them, his gaze never leaving Carthage.

"Where is Dorothy O'Brian?" she demanded.

Carthage laughed. "Have you already forgotten all I taught you, Grace? You have to work for knowledge."

Her hands tightened around her gun as fury built inside her.

Carthage looked over his shoulder at Omega Team, their guns trained on him, ready to take him out. "You think your precious snipers will be fast enough, Grace?" he asked. "Think *you* can shoot me before I shoot her?" The barrel of the gun skated across Zooey's temple.

"No," Grace gritted out, trying not to let emotion leak into her voice. She had to present a calm front. If he knew how much he was affecting her, how damn scared she was right now, he would be halfway to winning this sick game.

"I think you should tell your friends to leave us alone," Carthage said, drawing Zooey closer to him.

Grace jerked her head at Carter, the head of Omega Team. He glared at her, obviously not wanting to go.

"Now, Carter," she said.

The tac team retreated, the theater doors swinging shut behind them.

It was just Gavin and her now. She wanted to look at him, but she couldn't chance it.

Her gun was still on Carthage. His gun was still on Zooey.

Tears slid down Zooey's face, her Cleopatra eyeliner smeared down her cheekbones. She was breathing too fast—from the looks of it, on the edge of a panic attack.

"It's okay, Zooey," Grace said.

Carthage laughed. "It's most certainly *not* all right, Zooey," he said, and then he did something that made Grace's gut clench and her body shudder. He leaned over, his eyes still on Grace, and kissed Zooey on the forehead, the muzzle of the gun still pressing punishingly tight against her skull. She heard, rather than saw, Gavin let out a harsh breath. "Sweet girl, I bet you wish you hadn't blindly followed this one now, don't you?"

"Screw. You," Zooey said, through her gritted teeth. She was trying to stave off the panic attack with sheer bravado.

Smart girl. They had to get her out of here.

"You're surrounded, Carthage," Gavin said. "There's nowhere to run. Let her go."

"Now, why would I do that?" he asked. "We're having such a nice time, aren't we, Zooey?"

Zooey let out a hysterical sound, part whimper, part incredulous giggle. "Yeah, you sure know how to treat a girl," she said sarcastically.

"I do," Carthage said, and the way he said it made Grace's stomach heave. She just knew from the look on his face that he was thinking about her, eighteen-year-old Grace, who had been stupid and starved for affection from any father figure she could find. God, how she hated him. She wanted to put a bullet right between his eyes. But she couldn't. Zooey was at risk. Dorothy was God knows where.

She had to protect them both. Which meant

keeping him alive but getting him the hell away from Zooey.

"What are you going to do, Grace?" Carthage asked. "If you kill me, poor Dorothy will never be found. I can guarantee it. You could spend the rest of your life looking for her, and you won't find her. She'll just waste away, chained up, crying, starving to death, waiting for you. She's a tough one, that Dorothy. It took quite a while for her to start screaming when I cut into her."

Grace couldn't stop the sharp intake of breath as she imagined what horrors Dorothy was enduring. "I am going to kill you," she hissed.

"No, you're not," he said. "And neither is Agent Walker, over there." It made Grace go cold as he smiled mockingly and said, "How's the eye, Walker?"

"Barely needed stitches," Gavin growled. "You're gonna need a lot more than I did."

With an exaggerated shudder, Carthage turned to Grace, his eyes shining. "So macho. So coarse. You've truly debased yourself, Grace."

Grace didn't look at Gavin; she kept her gaze on Carthage, her pistol level, her hand steady. He didn't really think she was sleeping with Gavin, that much she knew. He was just trying to slut-shame her. If he truly thought she and Gavin had an intimate connection . . .

It might shake him enough to make him care-less. She needed *something* to get him to let go of Zooey. To give her some sort of window to grab her so Gavin could wound him.

"Sleeping with *you* was debasing myself," she sneered. She raised her eyes—just for a split, deliberate second—to meet Gavin's, before ze-roing back in on Carthage, who was turning a mottled red. She smiled, the kind of pleased smile that only the most sated woman would know how to give. "But sleeping with him? It was like finding myself." The truth in her words was there, raw and honest for all to hear.

And just like she suspected, it was his trigger. Rage filled his face, his body tensing all over as her words hit him.

"*Slut!*" he hissed, leaping to his feet, drag-ging Zooey in front of him. She was better than a bulletproof vest, and he knew it. He had her angled against him so that she blocked him from Grace's shot and made it impossible for Gavin to shoot him in the back without risk-ing a kill shot—with the bullet going through Zooey too.

It would be Carthage's ultimate dream if one of them accidentally shot Zooey in a bid to stop him and he managed to escape. That kind of victory would unhinge him. It would unleash a mur-derous rampage the likes of which they'd never seen. Dorothy would be dead within minutes of him arriving wherever he was keeping her.

"Oh, you're going to regret this," he spat. "You're *mine*. I'm going to make you pay."

"This isn't a game, you sick bastard," Grace said, advancing slowly toward them, Gavin following her lead. Carthage had backed up through the aisle, so now both she and Gavin were facing Zooey and him, their guns still trained on them, still unable to get a clear shot. Zooey was trying her best to be a deadweight, but Carthage picked her up, clutching her to him with little difficulty as her feet dangled in the air. Zooey was blocking any good shot, and Grace could see in her eyes that she knew it. Sweat slicked down her face, mixing with the mascara and tears.

"It wasn't supposed to happen like this," Carthage said. For a second, as he shifted toward the exit near the screen, Grace thought she'd find an angle, a shot that would wound him and leave Zooey unharmed—but no joy. Gavin shook his head when she glanced at him, telling her he was having the same problem.

"It's too early," Carthage went on. "I have plans, Grace. The circle isn't complete."

"Yet here we are," Grace said.

"She outsmarted you," Gavin said. "You can't run. We'll find you."

The *we* seemed to enrage him further. *"This isn't about you!"* he shrieked at Gavin.

He was almost to the exit. Grace tensed. This was the moment. Either he was going to drop Zooey and run, giving her just seconds to make a shot . . .

Or he was going to take her with him.

"Fool me once," Carthage muttered, "shame on me. Fool me twice . . ."

He shoved Zooey toward Gavin, and a gunshot echoed through the theater. The girl cried out in pain and Gavin caught her in his arms, lowering her to the ground while Carthage dashed through the exit.

"I got her!" Gavin yelled. "Go!"

Grace ran, hitting the theater doors with bruising force. They opened onto a long, dark alley. Her heart in her throat, her Glock at the ready, Grace frantically looked to the right, then the left.

There! She could see a shadowy figure ahead, just as he disappeared around the corner into another alley.

"Carthage!" she shouted, sprinting after him. She turned the corner, leading with her pistol. He was thirty yards away, obscured by the night and the shadows of the buildings looming above them. It was a risky shot—but it was her only shot.

She planted her feet, raising her gun, slowing her breath.

One.

Two.

Bang.

He let out a muffled grunt but kept moving, disappearing between the buildings.

Grace raced forward, questions flooding her mind as she splashed through a puddle, soaking her legs up to the knee. Had she hit him? Grazed him? Or was that too much to hope?

She rounded the corner and came to an abrupt halt.

It was a dead end, but there was no one in the narrow alleyway.

He'd disappeared.

Then she heard footsteps behind her. Her senses on high alert, she whirled, aiming her .45.

"It's us, Agent Sinclair!"

She lowered it slightly, squinting in the glare of the tac team's flashlights.

"He turned here," Grace said, stepping back to let Agent Carter lead, following right behind him. He moved slowly, sweeping the area back and forth with his semiautomatic, the light attached to it illuminating the space.

They got halfway down the alley when she saw it: a sewer grate.

When Carter shone his light on it, they saw

that the cover was askew. Someone had hastily pulled it back in place.

Fury filled Grace. She had *had* him. Right in her hands. Right where she wanted him! She wasn't going to get another chance.

And now he was gone. Hidden underground, in the labyrinth of sewer tunnels.

They'd never find him. Not unless he wanted them to.

"Should we follow, Agent Sinclair?" Carter asked.

Grace shook her head.

Gavin came running up, blood smeared on his hands. Grace's stomach sank.

"Zooey?" she asked immediately.

"She's fine," he assured her. "Flesh wound to the arm. Through and through. Very clean. EMTs are taking her to the hospital now. Carthage?"

Grace looked down the alley. "He got away," she said, feeling so small. The exhaustion and adrenaline made her feel like a match burned down to the end. There was nothing left of her.

He'd taken everything.

She kicked the dumpster in the alley, ignoring the pain howling through her toes, ignoring the fact that she was definitely *not* wearing the right shoes for it. She kicked it again for good measure.

"Son of a bitch," she growled.

She let herself have one moment. One moment when the anger and guilt flooded her, rushing through her body like a dam had broken. One moment when she let the doubt take hold of her.

And then she squared her shoulders and holstered her Glock.

"Let's go find a way to catch this bastard and save Dorothy," she said.

She would bring him down.

Even if it killed her.

CHAPTER 31

You fucking bitch,

You shot me. How dare you?

I couldn't see your trickery, just like when I first met you and was helpless against your allure.

I'm lucky to be alive. I could be lying in a pool of blood in that alley behind the theater, or in cuffs right now, marched in front of all those cameras.

A few inches to the right . . . and you could have won.

This is unacceptable. Absolutely unacceptable.

The blue-haired girl was too easy; I see it now. She was practically handed to me on a silver platter, and I overlooked it because I wanted so badly to make you pay—to break through those walls and crack the facade you show the world.

It isn't enough to humiliate you. It isn't enough to expose you.

You haven't learned your lesson. You're still pushing, still trying to outsmart me. You got close this time, you even put a bullet in me, but next time you won't.

I should've realized it before now.

The only way to teach you is to kill you.

CHAPTER 32

"G race?"

Grace looked away from the hospital room window, where she was watching Zooey, fast asleep after the doctors had stitched her wound closed.

Paul was standing there, looking somber. Dread filled her, because she knew that look. That was his time-to-break-bad-news look.

"What did he do now?" she asked, bracing herself for news that Dorothy was dead.

"I sent agents to Joann Taylor's residence like you asked," Paul said.

Her heart tightened along with her fists. "He got her," she said. It wasn't even a question. She was too tired to make it one. Because she knew.

He was completing the circle. He'd killed surrogates for her one female ally when she was in college, for her parents, for the TA who had brought them together. He'd killed Nancy because she represented Joann in the divorce and he'd killed Joann because she left him.

Grace was all that was left. The circle would be complete.

It began with her and it would end with her.

"There were no earrings found this time," Paul said. "But I guess that's beside the point at this stage."

"He doesn't need trinkets anymore," Grace said, staring at the ground. "The game is almost done."

"I'm worried, Grace," Paul said.

She took a deep breath, squaring her shoulders. "Don't be," she said. "I'm going to win."

"I'm worried because you're talking like that," Paul said, his eyebrows drawing together in concern. "He's in your head."

"I know," Grace said. "That's how I'm going to find him."

Without another word, she turned and walked down the hallway, to the lobby, where Gavin was waiting for her. He fell into step next to her as they walked out of the hospital and through the parking lot toward the SUV. Daylight was breaking across the sky. She couldn't remember the last time she slept. But it didn't matter.

Today it would end. She could feel it. It was the day of reckoning—and she wasn't sure if it'd be Carthage's or hers.

Once they got inside, Gavin finally spoke. "What's the plan?"

She looked across the car at him, something sweet and good and impossible to deny filling the parts in her heart she thought she'd long shut down. His easy acceptance, his stalwart bravery, the balance of steadiness and humor he approached everything in his life with warmed every part of her. It made her want to be better, to be brave enough to let herself fit in the place next to him.

"I don't know," she said. A quiet admission that she could give only to him, because she knew there'd be no judgment, just solutions.

"Hey, now," he said, reaching out to wipe away a tear trickling down her cheek. She realized, for the first time, she was crying. She blinked furiously, trying to hold it in.

"It's okay to cry," he told her. "It's been a really bad week."

She let out a watery half laugh, wiping at her eyes. "That's an understatement." She sniffed. "I don't know if she's still alive, Gavin."

She couldn't even bear to think of Dorothy, who was just getting started. Who had things so hard already. And was now enduring this hell because of Grace. Because she slept with the wrong man as a grieving teenager.

"She is," Gavin said. "I know it."

"How?" She didn't understand the unshakeable faith in his voice, but she saw in his face he believed it.

"Because she's a fighter," Gavin said. "Just like you. She'll survive this. And so will you."

"You don't know that, though," she said, feeling small and helpless.

"I do, though," he said. "Heart. Gut. Brain. They all agree." He reached over, taking Grace's hands in his. "You're the most amazing woman I have ever met," he said. "And it's not because you're beautiful," he added when she started to roll her eyes. "And it's not even because you're brilliant, even though you are. It's because no matter what happens, you keep going. No matter how many times he hits you, you pick yourself back up. You're stronger than he is, Grace. He knows it. That's why he took Dorothy."

"He wants to kill her in front of me," Grace said, realizing with a jolt what Carthage's plan was. "The circle," she said, looking up at Gavin with wide eyes. "He said 'the circle isn't complete.' Dorothy represents *me*. Younger me. The me he met all those years ago. She's almost the same age as I was. We don't look anything alike, but that doesn't matter, because of her personal connection to me. She's the perfect surrogate. In his mind, if he kills younger me in front of adult me . . ."

"He wins," Gavin finished.

Grace sat straight up. Carthage was all about re-creating the past. That meant the game had to end where it had started. She'd been thinking it had started with Janice Wacomb, but she was wrong. This had started years ago.

"I know where he is," she said.

CHAPTER 33

The University of Maryland's criminology department was housed in a large brick building with only a few windows—and only a few ways in. Paul had dispatched a team from headquarters to back them up, but as they pulled into the parking lot, Grace received a text saying they were stuck in traffic.

"We can't wait," she told Gavin.

"No way," he agreed, getting out of the SUV and going to the rear to open up the back. "Campus police?" he suggested as he flipped open the case, removed two guns, and handed one to her.

Grace snorted. "They'd probably end up getting hurt."

Gavin pulled out a pair of bulletproof vests, offering one to her. It was the standard-issue size, which was too bulky and big, but she strapped it on tight. Next, she hastily pulled her hair up in a bun, then took the extra ammunition Gavin gave her and tucked it in her pocket.

"It's a big building," he said. "Where are we going to start?"

Grace looked up at the building in front of them, assessing it like a SWAT team would, counting the entrances and exits, measuring the risks and rewards. If she came in from the north, she'd get to his office faster, and if he was keeping watch out the windows, he'd likely miss her. She'd have the element of surprise in her favor. But if she came in from the south, she had faster access to the center of the building, where the lecture halls were.

So, was he in his office, where they had their first in-depth conversation? Or in the lecture hall where they first met?

"Which would he choose?" she muttered. "The lecture hall," she said. "It's his stage. This is all a performance. He'd want to give what he considered his best performance there."

Gavin put his spare gun in his ankle holster and straightened, his hand settling on the gun on his hip. "Let's go get Dorothy back safe," he said.

They headed to the south side of the building, staying low and using the trees to their advantage to obscure their approach. Luckily, on a weekend morning in summer, the building would be nearly empty. He'd probably brought Dorothy in the night before, totally unnoticed.

He had the place to himself, just the way he'd want it. As much as Carthage loved grandeur and recognition, he would consider *this*—their confrontation, their final battle—an intimate, private thing.

Grace drew her Glock as they headed up the stairs outside the building, Gavin tight against her back. She opened the large glass door with one hand, then led with the gun as she moved down the hall at a fast clip. As she rounded the corner, she halted. A janitor was mopping the hallway, oblivious to her presence.

"Hey," Gavin hissed.

He turned, his eyes widening when he saw them, outfitted in bulletproof vests, guns drawn.

"FBI," Grace said, pointing to the badge at her hip. "Any other maintenance crew in here?"

He shook his head. "Just me," he said.

"You see anyone come by?" Gavin asked.

"Nope. I just started my shift ten minutes ago," the man explained.

"Okay, we need you out of here," Grace said. "SWAT is on its way."

He nodded and pelted down the hall. Grace waited until she heard the click of the glass doors so she knew he was gone. Then she squared her shoulders and motioned for them to continue. The lecture hall was at the end of the corridor.

He had to be there.

If he'd already killed Dorothy . . .

She couldn't think about that. She *couldn't*.

She needed to stay calm. She breathed in and out, timing her breath with her footfalls. If she was going to get the better of Carthage, she needed a steady hand and a cool head. She couldn't let herself imagine a scenario where Dorothy didn't walk out of this alive. It wasn't an option.

Gavin jerked the lecture hall door open, and Grace entered in front of him, swinging the Glock in a neat arc as she cleared the alcove that led to the stairs.

"Take the left side," she whispered. "I'll take the right."

He nodded and moved across the room toward the other set of stairs.

The lights were off. With her back to the wall, Grace peered around the corner of the alcove, down the hall, and into the darkness. The only light was from the high-set windows at the top of the room, giving the hall a cavernous feel.

From what she could remember, the floor was built at a deep slant, with rows of chairs set up in a semicircle like an amphitheater, the whiteboards and professor's desk at the bottom. She squinted into the dim light, trying to make out the shadows at the very bottom of the stairs, near the desk. As her eyes adjusted to the poor light, she realized someone was sitting there, tied to a chair.

Grace went cold. She had to lock her knees to keep herself from running down the stairs. It was hard to stop the instinct, the horror that rose in her as she realized she couldn't see if Dorothy was breathing or not.

She looked across the alcove at Gavin, who held up three fingers. She nodded and he started the countdown.

Three.

Two.

One.

They moved as one, down the stairs, guns raised. They were halfway down the lecture hall when light suddenly flooded the room. They both froze as a low whistle filled the room. Carthage was sitting right next to Dorothy, a gun in one hand, a knife in the other, held against her throat.

"Hands in the air!" Grace said, rounding on him.

"Ah, ah, ah," Carthage tutted, pointing his own gun. But he didn't point it at Grace or Gavin.

He pointed it at the large glass jar that Dorothy's hands were duct taped to.

"Careful," Carthage said. "That's hydrofluoric

acid in sweet little Dorothy's hands. One shot, and the jar will explode and it'll eat through her flesh. Chemistry really is a marvel. You can find any recipe on the Internet these days."

"God, you're a sick bastard," Gavin said.

"Grace," Dorothy whimpered. "Please."

"It's okay," Grace told her. "I'm getting you out of this."

"Don't listen to her, Dorothy," Carthage said, staring at Grace like he couldn't bear to tear his eyes from her even for a second. "She never keeps her promises."

He was sweating, his eyes lit with a manic fervor.

"You're going to need to put your gun down, Agent Walker," Carthage said.

Gavin glanced at Grace questioningly.

"LOOK AT ME, NOT HER!" Carthage bellowed, the knife in his hand pressing into Dorothy's throat. She stiffened, the jar of acid in her hands sloshing at the movement.

Grace flinched at the abrupt rise in volume and to her relief, Gavin slowly lowered his gun, holstered it, and raised his hands. "You're the one in charge," he said. "I know how important it is that you talk with Grace about your history."

The mention of her name caused Carthage's attention to snap back to her, much to her relief.

She needed him focused totally on her. It was the only way Gavin would be able to get close enough to act.

"Here we are," Carthage said, smiling viciously. "Finally."

Grace held her ground. She had no other choice. "What's the plan here, Carthage?" she asked. "You think we came here without backup?"

"I know you did," Carthage replied. "Your little lapdog will follow you wherever you ask. But that boss of yours is not too happy with you right now, is he?"

"He still has my back," Grace said. "SWAT's on their way."

"They're not here yet," Carthage said. "So in the meantime, unless you want Dorothy scarred for life, I propose that you do what I want."

"And what's that?" Grace asked.

"It's time to play a game," Carthage said, stepping forward.

Out of the corner of her eye, she could see Gavin move when Carthage did, getting closer to Dorothy as Carthage got a little farther.

"Maybe I don't want to play," she said, scared he'd notice Gavin's movement.

He tutted like a disappointed teacher. "Silly girl, what *you* want doesn't matter."

"I don't like your kind of games," Grace spat out.

"You'll like this one," he insisted. "It's very

simple. I ask you a question. And you tell the truth."

"And if I don't?"

"Then I shoot your paramour," he said, turning his gun abruptly on Gavin. Grace tensed, worried Gavin would react, pulling his holstered gun or one of his hidden ones. But he stood stock-still, his hands still raised, his eyes on Carthage.

"I mean, really, Grace," Carthage said. "A cop? Your standards have sunk to the bottom."

"Is this where I'm supposed to get offended and insist I'm ten times the man you are?" Gavin asked.

Grace glared at him. He needed to be *quiet*. She tried to communicate this with her eyes, but if he was cracking macho jokes, Gavin was clearly rattled.

Carthage laughed; it startled her because it was such a genuine sound. She adjusted her grip on the pistol just a fraction of an inch, unsure of the reaction. Was he offended? Or amused?

"Such a debased profession," Carthage said. "Why don't you stay quiet, Detective Walker? This is between Grace and me." He turned back to Grace, his eyes narrowing. "Maybe his life isn't worth much to you. But hers?" He stroked the knife down Dorothy's cheekbone, a thin line of blood trickling down in its wake. "You'd do anything for her."

Tears slipped down Dorothy's face, mingling with the blood. Grace tried to look at her reassuringly, but she knew there was no reassuring in this situation.

"I think it's time to stop wasting precious minutes and get back to our game, my pretty girl."

Grace gritted her teeth, tightening her muscles so she wouldn't shudder at the endearment. It sounded so wrong. So repulsive.

"What's the first question?" she asked. Dammit, where the hell was SWAT? Or campus police? They needed backup *now*!

Gavin stepped forward just a little, and Carthage's attention was so locked on Grace he didn't even notice. Just a few more steps, and he might be close enough. But the acid in Dorothy's hands . . . Grace had no doubt in her mind it really *was* acid. Carthage wouldn't leave that to chance. He wouldn't bluff.

He didn't need to.

"Now, remember, you can't lie," Carthage told her. "And I'll know if you do. I know you better than anyone, Grace. I made you."

"So you keep saying," Grace said coldly. "Just ask the damn questions."

"So impatient, always," Carthage said, reverting to his professor voice. It made her feel sick. She tightened her hands around her .45, steadying her stance.

"Who was the first person I ever killed?" Carthage asked.

Grace didn't even hesitate. "Martha Lee," she answered. "My mentor. What did you do, Carthage? Drive her off the road?" She stared hard at his face. His left eye twitched. "No, you don't have the guts for that. You might've got hurt. You messed with her car, didn't you? Did something that they didn't catch in the investigation."

"The police are woefully incompetent," Carthage sighed. "So, why do you think I killed dear Martha?" Carthage asked.

"You were jealous of her," Grace replied.

"She stole you from me," Carthage hissed, and there it was: the first crack she'd seen in his smooth, controlled exterior.

"She did nothing of the sort," Grace said. "She was a wonderful woman and a talented academic and a loving wife. She had a brilliant, creative mind. She was *truly* dedicated to her students. Selflessly dedicated. She gave and gave and didn't want anything in return, because she knew we were going to go out and do great things. She saw her students as her contribution to the world—not as an extension of her own ego, like you."

She stared at Carthage, daring him with her eyes to declare any of it false.

"She took what I had, what I'd created, all my hard work—and she got the credit," Carthage complained, sweat trickling down his forehead. The knife in his hand was back at Dorothy's throat. Grace wanted to shoot him in the head so badly, but she couldn't risk Dorothy. "*You* gave her all the credit, in black and white. She needed to be taught a lesson."

"You and your lessons," Grace sneered as Gavin took that moment to inch forward again. So close.

"I said *stay where you are.*" Carthage rounded on Gavin, the knife digging into Dorothy's flesh at the movement. "Another move and I will kill her *and* you."

Grace moved; she had no other choice. Four swift steps, and she was on the platform, just a few feet away from Dorothy.

Carthage turned to her, his eyes gleaming in the light. "You shouldn't have done that," he said.

"*You* did this," she said. "You did all of this."

"For you," he replied. "Another question, Grace," he added as blood streaked down Dorothy's neck. "Are you ready?"

She needed to get close to Dorothy. Yanking her out of the way seemed like the best option here. The jar in her hands was closed with a lid—she just had to pray it was shut tightly.

"This man." He gestured toward Gavin with his gun. Grace had to lock her knees not to fling herself forward.

And then Carthage asked a question that made her blood run cold.

"Do you love him?"

Grace froze, her eyes widening. What was the right answer?

Her mind raced, trying to sort through everything she knew about Carthage. Would he fly into a jealous rage if she said yes? Would that make Gavin more of a target?

If she said no, would it please him—or would he see through it?

Would he know it was a lie?

Was it a lie?

"Answer the question, Grace," Carthage ordered.

Grace licked her lips. "No," she said, but even she could hear the question in her voice.

"I told you not to lie," Carthage snarled, thrusting the gun at her.

Yes. The gun was back in play, but on her, not on Dorothy. That was progress.

"I . . ." She stepped forward, just one step. Carthage was so focused on her answer he didn't notice. "I don't know," she confessed.

It was the truth. Terrifying and exhilarating to contemplate on the surface. She'd save the deeper examination for a time when she didn't have a gun in her face and a teenager holding a jar of acid.

Carthage's shoulders visibly relaxed. Grace's eyes narrowed, noting it. "That's better," he said, almost sighing it. "I want you to be able to tell me the truth, Grace. It's very important."

"Are there any more questions?" Grace asked. She thought about taking another step in his direction but decided she couldn't risk it yet. She needed to get him more involved in the guessing game.

"Yes," Carthage said. "Why haven't you been able to stop me?"

"You've gotten lucky," Grace replied brusquely.

"Luck has nothing to do with it!" Carthage shouted, enraged. "I outsmarted you!"

Grace's trigger finger tensed.

"If I have to hand over my truths, Carthage, then you do too," she said, stepping forward again. She was so close. "This has never been a fair game. Just like ten years ago, we didn't have a fair relationship. You can't stand to be on equal footing with anyone—you always have to be the one in power. The one in charge. The smarter one. The older one. The admired one. I hung on your every word—and you loved it."

All his attention was on her now. Dorothy was forgotten between them.

She almost had him. If only she could edge just a little closer . . .

"Were you surprised at how easy it was?" she asked quietly, almost soothingly.

"How easy what was?" His shoulders, which had gone rigid again when he'd insisted on his superiority, started to relax.

"Killing someone," Grace answered.

Something in his eyes flickered—and Grace was disgusted to realize that it was lust.

"It was a relief, wasn't it?" Grace asked, risking another step forward. She was only three feet away now. She couldn't tackle Dorothy to the ground, but she could pull her away, as soon as she got rid of Carthage's knife. Gavin would jump in the second he saw the opportunity. She knew it.

It was a crazy plan, but it was the only one she had.

"You had something building inside you for so long," Grace said. "You watched Martha's car go off the road, didn't you? You needed to see it."

He smiled slightly. Thinking about his past crimes made him unwind the way a hot cup of tea relaxed a normal person. Revulsion churned in Grace's stomach, but she kept her voice low, inviting, nonjudgmental.

"It was . . . beautiful," he mused, his voice full of awe.

"And it just got better with each one, didn't it?"

"Yes," he whispered.

"And got easier."

"It was *so* easy," he said, the wonder in his voice making her want to shoot him then and there. But Dorothy was the priority. She glanced down at the girl, nodding slightly. Dorothy raised her eyebrows, showing her she understood.

"It's much easier to sow chaos than to maintain order," she said, her soft voice turning to steel.

His eyes widened immediately. "My kind of chaos is a work of art. I had you all fooled."

"You took the easy path, Carthage," Grace said, letting the disgust show on her face. She had to make him confused. To shift her moods, to keep him distracted and uneasy.

It made things more dangerous, but it gave her cover as she inched closer.

"I took the only path back to *you*," he growled. "I watched you that night . . . that night at the awards banquet. I know you saw me, but you never approached me."

"I didn't want to talk to you," Grace said.

"You certainly talked to everyone else," Carthage said, sounding like a neglected child. "I watched you the whole night. Watched you with them. How you handled them. Every person you spoke to, you gave them exactly what they wanted. You read them like a book and delivered whatever they needed on a silver platter. You smiled and complimented and joked. It was so calculated, and no one saw it but me. Because I know you, Grace. I was your first victim. We're all your victims. You make us love you, but it's a fraud. You don't love any of them. You don't love any of us.

"Did you hear that, Detective?" Carthage demanded, glancing over his shoulder. "She'll never love you—not really. She's not capable of it. Not capable of being real. Everything's an act . . . a game."

He stepped forward, the gun lowering for a split second. It was her window. Grace lunged forward, her hand closing around the blade of the knife. Carthage jerked it hard, cutting Grace's fingers and slashing it across Dorothy's throat before he turned and dashed toward the exit.

"No!" Grace screamed and threw herself forward. Her gun dropped as she scrambled for Dorothy's throat, pressing hard against the wound as a gunshot went off. For a second, she expected screams, the smells of burning flesh, the sound of shattering glass, but instead warm hands were pressing over hers, Gavin taking over the pressure needed to staunch the blood flow. Dorothy moaned, her eyes fluttering shut.

"Go!" Gavin shouted. "I missed him! I've got her."

Grace looked at the exit, then back at Gavin and Dorothy, torn.

"Grace, *go*!" he repeated. "I will get her through this."

She believed him.

She trusted him.

So she ran.

CHAPTER 34

Grace burst out of the lecture hall, facing a long hallway lined with doors.

Carthage was nowhere to be seen.

Grace gripped the Glock tighter. He wasn't getting away this time.

His luck had run out. She had to make sure of it.

Leading with her pistol, she made her way down the hall, checking doors—most of them locked, to her relief.

She needed to finish this—now. Gavin would take care of Dorothy, but that cut on her throat was nasty. It must have missed the artery, thank God, but the blood loss alone . . .

She gritted her teeth, speeding up. She could do this. She *had* to.

She was better than Carthage. A better person. A better profiler. A better shot.

Now it was time to play *her* game.

She moved swiftly, slowing when she approached the spot where the hallway branched off into a corridor. Her footfalls were soft—barely audible to even the keenest ear. She leaned back against the wall and edged down the corridor, her eyes tracking the shadows that stretched into darkness.

There. Her heart leapt as she saw a shadow at the end of the corridor flutter.

He was waiting for her, just around the corner. It was a good position. If she tried to advance, he had a clear shot.

Grace wanted to take a moment to think it through, but she was out of time. She had to decide—now.

He'd want to see her eyes. That was her first thought. When he killed her, he'd want to be looking at her. Maybe even holding her. It would be about the connection—for him, the ultimate connection, the ultimate power move: taking her life.

But he wouldn't advance. She had to make the first move.

She had to make him think he'd won.

Grace gritted her teeth, her stomach sinking. The last time she tried to trick him, she'd failed, horribly. The thought of trying again terrified her.

But she had no choice—she had to risk it.

If she didn't survive, Gavin would die too. Carthage would return to the lecture hall to finish him off.

He would make sure he'd truly won.

Grace swallowed, raising her Glock a fraction of an inch. It was now or never. She edged forward, her eyes fixed firmly on the corridor in front of her instead of to her right, where the hallways intersected. She walked past the corner Carthage was pressed against, her gun pointed ahead, her back to him.

She couldn't tense. She couldn't falter. A sudden movement, a stiff muscle, a tilt of the head, and he'd know.

She had to fool him. She took another step. Then another.

And she heard it—a scuffling sound behind her. *Now!*

She spun, firing. Once. Twice.

He stumbled backward from the impact, his hands flying up to his chest as he crumpled to the ground.

Grace hurried forward, her gun pointed dead on his heart. When he saw her looming over him, he struggled to sit up.

Grace planted a boot on his stomach, pinning him to the floor.

"Stay where you are," she ordered.

She stared down at him. Blood was quickly spreading from his chest wound, his breathing already slowing and unsteady. He coughed, weakly, his eyes fluttering shut. More blood bloomed at his lips, and his fingers loosened their grip on his gun, dropping it onto the tile floor.

He was dying.

She had killed him.

She hated that some part of her was horrified. But maybe that was what separated someone like her from someone like him.

"I—I *made* you," he gasped out, blood sliding from his lips.

With her Glock still trained on his heart, Grace's eyes narrowed as she lifted her blood-stained boot off his chest and kicked his gun away. Then she bent over until their faces were just inches apart.

"*I* made me," she said, her voice low and fierce.

For a moment, his eyes widened with terror and defeat as life faded out. The last thing he would ever know was the truth in her words and her voice—the truth that, in his final moments, he couldn't escape.

Blood pouring from his lips, Carthage let out a choked breath. It was his last.

Grace stood and stared down at him, still aiming her Glock at his chest, as if she was afraid he might sputter back to life. As if this was all part of his game.

But he was dead—the game was over.

And she had won.

CHAPTER 35

Hospital coffee was the worst, Grace thought, as she took another bitter sip from the cup Gavin had brought her.

He was waiting somewhere in the hospital, but the nurses had insisted only one person be allowed in Dorothy's room. Which was how Grace found herself keeping vigil by the teen's bed as she slept off her sedative. There'd been trouble getting hold of her mother—she worked third shift—so Grace wanted to make sure someone was here when Dorothy woke.

Just when she was about to doze off—her adrenaline rush had long faded—Dorothy's eyes drifted open. For a few moments, she just blinked groggily, her eyebrows drawn together as she swallowed. The cut on her throat was mostly superficial, but it had required quite a lot of stitches. It'd be sore for a while.

"Hey," Grace said softly, standing up so Dorothy could see her.

"Hi," Dorothy said, her voice cracking as her eyes filled with tears. "You found me. He said you wouldn't."

Grace reached out and grasped her hand. "He was wrong," she said. "You're safe. He's never going to hurt you again."

"You got him?" Dorothy asked.

"I got him," Grace promised.

Dorothy let out a shaky breath, wincing again as she tried to swallow, pulling at her stitches. She touched the bandage on her neck, biting her lip. "Is it really bad?"

Grace shook her head. "The doctor said you'd barely even have a scar."

"Well, that sucks—the least I could get out of all of this was a badass scar," Dorothy said.

Grace smiled, trembling, in awe of her resilience. She knew this was just the start for her and Dorothy. The teen had a long road ahead—recovery wasn't instant, even if she was already cracking jokes—but Grace was going to keep her on the right road. The one that led to college and security and a job she loved and a life she deserved.

"You don't need a badass scar when you're already a badass," Grace said. "And rest assured, you *are* a badass, Dorothy."

"You think so?" she asked. "Because I was really scared."

"That makes you human," Grace said, squeezing her hand. "But you survived. And you'll keep surviving. That's what matters."

Dorothy's eyes drifted shut. "I'm really glad you found me," she whispered.

"Always," Grace promised. "You and me? We're bonded now. Sisters."

"Profiler sisters?" Dorothy asked, making Grace smile.

"You play your cards right," Grace said, "and you'll be at Quantico before you know it."

"I'd like that," Dorothy said.

Grace kept holding her hand as she fell back asleep. Not long after she did, a nurse came in and shooed Grace out of the room.

Gavin was waiting for her in the lobby.

"How's she doing?" he asked, nodding toward the private room where Dorothy was fast asleep.

"Good," she said. "Thanks to you."

"Thanks to you," he said, as they both sat down in the lobby.

"The doctors said the scar won't even be that bad. She seemed a little disappointed by that. She said scars were badass."

"I'm hoping you think so," he said, gesturing to the cut on his head.

Grace smiled, reaching over and tracing the healing cut. "It's going to be a *very* dashing scar, I'm sure," she said.

"I got it trying to protect a girl, you know," he said, batting his eyes at her.

Her mouth twisted into a smile—the first one in days, it felt like. She hadn't left Dorothy's side since she was brought in yesterday morning. Which meant she hadn't slept in—she glanced at her watch—around thirty-six hours. She yawned, the physical and emotional exhaustion starting to catch up with her.

"You need to rest, Grace," Gavin said. "Let me take you home."

"I don't want to leave her," Grace protested.

"That's why I called in reinforcements," Gavin said, nodding to someone over his shoulder.

Grace turned around in the uncomfortable lobby chair and saw that it was Sheila, the director of the center. Relief flooded her when the older women smiled gently at her, enveloping her in a hug.

"I am so glad both of you are okay," she whispered against Grace's ear. "We're going to sit and talk everything through soon. But right now, I want you to go home with your very nice boyfriend and get some sleep."

"But Dorothy—" Grace said.

"I'll be with her the entire time," Sheila assured her. "Now go."

Grace was too tired to defy her. She let Gavin grab her arm and steer her out of the hospital and toward the car.

She dozed a little as he drove her home, but when they got to her house and he followed her up the steps, just a breath behind her, she felt like a live wire had been trailed across her skin.

They said nothing as they walked up to her bedroom and Grace pulled back the covers with aching arms.

"Did you want to . . . ?" She trailed off, biting her lip, unsure of how to do this.

She didn't want him to go. But she didn't know how to ask him to stay.

"I want to get in bed with you and hold you," he said. "And I want to *sleep*."

If she wasn't already in love with him, this might be the moment where she truly fell. "Me too," she admitted.

He smiled. "I guess we're on the same page, then," he said, his lips quirking in that playful tilt again.

"I guess so," she said.

She stripped down to her underwear artlessly, no decorum or care, but she could feel his eyes on her, a quiet sort of appreciation, as she slid into bed under the covers and he followed suit, pulling her close to him, her back pressed against his front as he curved against her, surrounding her with his warmth. His arm encircled her, his fingers interweaving with hers.

She sighed into the feeling of safety, of warmth, of *home*.

"You're an extraordinary woman, Grace," he said against her ear. "A badass lady in two-inch heels. And my heroine."

"Most of my heels are three inches," she said and he laughed, the vibration pressing deliciously against her back.

"You make me never want to let you go." It was an honest confession, spoken in the safety of a quiet room, just the two of them as witnesses. Instead of hanging there, it wrapped around her like his strong arms. Instead of scaring her, it made her feel brave.

"I'm not very good at this," she said, giving him her own confession.

"Hush," he whispered.

"No, really," she insisted, turning in his arms so they were nose-to-nose. "I've never done this, because it's always a bad idea. Even now, after everything, even when I want nothing more than to kiss you, I can give you a list of reasons why it's a bad idea—"

He kissed her, his mouth closing over hers,

driving all objection, all thought out of her head, until there was only him and sensation, his hand cupping her cheek, his fingers trailing down her neck.

When they broke apart, she was speechless, her protests fading like mist in the sunlight.

"Everyone's a little screwed up," Gavin said softly. "Let's take a chance. Make a go of it. What do you say?"

Grace looked at him. She could've lost him before she had a chance to even have him. What kind of woman walked away from a second chance?

She smiled and pressed close to him, her legs tangling with his under the sheets.

"I say *yes*," she replied.

If you can't get enough of Tess Diamond's
spine-tingling stories, be sure to pre-order
her next Avon Romance

BE A GOOD GIRL

Coming April 2018